DISCLAIMER

This is a work of fiction. Names, characters, businesses, places, events and incidents are either the product of the author's imagination or used in a fictitious manner. Any resemblance to actual persons, living or dead, or actual events is purely coincidental.

THIEF
BOSTON UNDERWORLD
BOOK FIVE

A. ZAVARELLI

THIEF © 2018 A. Zavarelli
Cover Design: Coverluv
Photo: Wander Aguiar
Editing: Jenny Sims

All rights reserved. This book or any portion thereof may not be reproduced or used in any manner whatsoever without the express written permission of the author except for the use of brief quotations in a book review.

PLAYLIST

ARCHIS— Bittersweet
Camila Cabello— Never be the Same
Halsey, G. Eazy— Him and I
Symon— Lonely Girl
Eminem, Ed Sheeran— River
Rita Ora, Liam Payne— For You
Zac Effron, Zendaya— Rewrite the Stars
Sia— The Greatest
Selena Gomez— Wolves
Imagine Dragons— Believer
Craig Armstrong, Lana Del Ray— Hotel Sayre
R.I.P.— Rita Ora
AWOLNATION— Sail
Bruno Mars— It Will Rain
Leona Lewis— Bleeding Love
Plumb— Damaged
Leona Lewis— Angel
Yiruma— River Flows in You

Leona Lewis— Take a Bow
One Republic— Apologize

GLOSSARY OF TERMS

Avtoritet— authority, captain
Boevik— warrior, soldier, strike force
Pakhan— leader, boss
Nika, Nikolasha, Kol'ka, Kolyan— diminutive forms of the name Alexei
Nakya, Tashechka— diminutive forms of the name Tanaka
Zvezda— star
Bratan— brother
Sovietnik—councilor, advisor to the pakhan
Vory v Zakone— thieves in law

CHAPTER 1
TANAKA

Let it ruin you. It's the only way.

  The words rush between my lips on a stolen breath, and in my mind, Vivi's face is still as lucid as the day she uttered that direction. She was loud and unintentionally poetic. Silky locks of raven hair, red lipstick, and cat-shaped glasses. These were just a few of the threads that stitched together my mentor and my inspiration.

  Every dancer at the Met tonight would sell their souls for a career like Vivi's. I was one of the lucky disciples chosen to study under her. I didn't let the opportunity go to waste. I was not under the delusion that I was special, and Vivi would be quick to remind me of it if I ever got the notion in my head. Every ballet student wanted to think she was special. That she was pure talent and natural grace. That she was the *best*. But every dancer's best was only as good as the dancer next to her, waiting to steal her shine in the spotlight. Vivi provided that lesson when she allowed another dancer to do exactly that. Her practice was brutal but effective. More than structure and timing, she taught me how to live and breathe my art. And most importantly, she educated me on what happens when a dancer becomes complacent.

I remember her warmly whenever I've put my body through hell, and I know that she would be proud. If she was here to witness the mangled state of my feet, she would tell me that I had gone to war, and I had won.

Flexing my toes, my eyes sweep over the desolate landscape of my thighs as I swoop forward in a meditative stretch.

There is no such thing as pain. There is only discipline.

Tonight, I will take the stage as a soloist for the New York Ballet Company, performing as Ceres in Sylvia. It is a hard-won role. A role I have fought and bled for. The years of study have not been kind, but there is no such thing as mercy in ballet.

The shelf life of a dancer is short, and for me, it's even shorter. I am fortunate that the ballet has always pleased my father because it is the one amusement he would not deny me. He told me as a child that a dancer embodies everything a woman should be. When he took me to my first ballet, I came to a quick agreement. The heavenly creatures floating across the stage in shades of pale pink and white were the most beautiful sight I had ever beheld. At the age of six, I resolved that I would be one of those dancers someday. My lofty aspirations brought amusement to my father's otherwise brash face, and he declared that if I wanted to be a true ballerina, it would mean accepting nothing less than principle. When I asked why, he explained that in the days of old, only the best dancers could earn the accolade of ballerina.

From that day forward, I resolved that I would earn the right to be called a true ballerina. And eighteen years later, I am closer than ever to my dream. Also, closer than ever to having it snatched away.

A muted whisper jars me from stillness, and when I open my eyes, the calm before the storm dissolves.

The standing agreement between my father and the artistic director of NYBC is that I must always have my own room to dress, even if it's only the size of a closet. My father likes to say that the guise of religion can buy you many things, but the truth is, his name is what affords such luxuries. The artistic director doesn't blink twice at the guards who shadow my every move. Unfortunately for me, the other dancers do.

I am kept separate. Hidden away and forbidden from socializing. The circumstances of my situation haven't bred the warmest reception from my peers, but I'm accustomed to the isolation. Which is why it is no small shock to discover that Gianni has infiltrated my improvised dressing room. I'm not even certain how he snuck in, and when I look at the door where my guard is waiting outside, a knot forms in my throat.

"What are you doing? My father will be here any—"

"Tanaka." He lowers to my level. We're eye to eye, and there's no mistaking his apprehension. Gianni is the poster boy for every Italian gangster costume that gets mass produced around Halloween. Slicked jet-black hair, gold rings on his fingers, and the stereotypical New York accent. I couldn't take him seriously on my best day, but I'm taking him seriously now.

"What is it?" I curl my legs under me and rise to my feet, my stretching forgotten. He can't be seen here with me and he knows it. So, if he's here, it can only mean something's up. I have the sudden urge to puke, and it has nothing to do with the impending performance. My stomach is a riot of nerves, and it's all his fault.

"You promised me." My spine sags forward as I clutch my waist. "You swore everything would be okay."

All I can think about is my dreams going up in smoke. Principal won't matter if I'm dead. Nothing will matter if I'm dead. The years of training, the countless hurdles I've overcome, they will have been for nothing.

Gianni glances at the door. "I came to warn you."

"Warn me about what?"

The conversation screeches to a halt when there's a knock on the door. The knock I've been dreading since his arrival. I knew it would come, and there isn't time to finish what Gianni started. He curses under his breath, bolting for a chair in the center of the room. I wave at him frantically while he pulls himself up through a displaced ceiling tile.

"Principessa," my father calls through the door. "Are you decent?"

The tile slides back into place, and I clear my throat. "Yes, Papà."

The guard opens the door, and my father enters. I meet him halfway as a sign of respect, and he kisses each of my cheeks. The ritual is predictable and familiar, but the uneasiness in his dark eyes is not.

Impeccably dressed in a suit and trench coat, my father remains steadfast in his old-fashioned ways. He will always look his best, and everyone around him should too. But even he can't hide the grimace in his step as he paces the perimeter of the room with a keen eye. It could mean one of two things. A business deal gone bad, or his debts are worse than I had imagined.

I don't ask, and he doesn't tell. A father does not discuss these things with his daughter. At least not in our world. My days, weeks, and hours are slave to a dancer's regime, while criminal activities consume his.

At first glance, the man is an improbable source for my paternal genes. He is a throwback to his Italian roots with dusky eyes and sooty hair. My complexion is far more coppery, and my eyes a more forgiving shade of amber. He is stocky in stature, and I am willowy like my mother.

I am grateful to have inherited her features, believing that in some small way, she lives on through me.

"*Sei Bella.*" Papà roosts on the chair that Gianni used for his escape only moments ago. "Tonight, the audience will see a genuine angel."

I smile at the compliment, but beneath his words is an undercurrent of despair, and it worries me.

"You know you must give this up soon, Principessa."

My answering nod is stiff and obedient. "Yes, Papà, I know."

Soon sounds quicker than I anticipated, but it is not entirely surprising. Dante has been making quiet preparations to marry me, and the moment I agree, my life will change entirely. Dancer's accolades are of no significance in a man's world. A mafia wife has one sole purpose, and it is not outside the home. I've been raised to know the challenges that await me. The sum of my life is only as great as the man's name that I take.

"Dante would like to have a word with you," Papà says.

I comply with a quiet, "Okay."

After one short command from my father, Dante enters dutifully. He greets me with a respectful kiss on the cheek and nothing more. It is as much contact as we ever have under the watchful eye of my father. I am to remain pure for my husband, and only on the wedding night will my virtue be taken. This is the way of my world, and one of the many reasons for my constant guard.

"You look like a goddess." Dante squeezes my hand. "I expect you will mesmerize the entire theatre. I am only disappointed I will not be able to see it."

My face crumples. "You aren't staying?"

Dante looks at my father before answering. "I wish I could, but business calls."

I nod because it isn't my place to argue. Business is business.

"Thing is," Dante says with undisguised bitterness, "the business is overseas. I could be gone for a couple of months."

A couple of months? This is news to me, and it's the first time I've ever known Dante to resent his marching orders. Orders undoubtedly handed down by my father. In a bold display of ownership, he slips his hand over my cheek and leans in to whisper in my ear. "When I return, I'll be making you my wife."

A shiver moves through me, and Papà clears his throat. "Time to go, Dante."

One last kiss on my cheek, and Dante does as he's told.

I give my father a weak smile, hoping he will go now. The show will start shortly, and my nerves have not abated. I need more time to warm up. I need to re-frame my thoughts and calm the chaos eating up my focus. My father's uneasy behavior. Gianni's unspoken warning, and now, Dante's swift exit. An atomic energy is building in the air with every passing second, and I don't like it.

I force my beating heart to calm when my father gestures for his men outside, and Gianni is the one to enter. He's here as a guard tonight, and his face is completely devoid of emotion when my eyes flash to his. He gives nothing away, and I know it's important that I do the same.

"Tanaka," my father says brusquely. "I'd like you to meet an associate of mine."

My eyes move to the door, a new threat lying in wait. The associate is introduced as Nikolai, but he is hardly an associate from what I can see. The man is from a different world entirely.

The first thing I always notice about a person is their posture. I was raised to believe that good posture conveys good manners, as well as respect for those around you. Nikolai carries his posture like a casual "fuck you." There is no decorum in his leather jacket, jeans, or his haphazardly laced motorcycle boots. Everything he wears is black, but the small glimpse of flesh beneath is a riot of colors. Tattoos cover every inch of his exposed skin, including his throat. I'm not sure which is more offensive—the ink or the fauxhawk atop his head. This is not the way you attend a ballet, nor is he the type of man I expect my father to keep company with.

"Tanaka." He reaches for my hand and kisses it in a way that few men would ever dare to do in my father's presence. "You dance beautifully."

The words are unmistakably accented. Russian. My composure wavers while I struggle to make sense of this situation. My father has always been protective of me. His own men know better than to speak to me or look at me, but for this stranger, somehow, it's okay.

At least my manners are still intact, so I reply as I should. "You've seen me dance?"

"I like to invest my time in the arts." The stranger flashes a boyish smile in contrast to the deepness of his eyes. Eyes as blue as an iceberg, and as enigmatic as one too. They invoke a feeling of shallowness in my chest. It's an odd sensation, but it feels as though he's laughing at me.

I look at my father, the most powerful man I've ever known. Everything has shifted as he stands beside Nikolai, suddenly dwarfed. I want to know the purpose of this meeting. Nikolai is not an Italian associate, and he has no business being here.

An assistant pops her head in to alert me to the time, and my thoughts are swiftly refocused. I have less than five minutes to be upstairs. Papà apologizes for keeping me and says they will leave me to prepare. But Nikolai doesn't heed my father's words. He lingers unnecessarily, his eyes examining my face with unsettling curiosity.

"Tanaka?"

"Yes?"

His eyes cut through me. "Break a leg, won't you?"

"*Merde*," I correct him. "You don't tell a dancer to break a leg."

He shrugs, and with that remarkable impression, he leaves.

My fingers tremble as I reach for my pointes. I've spent hours preparing these new shoes—burning, smashing, sewing, altering—and when this performance is over, they will be ready for the trash.

My feet are battered and swollen, calloused and on the verge of deformity. The severity of my practice has left me no choice but to use ouch pouches. But as I look around the room, I can't seem to find them. I know they were here, and I didn't forget them because I never come unprepared. But they aren't here now, and I have less than ten minutes to curtain.

The decision has been forfeited. I have no alternative but to go without, since there isn't even a cotton ball to be found in my bag. The other dancers would surely have some on hand but asking for them would be admitting weakness. I would rather suffer an eternity in hell than admit I was weak. A principal would do whatever it takes, no matter how much it hurts.

And it hurts mercilessly when I squeeze my feet into the toe box.

I take three deep breaths and push until my foot is in position. The beautiful shoes don't take away my pain, but they do hide the ugliness of the sport. I sever the mental connection with the agony of my body before joining the rest of the cast. My guard follows dutifully behind me, weaving through the chaos that is the Met. Throughout the halls, the structure is alive and buzzing with art in its many forms. In the basement, the Met orchestra rehearses "Mahler's Symphony No. 1," while on a separate level, a craftswoman paints hundreds of flowers for Madama Butterfly. Somewhere between the wig room and costume shop and the class where our ballet mistress whipped us into shape earlier, there is hair and makeup, which I skip since I always elect to do it myself. At one point, we pass by a statue being erected for Tosca, and a rapper/drag queen who is more well known for his role as Prince Coffee.

Upon arrival at our final destination, the stage is already abuzz with energy. Dancers in costume whip out the moves they struggle with most, practicing tirelessly while they still have the chance. Also busy at work are the conductor, lighting manager, master carpenter, and stage manager. Just a few of the cogs that make this giant ballet machine purr.

There isn't enough time to prepare. The only faith I can subscribe to is my unwavering practice. I have lived, breathed, eaten, and slept with this ballet. My mornings are spent with the company. Warm-ups at the barre. Rehearsals and exercises followed up with more training on my own time. Yoga and Pilates for strengthening any of the perceived weaknesses jotted into my journal. I have subsisted with the intent that this moment would be perfection. That every chance I seize to shine will be perfection. If I am to be appointed principal, I must be faultless. Every role, large or small, is an opportunity to prove my worth. Time is not a dancer's friend, and when you are the daughter of Manuel Valentini, it can only be your enemy. I have a dream, short lived as it may be. As long as blood warms my veins, I will fight for it.

There are no excuses.

So when I am called upon, I float onto the stage, and I dance. Sometimes, false bravado is all you have. You can only hope and pray that you've done everything right. I slept for nine hours. I ate some light protein. I've stretched, though not as much as I would have liked. Now, I have only my skill to rely on.

The initial shot of adrenaline flooding my veins buffers the pain, gifting me false confidence. But upon stepping into my first *croisé* position, I become aware that something isn't right. The toe box is cramped, and I blame myself. I should have been better prepared. I should have tested the shoes one more time backstage to ensure everything was correct. But my duty was to my father. I must always do what's right.

The choreography lives on, and so do I. Regardless of the distraction, my moves are flawless, but I don't allow myself an ounce of arrogance. Every position is performed with care, each step precise and light. My father is watching from the audience, of that there is no doubt. I can't disappoint him. Every performance is a justification for the countless years I have dedicated to my practice.

I need ballet like I need air to breathe. It is my life. My heart. My soul. And the thing I fear most is what will become of me when I am no longer a dancer. I'm on track. For as long as I can remember, this train has been moving in one direction, and I'm going to get there. It's in my bones. It's the only thing I know for certain.

But Vivi would be quick to tell me that nothing in life is certain.

The first blow comes when I rise *en pointe*. White-hot agony pierces through my toes without warning, and warm, sticky blood fills the toe boxes.

I close my eyes and attempt to breathe through the pain while I come to terms with one unwavering certainty. My shoes have been sabotaged. There is nothing I can do but go on with the performance and pray I don't bleed onto the floor. Whatever tore through my flesh is already embedded there, and I don't care. I must finish at any cost.

I must not falter.

It is with this grand intention that my entire world topples in a matter of seconds. One leap and one failed landing, and it's all over.

As I crumple to the floor, the fear at the forefront of my mind is the snap I felt in my ankle. Logically, I'm aware an entire audience is present for the worst moment of my life, but I have disengaged. Clouded by disbelief, I attempt to get up, only to collapse again. My ankle no longer functions. It doesn't move.

I could think of a thousand ways I would rather die before someone finally takes pity on me and carries me off the stage.

"Have some mercy, won't you?" Papà's shadowed figure whispers from behind the curtain.

"Were you under any illusions that this might end differently when you made the agreement?"

"She is my only daughter."

"Ahh, yes. That does pull at the heartstrings, I suppose. But I believe she was also your only daughter when the matter of collateral was explained to you. If you are not happy with this solution, then perhaps you should pay the debt and be done with it."

"You know very well that I can't," my father says. "She is injured. At least allow her to heal, and then perhaps we can work something—"

"She can heal just as well under the supervision of my doctor."

"But the bills," Papà protests.

"You wouldn't be able to pay them anyway. They will be added to your debt. And when you come to collect, as I know you will, she will be good as new."

"I cannot stand for this. This is not the way she was raised. She is a good girl. Her reputation will be ruined—"

"What choice do you have?" the unforgiving Russian asks. "It is you or your daughter. And I'm afraid I have little use for you."

Silence follows.

THIEF

My eyes are still and closed, but sleep has evaded me. The trauma of this evening has drained me of my will to think, feel, or even breathe. I have pleaded with every deity I could think to summon. I have prayed. I have cried. I have swung violently between hope and despair.

Intellectually, I'm aware of what's taking shape right now between my father and Nikolai. But I can't find the presence of mind I require to care. What does anything matter when the only thing I ever wanted has been so viciously taken from me?

It still feels like a nightmare I can't wake up from. No matter how many times it goes round and round my mind, I can't force it to make sense. Certainly, incidents like these are not unheard of. Life in the world of ballet can be a blood sport. Jealousy is rife, and the competition is ruthless. But I never once thought anyone in my own company to be capable of such viciousness. The most I have ever been victim to is a dirty look or catty comment. Such an extreme measure has blindsided me, and I'm left to wonder how I didn't see it coming.

A hand grazes my arm, and when I open my eyes, my father is at my side, his face grim. Beside him is Nikolai, unnervingly quiet. He doesn't belong here, and I don't know why my father allowed it. My world has always been small, but the only thing I've ever known my Papà to be is powerful. His men do what he tells them. I do what he tells me. Everyone falls into order when he speaks. But not Nikolai. In this new chain of events, Nikolai is the one giving orders.

"Tanaka." Papà's voice doesn't waver, but it's softer than I've ever heard it. "There has been a change of plans. You must be a good girl and do as I say. Do you understand?"

My only response is to blink. I'm too numb to argue. I'm too wrecked to give him a verbal response. Something he would chastise me for at any other time.

"Nikolai has graciously agreed to provide some accommodations for you while I am away on business. There is no need to worry, though, little lamb. It will only be for a short while."

I don't have the emotional capacity to accept this as my reality right now. For years, my life has been on a straight course that never deviated. Principle and ballet. Those were my only goals, and I had such little time to make them happen. I was supposed to marry Dante. That's what I've been told. That's what I've been preparing for. For my entire life, I've been sheltered. Schooled at home. Forbidden from having friends or leaving the house. I could not be alone with a man, ever. It's what I've been taught and what I've always abided by. My father arranged my marriage, and it was set in stone. But now, he tells me he is sending me away with a man I don't know at all. One who appears to have none of the values instilled in me.

For a fleeting moment, I wonder what Dante will say. And then my thoughts gradually drift back to my company. A tear leaks down my cheek, followed by another. I don't know anything other than one unalterable truth. I'm a dancer. It's all I have. It's all I am.

When the doctor returns to discuss my fate, his face is clinical. Detached. And he barely glances at me before addressing my father as he's been instructed to do.

"Mr. Valentini, your daughter has ruptured two ligaments in her ankle—"

"No." I try to move, but one look from my father halts me.

"I'm sorry." The doctor looks at me now. "Your injuries will require surgery to repair the ligaments and remove the glass still embedded in your toes."

"But I'm a dancer," I whisper.

His eyes betray the words his bedside manner won't allow.

Not anymore.

CHAPTER 2
NIKOLAI

Kosmos—our Vory owned club—is a no-frills establishment. Women and booze are the main attractions up front, and in the back, we run our operations. Today is the 3rd of the month, which means I am due to report for our monthly meeting.

I arrive early to socialize, as is custom, but the man I'm really seeking out is later than usual. Alexei has been preoccupied with his new blonde toy as of late. I think we have all cut him some slack since he's long overdue for a female companion, and Talia seems to suit him.

Viktor approaches me during the social hour, his face drawn and his eyes tired. Many things have been weighing on his mind in recent weeks, and I can only hope I have not contributed to his worries. The *pakhan* to our Vory brotherhood, Viktor is the boss and our leader. He is mature in age and harsh in character, but overall, I find him to be a fair man.

"Kol'ka," he greets me. "How are you?"

"I am well. How is your family?"

He nods and takes a sip of his scotch. "Well enough."

There is a strained moment of silence between us in which I know what will come next, but I do not show weakness or make excuses. During our last meeting, I was promoted to the rank of *avtoritet* in my father's stead. An honor on any other occasion, but I am certain my father does not see it that way. Especially not after I cut off his ear at the order of Viktor.

"Have you heard from Sergei?" Viktor scans the room for the man in question.

"No, we have not spoken since our last encounter."

Viktor's brows knit together. "I don't suppose the events that took place that day bred good will between father and son."

"I understand why it had to be done."

"I will not stand for such behavior in our organization. Sergei took too many liberties with his position, and he did not deserve the title he bore."

"I agree."

I'm not saying so for the sake of pleasing Viktor. Sergei has always had a head too large for his shoulders, and it gets the best of him often. Familial blood or not, my loyalties lie with the Vory. If Sergei cannot live with our rules, then he is undeserving of the stars we bear.

"Any word on the Rembrandt?" Viktor changes gears.

"No," I admit reluctantly. Lately, my time has been preoccupied with other pursuits. Most notably, the acquiring of Tanaka Valentini. The time and effort I have spent to bring her into my possession have become a distraction, and my Vory duties have fallen by the wayside.

I could describe what I do in many ways, but the truth is the most simplistic. I am a thief at heart with art being my specialty. I steal it, and I create it, and sometimes, I even destroy it. It is a job unique to someone with my talents. Gone are the days of gangsters shaking down local businesses to earn a nickel or two. In the modern world, times have changed and so have our practices. Priceless art has a large collateral value in criminal organizations, and it is often used for bartering. However, with Viktor's blessing, I've chosen less primitive methods of utilizing the items in our possession to turn a profit.

Typically, the pieces I deal with are opportunistic ventures, but on occasion, I don't mind a challenge. At some point, Viktor determined a stolen Rembrandt would make a lovely gift to his eldest daughter, should I be able to track it down, but he's recently become more persistent.

"I don't suppose she would settle for a forgery?"

Viktor smiles. "Don't be daft, Kol'ka. She'd never know the difference, but I would."

"Indeed," I answer. I can respect that he only wants her to have the best. Something rare and priceless. And the hunt has always thrilled me. Finding something rumored to be lost for so many years gives me an adrenaline rush like no other. My travels have been extensive, and my recoveries worthy of a museum in my honor. But my position requires me to remain humble, no matter how big the score. Our clients value anonymity, and they would not pay such steep prices for something anyone could own. The stupidly wealthy are just another form of crooks, and they get off on the thought of owning stolen artwork, too. To be in possession of something so valuable they can only share it with their most intimate and trusted friends is a thrill that expensive trips or flashy cars can't replicate.

Viktor glances at his watch. The meeting is due to start in several minutes, but he is not finished with this conversation, and already I am weary of what comes next.

"I'm sure it will come as no surprise that I have some questions for you," he says.

"Of course."

"Tell me about the girl."

I drain the rest of my vodka and lime and dispose of the empty glass on the table. I have only been a*vtoritet* for several weeks. What I did was ballsy, and some might say stupid, but in my eyes, I have earned my title and the power that comes with it. This was not an impulse decision. I have been waiting my whole life for answers.

"She is the daughter of Manuel Valentini."

"I'm aware," Viktor muses. "He has requested several meetings with me already. What I want to know is why she is with you."

"Her father owes us a great deal of money. I am merely motivating him to pay it back in a timely fashion."

Viktor's dark eyes move to mine, lancing right through the half-truth. "Do not trifle with me, Kol'ka."

My eyes move over the room and land on Sergei, who has finally made an appearance. His head is still bandaged where his ear used to be, and he is absent of the smug expression he typically wears. It's safe to say he has come back with his tail between his legs.

"Does this have any relation to your father's business dealings in the past?"

I return my attention to Viktor, affronted by the observation. Discretion is a quality I take great pride in possessing, and it never crossed my mind that he would so clearly guess my intentions.

"There have been many rumors over the years." Viktor retrieves a cigar from his front pocket, pursing it between his lips as he speaks. "He once said himself that your mother ran off with an Italian."

"That isn't true." My tone is careful and deliberate, but it makes little difference. The fact that I am defending my mother at all is the answer to his question. When she disappeared from my life at the age of ten, the only explanation I was given was that she was a liar and a whore, and I was never to speak her name again.

Viktor gestures for my lighter, and I hand it to him. He lights up and takes a few puffs of the cigar while he settles on the right words. "The truth is, I'm not certain what happened to your mother. She was a good girl. Too sweet to be caught up with the likes of your father. If you do discover the truth, Kol'ka, I would like to know myself."

His words ground me. I did not ask for his blessing, but in his own way, Viktor has given it. He is aware of my true intentions, and I can do what is necessary now that we have come to an understanding.

Viktor checks his watch and abruptly decides this conversation is over. He announces that the meeting is about to start, and social hour is finished. The brothers file into the meeting room, and I walk beside the *pakhan*. Before we reach the door, one last thought occurs to him, and he halts me.

"There is just one thing I must insist on."

"Yes?"

His nose wrinkles in distaste. "The girl is not Russian."

"I'm aware."

He flicks a piece of lint off his jacket, the gesture symbolic of a warning. "So don't get attached to her."

"Do you like?"

The Russian dancer leans forward to show off her new pair of tits while I smoke a cigarette. Her name is Mara, and I fuck her on Tuesdays. Lately, she's been out of commission on account of the surgery. I haven't seen her around for a while, and now I know why. Beneath her tiny bikini top, the implants look like grapefruits. They don't move at all. I know because it came to my attention when I fucked her ten minutes ago.

Mara's wondering why I didn't touch them. She's pursing her lips, and those look a little swollen too, if I'm not mistaken.

A wisp of smoke coils out from the corner of my mouth. "They're lovely."

Sometimes it's better to lie. I'm a man who prefers sins of the flesh, not silicone. This will be the last time Mara and I meet. But while she's here and it's easy, I gesture to my dick, which is hard again.

The beautiful thing about a woman like Mara is that's all it takes. We are both too jaded to believe in love. She uses me for the void that Daddy left her, and I use her because it's uncomplicated. She does her best work on her knees, and there's no shame in that.

Long red fingernails scrape up my thighs. When she sucks my dick into her mouth, I lean back on a sigh and finish off my cigarette while she bounces up and down between my legs.

I like a room with a view, which is why I requested her presence in the gym today. Around us, her work is broadcast and reflected by mirrors on all four sides. But my eyes aren't on the mirrors or even her. They are on the door. And when it opens at exactly three o clock, I am not disappointed.

Honeyed eyes rake over me with contempt before settling on Mara's head in my lap. Tanaka makes a point to look at my dick, and then she makes it a point to appear unimpressed. She is a liar and a snob. When my eyes dip to her chest, two hard nipples scrape against the thin fabric of her white leotard. Pure like her virgin pussy. I'd be willing to bet my left nut that she is soaked for me, but she does well to hide it behind her disdain.

Frustration drives me to fist Mara's hair and shove my cock as deep as she can take me. I fuck her mouth while my eyes fuck the uptight ballerina across the room. The release is violent, and it happens sooner than I would have liked. Tanaka lost interest in my games before I could even get started.

My head falls back against the chair while my dick convulses in Mara's mouth. She tries to draw it out, but I am well and truly done.

Across the room, Tanaka sets up camp with her water bottle and tote bag, making it apparent she has no plans to evacuate anytime soon. For such an obedient Italian girl, she seems to have no trouble defying me. Her ankle is immobilized with a brace, and she is still hobbling around on crutches, yet she attempts to maintain an exercise regime worthy of a concentration camp.

"What is she doing?" Mara scrunches her face in bewilderment when she spies my new toy stretching her leg on the padded floor.

"Who knows." I zip up my pants and toss Mara her skirt. "But I have business to take care of."

Tanaka dutifully ignores the spectacle as Mara dresses unabashedly. When it's time for her to go, I do not give false assurances of another reunion, and she doesn't ask. I retrieve some cash from my wallet, not for sex, but because she's used to men taking care of her. She thanks me in Russian and leaves.

I should go too, but I find myself rooted in place, eyes on Tanaka. For two weeks, we have carried on this routine. There are no words exchanged between us. I spend my days with Vory business, and she spends hers chasing impossible dreams in this gym.

She came here without a fight, but with each day that passes, her resolve glows brighter. Ballet has been her life until now, and she has not yet come to accept that her old life is dead.

I lean against the doorframe and flick the lid of my lighter between my fingers. "Why don't you find a new hobby?"

Her golden eyes flash with fury, and to my own irritation, it stirs my dick back to life.

"Find a new hobby?" she clips.

"Yes."

"Are you truly that oblivious to the amount of my life I have dedicated to this 'hobby'?"

I make a flippant gesture to her useless ankle. "Does it matter now? I think it's time to stop beating a dead horse."

Her nipples are hard again. Almost as hard as her jaw when she's nettled. My eyes carve a path up the curve of her neck to the spot where her pulse thrums in staccato. She catches me staring and makes an unconscious effort to remain modest, tugging her skirt lower and the straps on her shoulders higher. A smile tugs at the corner of my lips, and she lays into me with a voice like a whip.

"From the age of six, I have trained as a dancer. You think your mafia is exclusive? Try the ballet, Mr. Kozlov. I attended summer intensive programs that most could only ever dream about. The corps de ballet offered me a contract before I even finished high school. While other children played outside and experienced all that childhood had to offer, I was in the studio. I have ascended the ranks of this hierarchy in spite of significant odds, and if we were to compare our worlds, then you and I would be equals. My entire life, I have bled for this dream, and you believe it is your right to casually suggest I find another hobby?"

A forceful exhale concludes her rant, but it seems to have stolen her precious energy along with it. Perhaps it is the recovery, but regardless of her fiery temper, she appears almost lifeless after the smallest exertion. Her present state is at odds with her mind, considering the girl is anything but weak.

From the moment she laid eyes on me, she believed herself superior. But the reality is that she is a spoiled little bitch who has been locked away in her castle too long. This girl who compares her ballet to my mafiya is completely ignorant of the world and how much power I hold over her fate. I expected as much of her.

What I did not anticipate was that she would be so lovely to look at. When Manuel offered up his prized daughter as collateral for a debt, I had decidedly painted her as a gargoyle in his image. But in truth, she looks nothing like him.

A waifish girl, she is too thin for my tastes. Her body is the testament of a struggle between femininity and girlishness. Caught in the clutches of both, it's undecided of which she wants or needs. But there is no denying the unnatural grace she carries. Whether it's the subtle flip of her hand or the curve of her leg, she is almost inhumanly beautiful. She is elegant, manicured, and well groomed. In short, she is everything I am not. Yet when I first saw her, I was admittedly captivated to the soft-spoken beauty in a way that was unfamiliar to me. She is nothing like the Russian girls I am accustomed to. She is nothing like any girl I am accustomed to.

She is undoubtedly intelligent, but the level of her naivety gives me whiplash. There is an innocence about her that provokes doubts in me. Doubts that are at odds with every value I stand for. The longer I endure her presence, the clearer it becomes. I would do well to stay away from her because she is of no importance to me. And as shameful as it may be to see something so lovely destroyed, it might come to that in the end. I must remember this. Whatever fate befell my mother, so too will Tanaka's be.

CHAPTER 3
TANAKA

There is no such thing as pain. There is only discipline.

My leg comes off the floor, only to collapse again a moment later. The defunct limb has failed me, just as the heartless Russian so rashly observed. Even the slightest movement produces a backlash of agony throughout my ankle. The muscles I have painstakingly forged over the years are dying. After a lifetime of abuse, the reckoning has finally come, and in turn, the dark cloud above looms larger.

Illogically, my deepest fear takes root in my gut. A vision of me crippled, unable to move or walk at all. I may as well be, if I can never dance again. My eyes burn with repressed emotion, but I don't give into it. Tears are a weakness I seldom indulge, and I'm not about to start now.

"Tashechka."

Nonna is in the doorway, hands tucked into the sides of her plain gray dress. Nikolai's housekeeper is a modest, quiet woman who favors simplistic dresses and headscarves to perform her duties. Since my arrival here, I have come to understand that those duties also apparently include me.

"Your lunch is waiting for you in your room." Her Russian accent is thick, but discernable.

Lunch, as she calls it, will likely be soup with a hearty meat dish and sometimes potatoes. Often, she includes a fruity drink with berries inside, the calorie content of which I don't know, but the sugary taste swiftly dissuaded me from consuming it. Already, in my time here, I have packed on five pounds, and the numbers on the scale from this morning's weigh-in still haunt me.

"I'm not hungry."

Nonna frowns, and I look away. I don't mean to disrespect her. She has been nothing but attentive. Too attentive, in fact, and it's the only reason for my ire. At home, I have a strict routine with my meals to keep me centered and focused, but here, food has turned to chaos. I am accustomed to providing my own meals. Often, I would be expected to cook my father's dinner. It was one of the many things he deemed necessary to prepare me for marriage. But my father stuck to the business of eating the food provided and scarcely paid attention to my plate. It was a system that worked for both of us. But since being under Nikolai's care, my meals appear like clockwork. Meals I have no right to enjoy when I'm not dancing. Even if I were, I'd rarely allow myself to indulge so often.

To my relief, Nonna disappears without a fight, leaving me to focus on my practice. It is the only thing I can focus on, present circumstances considered. Though it's sometimes tempting in my moments of despair, I refuse to ruminate on the stark reality of my situation. After only two short weeks, dancing feels like a distant memory. The blood, sweat, and tears I have devoted to my craft cannot have been for nothing. My position in the company will surely be at risk. I would be surprised if they haven't replaced me already. But these are thoughts I won't be a slave to. Abandoning hope now would mean sacrificing everything I have worked for merely because I do not possess the strength of will it requires to succeed.

It makes little difference that I have been traded for a debt. It is of no consequence that my father has betrayed me, and Nikolai will likely kill me if his demands are not met. I am intimately acquainted with impossible odds, and I have always resolved that, regardless, I would prevail. Vivi always told me that my mind was the most powerful weapon at my disposal, and she was right.

It is with this intention that I close out my practice and exit the gym. I tend to avoid Nikolai if I can help it, and so far, it hasn't been difficult. It's only on rare occasion that we come in contact since he dumped me in my room and informed me it would be in my best interest not to attempt to escape.

He should have saved his breath. Just like my father, Nikolai lives his life under lock and key. From everything I've observed so far, it's also apparent that his system is light years ahead of my father's as far as technology is concerned. Between the fingerprint scanners and pin codes and voice recognition systems, I am not entirely sure how anyone ever leaves. By challenging me to escape, he was merely indulging himself in a good laugh at my expense.

Even if those things weren't in place, there are other fail safes. Nonna is always watching me, aware of my movements. Her loyalty to Nikolai is unwavering, and I don't doubt for one second that she'd throw me under the bus the moment she got a whiff of trouble. More dangerous than Nonna are the guards who work for him. Vory members who come and go, speaking to each other in their native language and dutifully ignoring me.

Life at Nikolai's compound is familiar to the one I have always known, but I am still a prisoner. In that regard, nothing is new. The only variance is the scenery.

Nikolai's stone fortress is tucked away in the wilderness known as the Berkshires, which is just a hop, skip, and a jump from Boston. It is secure. Decadent, but built for function. Though I am free to roam the house, I have not made it a point to venture far from my bedroom or the gym. Nikolai often utilizes an office on the second level, and so far, I have done my best to avoid it. Dotted along the same grand hall are several bedrooms, including my own, and two bathrooms. Oddly enough, these are the most extravagant areas of the home, with heated floors and open stone showers.

Overall, I find Nikolai's tastes to be uncommonly old fashioned. In stark contrast to the modern technology that rules his security, the pieces in his home are highly individual and antique. Every chair, lamp, table, and rug are solidly built and well utilized with a long history behind them. While I hardly want to credit the man sporting the disorderly fauxhawk and motorcycle boots with choosing such fine, artistic furniture, somehow, I just know that he did.

Admittedly, certain qualities about him have blindsided me. He exudes an authoritative presence. The kind who could command an audience with one sweep of his glacial eyes. Rather than using this power for the greater good, it seems he chooses to deploy it on a large percentage of the female population as an expression of his virility. His omnipotent energy is a wasted gift on a soul devoid of even a speck of light within the shadows.

These are thoughts I will keep to myself. What he does or doesn't do with his life is of no importance to me. I only wish that I was not forced to witness the conquests so casually broadcast throughout the house. During my time here, I have been privy to a multitude already. One thing I can say with certainty is that Nikolai is not singular in his tastes. Brunettes, blondes, redheads—he partakes in every flavor. Why he chooses to display these activities openly remains a mystery I have no ambition to solve.

I may be untainted by the sins of the flesh, but I am not ignorant to the ways of men. In my world, it is an expectation that men indulge themselves at the end of a long day. Dante was no different, and I was brought up with the understanding that it was my place to turn a blind eye when my eventual husband sated his desires elsewhere.

It was not a difficult task—perhaps because he had not yet taken me—and I felt no ill will toward the women I didn't have to see. But Nikolai chooses to flaunt his escapades, and for reasons I can't understand, it bothers me more than it should.

THIEF

Today, however, I am lucky. When I stop at the threshold of his office, it isn't a woman I find, but another man. A man with startling blue eyes and a striking resemblance to Nikolai's build. He is also heavily tattooed and unmistakably Vory.

"Nakya." Nikolai addresses me with stiff familiarity. Diminutive forms of names are common in his culture, and even Nonna addresses me with one, but this is the first occasion Nikolai has done so. In any case, he makes it clear that this new terminology does not make us friends. His eyes pass over me with little interest in the cause for my intrusion. He merely wants me gone.

"I would like to make a phone call," I announce.

The blue-eyed stranger speaks to Nikolai in Russian, and in return, Nikolai murmurs a quick reply. From a young age, I was tutored in three separate languages, all of which would benefit my father in some way. Although Russian was one of them, my skills still leave much to be desired. Without speaking it often, I can only distinguish a few of the words between native speakers, who tend to converse much faster. From what I'm able to gather, the blue-eyed stranger is asking about me. He seems surprised by my existence, and in turn, Nikolai appears increasingly anxious to rid them of my presence.

"Nakya, this is Alexei," Nikolai states perfunctorily.

"Hello." I bow slightly, as I have been trained to do, only to realize the absurdity a moment later. These men are not of the same culture.

Alexei pierces me with an unrelenting stare. It occurs to me now that in my rush to make my sudden request, I didn't take the time to change into something more appropriate than a leotard and leg warmers. At home, my schedule is such that I tend to live in my ballet clothes, only dressing appropriately at night before my father returns. And at the company, it is not uncommon to see many of the dancers parading around naked. In ballet, you learn quickly that modesty comes second to necessity. Most of the costumes show everything anyway.

25

But the sudden flash in Nikolai's eyes alerts me that I am out of turn. When only a moment ago I told myself it didn't matter, now I can't seem to calm the erratic palpitations in my chest. By some sort of divine grace, I maintain my composure, hoping that Nikolai will dismiss me. The urgency of my phone call now forgotten, I am eager to return to the sanctuary of my room.

Nikolai grants my reprieve with a cool inflection in his tone. "I am busy, pet. Go to your room, and we will discuss this later."

I retreat as I've been ordered. But the entire way back, I gulp mouthfuls of air, dreading the turn of events my actions will bring.

"Nakya."

The chill of Nikolai's voice startles me, and when my eyes rise to meet his, a weighted awareness returns to my chest.

"What do you think you're doing?" he demands.

The magazine in my hands falls together. I was right to worry. His energy is dark and distinctly volatile. It was out of line barging into his office when he was in a meeting, but to admit it would be a mistake.

"I'm not doing anything." My voice is too soft, barely audible, but it does not tame the harshness of Nikolai's features.

"What do you mean to do, coming into my office dressed in ..." He gestures to my clothing. "It's not appropriate."

If he weren't so nettled, the irony of his declaration might be humorous, considering there are women leaving this house at all hours of the night in various states of disarray. What unspeakable offense I've committed by wearing a leotard is a puzzle only his mind can solve.

When he stalks toward me, instinct triggers me to hunch down and protect my head by curling into myself. My heart is sluggish, and my palms clammy as I wait for the inevitable. But when it doesn't come, I dare to peek up at him, only to find him frozen midstep, his expression uncertain and his eyes dazed.

His actions are at odds with the certainty I feel in my gut. Life has taught me well that when the storm comes, you take whatever shelter you can find. When he doesn't move, I dare to try.

Scrambling from the chair with feverish limbs, I hobble desperately in the direction of my only sanctuary—the bathroom. Deprived of my crutches and too far gone to reach for them, I'm nearly immobile. Even with the brace, pain splinters every step, and tears prick my eyes. Before I'm halfway across the room, my legs give out, and I collapse to my knees.

Nikolai watches wordlessly as I totter forward onto my elbows, clutching the carpet between my fingers as I crawl away like an injured animal.

"Nakya," he bellows. "Stop. Stop this right now."

Logically, I know I should, but I can't. I'm too terrified of what will happen if he catches me. And so I go on, dragging my body forward until my fingertips cross over the threshold of the cold bathroom floor. The marble gives me something concrete to grab onto, but it's of little use when Nikolai's iron grip catches me around my good ankle.

A strangled cry squeezes from my lungs when he flips me over and pins me down with the overbearing weight of his powerful body. There isn't a chance in hell that I could fight him off now. His pulse is strong and steady, his muscles unyielding. I'm out of breath and out of hope.

His hand hovers over my face, and I shake my head frantically, pleading to a higher power to save me. Calloused fingers come to rest on my jaw, contracting in warning.

"Stop," he repeats.

It's another wasted command, considering I couldn't move even if I wanted to. The wall of his chest has me trapped. My head spins and my pulse thrashes in my ears. Every breath is a labored struggle, and I think I might pass out.

"I'm not going to hurt you, *zvezda*. Breathe. Relax and breathe."

My hands come to rest on his biceps, determined to push him away. I can't take false comfort in his honeyed assurances. I don't want to. But right now, it feels like that's exactly what's happening.

He's a liar.

But if it's true, he's a convincing one. More skilled than perhaps even me. When my eyes clash with his, the fight in me dissolves.

He is blue. Hazy blue. Electrifying blue. Blue like the sea and the sky and the storms that rule my life. And right now, his blue is ruling over me. In a matter of seconds, he's rendered me a servant to the breezeless ocean in his eyes. They are soft around the edges, unmarred by the lines of time. Everything about him is harsh, but I did not realize his eyes could be so sedating.

I'm hyper aware of him now. The way he smells of tobacco and cloves and vanilla. His scent is smoky, dark, and faintly sweet. His body is warm and rigid. And I have witnessed men in all their muscular glory on the stage of the ballet, but I have never been so close to one. I have never felt a man's weight pressing into my body, making me feel small and soft in contrast. I have never stared so intimately into eyes like these while he touches my hair, untangling it from my face the way I imagine a lover would.

I've never had a lover. I've never been touched by a man or even a boy. But there is no mistaking which side of the spectrum Nikolai falls on. He is all man. And his domination of my smaller, weaker frame has left me feeling drunk and slightly disoriented. A battered driftwood wrestling with the tide. Rocking against the waves, desperate for solid ground, he's pulling me farther and farther from the shore. I'm going to drown in his energy.

"Stop." The word rushes from my parted lips, reeking of my desperation and confusion.

Nikolai halts, his hand still tangled in my hair. The air between us is thick and sticky. Hot and humid like an East Coast summer. His ocean eyes carve a path to my lips, and he is so close I can taste the cinnamon on his breath. I think that he might kiss me, and it horrifies me that I want him to.

I feel like I've been doused in ice water when he yanks away abruptly and without explanation. In the time it takes me to blink, his face has neutralized, the dangerous chemistry between us expertly defused.

"I'll carry you back to the chair."

His voice is without color or emotion. A man without feeling. Somehow, I am the one left feeling wrecked when he lifts me without effort and deposits me into the chair like a child.

This isn't right. None of this is right. When Nikolai stalks out the door without another word, my ankle throbs, and my chest does too.

I knew my captor was dangerous.

I just didn't realize how dangerous he was to *me*.

CHAPTER 4
NIKOLAI

"Were you able to find anything?"

Alexei glances up at me from his desk, his eyes cataloging every micro expression on my face. Born of necessity, the habit has become second nature to him. It's just one of his talents, but I am yet to find something Alexei does not excel at. Driven by an insatiable hunger to prove his worth, he is an overachiever in all things Vory related, bearing the title of cybercriminal genius and unrivaled master of the chess board.

While his achievements are many, his sacrifices are greater. For all the years that I've known him, I've known him to be a recluse. He chooses the safety of his home over the potential exposure of his secret. Though his seclusion is hardly necessary, considering most would never suspect he is mostly deaf. He learned to read lips after he lost his hearing as a boy, and if it weren't for Sergei making me aware, I would have never known myself. Even so, he is justified in hiding his affliction. Such an impairment is a weakness in our line of work. And though his condition makes little difference to me, Alexei does not see it that way.

Bad blood has tainted our relationship for as long as I can

remember, but our duty to the Vory brotherhood obligates us to civility. As far as any of the Vor know, the only common link between us is the stars we bear on our chest. They would never suspect that we also share DNA. I find it difficult to believe it myself sometimes, but the rivalry that lives between us can only be born from blood. He has always been jealous that I had our father's approval, and I have done well to nurture my own resentment of his freedom from Sergei. Brotherly affection has not grown with time, and especially not after the unforgivable offense I committed against him.

"Your answers are in the file," Alexei tells me.

He wants me to leave. He would like nothing better. And perhaps, I should. It's the easy thing to do. But each encounter only reminds me that we are not so different. Alexei would not have followed through on this favor if all hope were truly lost.

What my pride won't allow me to admit is that I do regret the actions that severed the trust between us. Had I known how much it would hurt him, I would have reconsidered my position on the subject. Some might say it is better to be blissfully ignorant, but in our world, it is a costly luxury. If a Vor is disrespected, he must be given the opportunity to reap his vengeance. Someday, I hope that Alexei will come to see it that way too. However, today is not the day to rehash history. Today, something else weighs heavily on my mind.

"What did you discover about her mother?"

Alexei's disposition remains flat. He could easily dismiss my questions. Already, he has granted me more than I expected, but I have a disturbing need to discuss this with someone. And regardless of the fact he hates me, I know my secret will be well kept with him.

"She died when Tanaka was twelve," he answers. "Suicide."

Retrieving the cigarettes from my pocket, I rap the packet against the desk. "I assumed she had left."

"You would be a fool to believe that," Alexei scoffs. "And you can't smoke in here."

I stuff the packet back into my jacket to appease him. "Perhaps.

Or perhaps it was that Manuel did not put up much of a fight when I volunteered to take his daughter instead of his throat."

Alexei's brows draw together as he leans forward. "Tell me what this is really about so you can stop wasting my time."

The answer gets lodged in my throat. It shouldn't matter what happened in Tanaka's past. The only thing that matters is what happened to my mother. Alexei is right. This is a waste of time. I reach for the file and push back from the seat.

"What purpose does she serve to you?" His question stops me, and when I look at him, a restless worry has taken root in his eyes. He has always been soft when it comes to women. The same was true with Katya. She was a whore and a liar, and Alexei could not see it for himself until I helped him along.

"What difference does it make?" I ask.

He doesn't answer, but he doesn't need to. His judgments dictated long ago that I'm cut from the same cloth as our father. Sergei can be vicious, and perhaps, I am like him. But the truth is I don't know.

"She is just a girl," I tell him. "Collateral."

Alexei moves his attention to the chess board always present on his desk while he contemplates my answer. I have little faith he believes me, but after picking his thoughts apart against the space that he knows best, he gives me the benefit of the doubt.

"There is one detail I didn't include in the file, if it interests you. I have been told that Mrs. Valentini wore a head scarf to hide her face."

"And why would she do that?"

"I suppose it was because she was horribly disfigured. Or so her maid tells me."

Upon my return to the house at midnight, I am surprised to find Nonna waiting up for me. Unconsciously, my eyes move up to the ceiling where Tanaka should be sleeping on the second floor. The first thought that comes to mind is that she has escaped. Her slimy mole of a father has come for her, and she has escaped.

"Nika, I am sorry to disturb you," Nonna sighs. "But something is troubling me."

"What is the problem?"

She gestures to the ceiling. "This girl, there is something wrong with her."

"What is it?"

"I try everything." Nonna purses her lips. "She will not eat. Picking at food like a bird all day. Very little. And sometimes, I hear her in the washroom, vomiting."

The vein in my neck throbs, stabbing against my skin as white heat congeals my blood. I will not stand for this behavior. She may have escaped punishment under her father's watch, but it won't be tolerated here. If anyone is going to destroy the girl, it will be me.

"I will take care of it, Nonna."

She reaches out to touch my arm. "Perhaps tomorrow?"

The concern on her face is sobering, but also frustrating. "Do you believe I would hurt her?"

Her mouth falls open, and she shakes her head quickly. "No, Nika. I meant no disrespect. It's just that she startles so easily—"

I leave her in the entryway, her words affecting me in a way they shouldn't. It is, in fact, the intention I set out with. I took possession of Tanaka with the understanding that it might eventually mean taking her life. These are the rules our Vory abide by. An eye for an eye is only fair and just. But admittedly, I did not expect Manuel's daughter to be so innocent and pure. And with every day that passes, her exotic beauty seems to infect my mind.

Being a Vor means never showing weakness, and I'm not of the mindset to start now. Despite my confliction, my course does not deviate as I move toward her bedroom. When I open the door, she startles, just as Nonna predicted, shooting up in bed and clinging to the sheet. A sliver of moonlight falls from the curtain, bathing her in soft light, and it gives me pause. She is too beautiful to wreck herself this way, and I have the sudden urge to question the authenticity of Nonna's words. But regardless of my uncertainties, the signs can't be ignored. She is weak and too thin. Something I credited to her endless routines was a misconception on my part.

"Hello?" Her voice is timid and frail as she attempts to make out the shadow in her doorway. This little mafia princess is always expecting wolves at her door, and it leaves me to wonder how often she has encountered men like me before. When I flip the light switch, her sleepy eyes adjust in phases, relaxing as they move over my features.

Irritatingly enough, her sudden comfort in my presence causes my dick to stir to life. She should not be relieved when she sees me. But what's worse is that the warmth of her feminine scent eases me too. I could think of nothing more relaxing than bathing in her scent right now. I would like to bury myself in it, fuck it, and douse my body with the fire of her skin to carry with me always.

These thoughts are dismissed the moment I realize the absurdity of them.

"Until you can show some respect for my hospitality, you are to remain in this room."

Her brows draw together, and she pulls the sheet tight around her, obscuring her hardened nipples and white camisole from my view. "What did I do to disrespect you?"

"It's your body you are disrespecting." I gesture to her willowy form beneath the blankets. "I have provided you with three nourishing meals a day, and you choose to waste them or deposit the contents in the toilet?"

Her eyes widen, and her hair falls loosely around her face when she shakes her head. She is embarrassed, and she is a liar.

"I forbid you to use the gym until you can show me that you have learned to eat properly."

"You can't do that," she cries out. "I'm still rehabilitating."

Desperation claws at her features, transforming her from a

sleeping beauty to a simpering child. Whatever relief existed before has now morphed into hatred. It's better this way. She should hate me, and she should know better than to defy me.

"The doctor will come to your room to continue physical therapy, but you can forget dancing until you are healed."

Her lip quivers, and for the first time, I think I might see real tears from her. This girl

is skilled at hiding her true emotions, but this seems to be the thing that will break her. How she can cling to something so violently troubles me deeply. It isn't normal behavior. Certainly not for someone who was aware that she would be forced to give it up once she married. Her reaction only fills my head with more questions and doubts, but I can't give voice to them.

I've established the boundaries, and I'm prepared to leave her to her sorrow, but she is not willing to let it go so easily.

"It was you," she sneers. "Wasn't it?"

I arch an eyebrow at her, waiting patiently to hear the crime I am accused of.

"I have gone over it so many times," she says. "The events of that night. It's no coincidence that you showed up to take me away the same day someone sabotaged my shoes."

I smile at her naïvety. "That would be the easiest thing to believe, I suppose. Wouldn't it?"

"It's the truth," she insists.

"Ahhh but, Nakya, the truth is I think you know who sabotaged your shoes. I had nothing to gain by doing so, and I would have taken you regardless. But I was not the one who wanted you to give up nonsensical dreams, so you could marry in the traditional way."

Her lips slam shut, and she doesn't say another word on the subject. But it's just as well.

I've made my point.

CHAPTER 5
TANAKA

With the light of morning comes a renewed sense of hope. When I slip from my bed, the house is quiet, and my breakfast is waiting on the dressing table. Everything is as it should be. I'm confident that when I walk to the door and turn the knob, I will laugh at the absurdity of my dreams last night.

But the knob doesn't move regardless of how I turn it because it wasn't a dream and he's locked me in here. My palms lock into fists at my sides, and I resist the urge to slam them against the door.

I have always been a prisoner, and in that regard, nothing has changed. But the cruelty lies in the small taste of freedom Nikolai granted me before he snatched it away. He thinks he can alter my strength of will by challenging me in this way, but he doesn't know that I've already walked the streets of hell and dealt with devils worse than him.

His attempt to blame what happened on my father or Dante is weak and pathetic. He is a liar and a thief, and there is no honor in his word. I refuse to believe anything other than what's obvious. As my mother always used to tell me, the simplest answer is usually the correct one.

THIEF

The room isn't ideal, but I can still make the situation work. I can continue to practice and work on strengthening my ankle. But now that I'm aware of Nikolai's intentions, I must stay ahead of them.

I chop up my breakfast to dirty up the plate. It's a trick I learned long ago, and it's never failed me yet. When I'm done, I scrape all but a few small remnants into the toilet and flush with a resounding sense of victory. This has always been the one area of my life where I've had complete control, and I'm not about to let him change that.

With the ruse complete, I take to the floor for warm-ups before moving on to some makeshift barre exercises in the closet. For the entirety of the day, it's rinse and repeat. Work and rest. Work and rest. When my body breaks down and can go no further, I take a small amount of nourishment to fill my tank. Sometimes, when I go too far, I purge it all back up with a healthy dose of self-hatred.

It's a cycle I learned from watching my mother as a child. I once heard her mention that my father thought she was fat, and that was why he didn't love her. In a drunken slurry of words, she uttered something I could never forget. *You have to stay pretty, Tana. You must be pretty and thin, so love won't evade you too.* It scared me to witness her breakdowns, and I decided at a young age that she was probably right. The best ballerinas were thin and pretty, and I wanted to be loved just like them.

Some might say it's not healthy, but until Nikolai, nobody has ever complained about my eating habits. He has falsely deluded himself into staking a claim over my body. The body I have worked so hard for. He can have my life. My freedom. Even my hours in the day. But he will never have my body.

As a testament to that, I'm prepared to continue my routine as best as I can within the confines of my room. I need to warm the muscles in my body before moving onto static stretches, all of which can be difficult with the brace. A few of my favorite dynamic movements are shoulder rolls and leg swings, now aided by the assistance of the dressing table. But before I can even begin, the lock disengages on the door.

Ice blue is the first thing I see, and subsequently feel when chills crawl over my body. My captor doesn't need words when his energy is dark like this. It billows into the room like smoke and chokes the life out of everything inside.

Running is not an option, and I am not one to quickly forget difficult lessons learned. My first instinct is to curl into myself. But the wolf at my door doesn't move. He doesn't even appear to breathe. His legs are planted wide, his nostrils flared, and his eyes are so flinty I'm desperate for the sanctuary of my bed.

"*Zvezda*." His irises track the lines of my body like a true hunter, indexing my weaknesses. "Your father took specific care to inform me that you were a good, obedient girl. He said you had been raised to do as you were told and would not be any trouble."

I swallow, and the lie comes out with a choked quietness. "I am."

Nikolai tilts his head to the side, his lips curling into a cruel smile. "Yes?"

"Yes."

"Do good girls lie, Nakya?"

My heart thrashes against my ribs, and my stomach churns. I don't know what he knows. He is toying with me, and the unpredictability scares me more than anything. In my own environment, I have come to know what to expect. But this is not my natural element, and I truly don't know what this man is capable of.

"No." The word is a whisper. A hope that the simple acknowledgment will make him disappear.

"No," he agrees. "They do not."

The space between us looms quietly. Nikolai is not in any hurry to break the silence and the long stretch of time only compounds my nerves.

"You seem intent on defying me," he finally says. "And naturally, I am left to wonder why you are obedient to your father but not me. Do I look like the kind of man you want to trifle with?"

I shake my head.

"Use your words, princess."

THIEF

"No," I say, too loudly.

And again, my instincts urge me to run. But Nikolai won't allow it, and he makes it known when he stalks toward me. I screw my eyes shut because it's always better not to see what's coming. But the draft moves past me, and curiosity gets the best of me. When I open them again, he's disappeared into my closet.

He's touching all my things. I am left to bear witness as he jerks my ballet clothes from the racks and bundles them into his arms.

"Those are mine!" I move on autopilot, stealing what I can from the racks, tossing each piece into the corner and guarding them with my life.

Nikolai turns and sizes up my pathetic little pile to the one he has already claimed. "It appears I haven't made myself clear, pet. So let me do so now. I own you, and I can do whatever I like."

My head rattles, and I'm at a loss. It feels like he's stealing my soul. I don't know how to deal with this kind of insanity. "Please—"

"You have disobeyed me. Save your begging for someone who might listen. Right now, you are wasting your breath."

"I've done nothing wrong," I declare.

His eyes tell me otherwise. "You flushed your breakfast down the toilet, did you not?"

I flinch, and that's when it occurs to me. He has cameras in my room. Possibly my bathroom. *And he's watching me.* I can't believe I didn't think of it before.

The truth is too raw to accept. I don't want to know what he's seen. My private moments. My grueling workouts, followed by the horrific breakdowns. My obsession with food. These struggles are mine, and they are intimate.

"You are sick!" I yell. "How dare you watch me in my private moments? How dare you spy on me? You are filthy, and disgusting, and it's no wonder you fill your life with meaningless encounters. Who could want you—"

My tirade is cut short when Nikolai tosses my clothes onto the floor and produces a flask from his jacket pocket. I watch noiselessly as he douses the pile of leotards and tights in fluid and strikes the wall with a match.

For a few stunned moments, I'm immobile, unable to fully comprehend the sight before me. He truly is a madman. He is without mercy, tossing the match onto the pile and igniting my life in flames. My thoughts are scattered and disconnected, and all reason has escaped me when I fling my body toward the flames in a desperate attempt to salvage what I can.

Nikolai intercepts, capturing me around the waist and pinning me against the wall. I claw at his hands and then, when that doesn't work, his face. I'm not thinking about the consequences. I'm only thinking about the crime he has committed against me. His actions have inexplicably split me wide open, stirring to life the dormant rage that lives inside me.

When I draw blood, I'm quick to discover that I have the capability of stirring Nikolai's rage too. All men want to be powerful, and my captor exerts his by collaring me around the throat with the meaty flesh of his palm. His methods are brutal and effective. I fall limp in his arms, waving the metaphorical white flag. He's made his point, and I have learned my lesson. But he isn't done. He isn't even reachable right now. His dead eyes are looking right through me. My hands move to his, feebly attempting to remove the block against my airway.

It occurs to me that I should beg. I should plead. *Keep fighting*. But between those thoughts, there are other, darker thoughts. What is there to fight for? My ankle is ruined. My losses and agonies have been greater than any contentment I've ever known. I would be a fool to withhold hope that I can control my destiny. I am bone-tired of facing each new day and the challenges it brings. And when blackness creeps into the edges of my vision, the decision is made for me. My body doesn't have the strength to fight, even if I wanted to. All that I'm capable of now is watching the dying embers fade from the monster's eyes before me.

THIEF

Fragments of reality pull me back into the world at a sluggish pace, stealing any hope I held for a peaceful death. My mouth is dry as cotton, and my head is thick with fog. Light flickers in and out of my vision, and when I see the blue of my monster, acidic tears burn the back of my eyelids. How could I ever believe in heaven when I am stuck in hell with him?

I'm uncertain how much time has passed since everything grew dim, but Nikolai is still here. Only this time, he is beside my bed, wearing a tortured expression on his face.

"*Zvezda*, I—"

What sounds vaguely like the makings of an apology tapers off to nothing. Just as I suspected, he is a coward. I don't want his wasted words. I want nothing further to do with him, and I find a bitter satisfaction in the claw marks left on his brutishly striking face.

I meet his gaze and hold it. "You may burn my clothes, Mr. Kozlov, and I will still dance naked. You may beat me or touch me in ways you have no right, and still, you won't break me. I'm telling you this now, so if it is your intent, then go on and do your worst to me."

Nikolai shows no visible reaction to my statement, and if he weren't looking directly at my face, I might not even be certain he heard me. I wish he would just leave so I could get back to my work. But he doesn't. He lingers wordlessly, his eyes moving over my tender throat with painstaking precision.

It's only when I attempt to sit up that the muddled situation becomes clear. He has no need to argue. When I struggle with the imprisonments on my limbs, I feel as though I'm being strangled all over again. He has bound me from moving at all. I jerk against the restraints in vain, and Nikolai flinches.

"You can't do this!"

But he can, and he has. He won't look at me. Why won't he look at me anymore?

He issues a subdued request in Russian, and a woman in a white lab coat wheels in an IV stand.

"What are you doing?" I thrash against the restraints. "You can't do this!"

Nikolai speaks to the woman in Russian, and it doesn't take me long to understand that she is a Vory doctor. He issues his orders, and she obeys.

When her eyes fall on me, I shake my head and plead for any scrap of mercy she might possess. "Please, you can't."

She purses her lips and reaches for a medical bag. "Is for your own good. You will see."

A high-pitched sound vibrates off the bedroom walls, and the shock on Nikolai's face is the only indication I have that it's originating from me. I'm screaming. Crying and begging and kicking, desperate to break free.

This time, it's the doctor who issues a command to Nikolai. Across the room, his eyes move to mine, and for a few fleeting seconds, he spares a glimpse of his humanity. He is hesitant. It's fast, only a flash in time, and if I blinked, I would have missed it, but I didn't. I saw his moment of weakness, and I'm desperate to nurture it.

"Please," I beg.

I become nonexistent to him again when he falls into order and holds my arm firmly in place as the doctor establishes the IV. I stop thrashing, but only because I'm afraid of the needle.

"What are you giving me?"

They both choose to ignore me, but their responses aren't necessary. The effects of the sedative make themselves known around the time the doctor begins making her preparations and understanding dawns on me slowly. It isn't just a sedative I'm getting today.

It's a feeding tube.

Chapter 6
Nikolai

In the Charlestown neighborhood of Boston, my Audi R8 idles just down the cramped street from the address written in my file. Standard and unassuming, the apartment building on Essex is about what I would expect.

My fingers drum a solo over the steering wheel as I contemplate turning around. There are other ways. I could send Tanaka and her emotional baggage back home to her father. Torturing him for answers would be just as effective and less of a headache than dealing with her obvious mental issues. It would save me from the constant frustration I have felt since she entered my life.

But it would not be justice served. Manuel can't comprehend suffering until he experiences it for himself. This is the whole point of vengeance. Since I was a boy, I have vowed the day would come when I would discover the truth about my mother. If she was a liar and a whore who abandoned us, then so be it. But if she wasn't, then I would avenge her and know for certain the true nature of my father.

If Sergei knew my intentions, he would laugh in my face. He

would say that I have never forgiven her for leaving and I am only clinging to the hope that she loved me when she never truly did. Like my father, he raised me to believe that he would always be honest with me, even if it hurt.

His words didn't inspire warm feelings, but as a boy, I accepted the only reasonable explanation for my mother's abrupt departure from my life. I admired my father for his strength. For his ability to carry on without her when inside I felt as though something had shattered and it would never be put back together again. But with age came perception. Over time, I came to understand that Sergei was not exactly the hero I had always painted him to be.

Carrying on without answers is no longer an option for me. The torturous dreams that visit me in my sleep demand to be solved. Her ghost has long haunted me, tainting every aspect of my life. Triggering fears that no grown man should have inside.

You are filthy and disgusting, and it's no wonder you fill your life with meaningless encounters. Who could want you?

Perhaps, the beautiful little dancer was right. Perhaps, there was truth in her words, and that was why I was so desperate to silence them.

I shut off the engine and look up the street.

The maid's apartment is not far removed from Nonna's living quarters at mine. Sparse, with only the essentials for a comfortable living and little else. The space is absent of the usual racket in modern homes, and it smells like tea and freshly baked bread.

I find her rocking in a chair at the end of the hall, her hands making quick work of two knitting needles and some yarn. The woman who I'd estimate to be in her seventies barely blinks when she notices me looming on the threshold of her room. The bedside lamp illuminates her pajamas and the pistol she keeps beside her.

THIEF

"What do you want?" she asks.

She doesn't care to know who I am, and I don't imagine this is the first time she's had an unexpected guest. Nor will it probably be the last. If Manuel Valentini had any consideration for his former employee, he would have sent her off to a warmer climate where nobody knows her name and she could enjoy her retirement properly. But as it stands, it doesn't look like this woman received much of a severance package.

"My name is Nikolai," I tell her. "You have no reason to fear me."

Her hands pause long enough for her to look up and study my features. And more notably, my visible tattoos.

"You are Vory," she observes. "*Thief in law*."

I nod, unfazed by her sharpness. Her many years of service to Manuel undoubtedly gave her an intimate education of the many different criminal factions on the East Coast. The answer to be determined is where her opinion falls on my brotherhood.

"So, *thief*?" She squints at me in the dim light. "I will ask you again. What do you want?"

"Answers."

Her attention once again diverts to her knitting, effectively dismissing me. "Then you may as well leave. Or kill me if you intend to try, but I will warn you not to judge me by my size or age. I am a quick draw, and I will not succumb to torture, try as you might."

Her response warrants respect, and I intend to show it. While there is a time and place for violence, it isn't with elderly women. Or women, in general ... *if I can help it.*

The pretty broken doll haunts my memories, her body limp in my arms. She is so strong of mind that I did not anticipate her body to be so frail. The incident further proved the need to rectify her behaviors before she dimmed her own light forever. It also proved that I am incapable of defending myself against the toxic words she flings my way so carelessly.

Filthy. Disgusting.

Who could want you?

My fingers itch for a cigarette, but it isn't the time. I need to focus. I need to remember why I'm here.

"Your name is Aida, yes?"

The maid doesn't answer. Her hands are absorbed in her knitting, but I have no doubt her mind is conscious of every movement I make.

"I believe you worked for Manuel Valentini for a number of years, and I have some questions about his mistresses."

She snorts. "Then you are better to ask him yourself."

The creaking of her chair is the only sound left between us, but it does not deter me. I understand her reluctance to talk. If she even entertained the idea of snitching on Manuel, she could easily be dead come tomorrow.

It is not often that I change my approach. If a Vor wants answers, he simply commands them by any means necessary. But women are softer, and I know I must find a way to appeal to this side of her. If I had to venture a guess, this woman would have been in Tanaka's life at the time she needed a mother figure most. It's not the thing I want to discuss, but for now I will entertain the notion.

"Perhaps you can assist me with something else. What about Tanaka Valentini?"

Aida stops knitting. "What about her?"

"She is a temporary guest at my home," I answer. "But it has come to my attention that she doesn't like to eat."

It's minor, but I don't miss the drooping of her features. Tanaka was special to her. There was a connection there. And I need her to tell me everything about it.

She sets her knitting aside to rest her hands in her lap. "How do I know you are telling me the truth?"

I fish the phone from my pocket and access the live feed of Tanaka's room. The doctor is gone, and she is resting, the trauma of earlier events forgotten in her sleep. She looks like a goddess on her white satin sheets, but it pains me to see the tube taped to her nose.

THIEF

I show the image to Aida, and she studies it for a few moments to be sure. When she has drawn her own conclusion, her attention returns to my face.

"What is she doing with you?"

"It's only until her father pays his debts. But I can't in good conscience allow her to desecrate her body."

Aida shakes her head. "Then you will try until you are blue in the face. If you want her to eat, I am not the person to ask. To be frank, I'm amazed she has survived for this long."

"Then perhaps you can tell me why she does it."

"What difference would it make?" She shrugs. "The girl is sick. She needs help. But her father never allowed it."

Her indifference is forced. It would be a weakness to admit she cares, but her will is close to bending. I need her to keep talking.

"Why wouldn't he allow it? I was under the impression that she was special to him."

Aida purses her lips. "She is a mafia princess. You should know these things, *thief*. Her life has been sheltered. No outside influences. That is the only way, I suppose, to keep her safe."

"I am open to suggestions."

The old woman sighs, shoving her bottle thick glasses up the bridge of her nose. "Try minestrone. Her mother used to make it for her as a child. She would always eat it when I made it too."

My lungs expand, and I feel lighter. Perhaps it's relief, but every scrap of information I gather about Nakya only fuels the fire inside me demanding to know more.

"You can't force her," Aida adds. "It's not the way with her. She is obedient but stubborn. If you tell her she must do something, it will only encourage resistance."

There is no question I forced the feeding tube on her. But after the doctor's examination and report, we both agreed it was necessary. I don't like forcing nourishment on Nakya, but if I must do it to keep her alive, I will.

"Can you tell me more about her mother?"

Aida's brows knit together. "What does that have to do with anything?"

"I have heard rumors, and I am curious what happened to her."

"The same thing that will inevitably happen to Tanaka," she says. "It's the mafia way."

"Her mother killed herself," I argue. "Tanaka is not of such weak disposition."

"If you know already, then you have no need to ask these things of me."

"I only want to know more about her so I can help."

"Sure, you do." Aida snorts. "You want to help as long as it benefits you."

She is right, and to deny it would be an insult to her intelligence. Aida is done with this line of questions, and I'm out of angles. There are other avenues. It will take more time, but she is not the only possible lead.

I turn away, and her voice fills the silence.

"I'm an old woman. I just want to live out the rest of my days in peace."

"Nobody will know I've been here," I assure her. "You have my word."

"What good is a *thief's* word?"

I pivot to meet her cloudy gaze. "You tell me."

She points down the hallway. "Go to the kitchen and I'll make us a cup of tea."

I do as she instructs, and Aida is not far behind, shuffling along in her robe and slippers. She busies herself with the preparations while I take a seat in an uncomfortably small vinyl chair at the kitchen table.

While the kettle warms, Aida sets the table for tea. Cups, saucers, sugar cubes, and creamer. She adds a plate of freshly baked banana bread from the microwave, and I eat two slices while I wait. Throughout the process, her eyes move to me often. She is still uncertain of my motives, and when she comes to sit across from me, I think she is undecided how much of the truth to indulge.

"Tanaka was a bright little girl," she tells me. "Smart and inquisitive. Her studies taught her everything that a girl of her stature should know, but it was never enough. Her mind was always full of questions, and that curiosity would sometimes get her into trouble."

My lip curls at the corner, though it should make no difference to me what the little dancer was like as a child.

The kettle whistles, and Aida brings it to the table, pouring it over the tea bags before resting it on a hot pad. She resumes her seat, the steam fogging her glasses as she stares into the cup.

"I have never in all my years witnessed such a determined child. When she went to her first ballet, that was it for her. It was the thing she wanted to do, and nothing else could captivate her attention from that day forward. Not even her studies. She wanted to set her own course. She wanted to perfect every move before she even learned the basics."

I remove the tea bag from my cup and add a cube of sugar. "It sounds like very little has changed. She never seems to think of anything else."

Aida prepares her own tea with sugar and cream. "It was an escape for her. At first, I thought it was good for her to have a childhood dream. It allowed her a space away from her life. I could see it on her face when she danced that she was in another world. But when her mother died, it became her only world, and she retreated there far too often. I tried to find other outlets for her, but it did not work. Nothing ever worked. The only time she was happy was when she danced."

I venture another try at the question that continues to plague me. "What happened to her mother?"

This time, Aida doesn't hold back. "Manuel happened."

"I have heard that she often wore a veil."

"She never took it off." She shakes her head. "Not after—she was horribly disfigured."

"By Manuel?" I press.

She hesitates but nods. "He carved her face up with a knife so that no man in his employ would ever be tempted by her beauty."

My blood burns, and it only serves to bolster my case against him.

"And what about Tanaka? Did his violence touch her as well?"

Aida's brows come together, and she pauses to take a sip of her tea. "I never witnessed it."

"She flinches at the slightest movement. There must be a reason."

"I never witnessed it," Aida reiterates, "but it doesn't mean it didn't happen. There were times she would be locked in her room for days, and I was not permitted to see her. But I saw the bruises, and that was enough. She blamed it on the dancing."

Her response satisfies my suspicions, but there is no satisfaction in discovering the true nature of Tanaka's father. Manuel Valentini destroys beautiful things. Manuel Valentini doesn't deserve to breathe. And one day, when I am certain I have wrung every ounce of suffering from his soul, I will destroy him too.

"You inquired about his mistresses," Aida observes. "There must be a reason you have kept Tanaka alive. So, who is this woman you seek?"

I finish my tea and move the plate away. There is no point skirting around the topic. This is what I came here for.

"Her name was Irina. I believe she came into Manuel's life around fifteen years ago."

Aida folds her wrinkled hands across the table and studies me. "And who is Irina to you?"

I could lie, and I probably should. But like me, Aida is not a woman to be trifled with. She values honesty, and I respect her enough to admit the truth.

"She was my mother."

Her face wrinkles, and she hunches forward with a sigh that I suspect she's withheld for years. "I don't know of an Irina, but that doesn't mean anything. Manuel had many mistresses who he kept outside the home. I only hope for your sake that you are mistaken in assuming she was one of them."

My pulse throbs as I look at her for the answer. "Why?"

"Because they are all dead now."

CHAPTER 7
TANAKA

For seven days, I have remained captive to my newly acquired NG tube. Every morning without fail, the doctor comes to my room at six to begin the all-day ordeal that is my feeding schedule. In the blink of an eye, my life has been reduced to a series of nutritional shakes and nothing more. Today is no different, and I have the urge to retch when she appears with the meal replacements and syringes I have come to hate.

Dr. Shtein tells me it could be worse. She explains that this is the least invasive option as far as tubes go, having it inserted directly through my nasal system and down my esophagus. Her words came with a warning that if I had any bright ideas about pulling it out, the tube could also be inserted directly into my stomach through surgical means. Needless to say, I haven't had the courage to remove it.

The tube irritates my nose and it feels like I have a garden hose stuffed down my throat. The liquid nourishment she forces into my stomach disgusts me and makes me wish I could vomit at every meal.

I've been granted no other choice than to accept the complete loss of control over my body. As a skilled liar and manipulator, I thought I had a wealth of tactics at my disposal. But Dr. Shtein is not one to be easily swayed. My pleas have gone unanswered, and bartering only makes the doctor shake her head. She can't be won through false claims of illness, and it seems there isn't a circumstance in the world that will get me out of the constant feedings.

Since her abrupt seizure over my life, I've had little else to do but wonder who this woman is. The amount of time she spends with me throughout the day indicates she has no other post. She is a doctor for the sole purpose of being on the Vory payroll. The array of medical equipment at her disposal dictates that she has a long leash as far as finances go, and since our first encounter, I have found myself subject to a host of tests under her direction.

Outwardly, I hate her. I want to curse her name and subject her to as much pain as she has given me. But inwardly, she is my only source of comfort. Nikolai has not returned. In his absence, there is only Nonna, who speaks very little. When she comes to my room, she will not meet my eyes, and I know it's because she betrayed my secret.

I am restless and irritable and on the verge of fracturing. If I allow my thoughts to drift to the weight I've gained over the past week, it will break me. If I ruminate on the length of time it's been since I've trained, I will lose all hope completely.

While I seek asylum from my own mind, the doctor checks my vitals. Pulse, temperature, blood pressure. It's more than I ever had tested as a child. Other than my childhood vaccines, I never had the occasion to visit a regular health clinic. I can only remember that when I was sick, the doctor on my father's payroll would write a prescription without even seeing me. My father ruled his kingdom with an iron fist, and outsiders were strictly forbidden. But such does not seem to be the case with Nikolai. His home seems to be a revolving door of outsiders, which has now come to include my physical therapist and Dr. Shtein.

"When will I be free to eat on my own again?" I ask.

Dr. Shtein looks at me, and her face is blank. This is business for her, but I know from the conversation I overheard with Nikolai it was her idea.

"When you can prove you are capable of doing so on your own," she answers.

"How can I prove it if I'm restrained?" I argue.

She wheels one of the machines out of the way and pulls her chair closer to the bed. "How long have you had this behavior toward food?"

"I don't know." It's a lie, and she knows it.

Her phone chimes, and she checks it discreetly before turning her attention back to me. "If you aren't ready to be honest, then I have no reason to reconsider my treatment."

I swallow, and it feels like there's a clump of flour lodged in my throat. I don't want to live another day strapped to the bed and subjected to feedings like a child. It's inhumane and humiliating. Over the course of a week, I have lost every ounce of dignity I possessed.

"I can't remember when it started," I admit. "But I was very young when I learned to choose foods that had the fewest calories. I filled my diet with those and little else. It was what my mother did."

"So this is a learned behavior," she observes.

I don't answer because I don't want her to think badly of my mother. My mother was a good person. She did the best she could to raise me in her circumstances.

"Have you ever been treated by a doctor before for this condition?" she asks.

"No."

"So you are not aware of the damage you have done to your body?"

I try to swallow again, but I can't. My throat is too dry, and I'm afraid of her cruel words. It can't be that bad. I feel fine.

"You are just trying to scare me."

"Do you know what osteopenia is?" she returns.

THIEF

I shake my head, and I want to tell her to stop because it doesn't matter what it is. I don't have it.

"You have not provided your bones with adequate calcium for a very long time," she says. "The progression of damage is a very simple one, with osteoporosis being the next award for your starvation. At which stage, it would be highly unlikely you would ever dance again."

"That isn't true." At least, I don't want it to be true, but she takes no mercy on me.

"You are an athlete who does not provide your body the necessary fuel to maintain the muscles required for your sport. In essence, your body is eating itself alive. Your heart is under extreme duress, and the only possible result of such continued behavior is heart disease and inevitable death. Do you understand that without treatment, it's very possible you could be dead before you ever see your thirtieth birthday?"

Moisture fills my eyes, but I don't want to believe it. It isn't true. It can't be. Only to prove her point, the doctor takes the discussion a step further by showing me the results of the many tests she has run and explaining them as if she's speaking to a child.

"Mr. Kozlov will not allow this behavior to continue while you are under his care. Without your cooperation, I can provide the nourishment you need, but it will only last as long as the treatments. In the end, it's up to you. You must make the decision whether you want to live or die."

"It can't be that simple," I maintain. "I feel fine."

"You feel fine because your body has only known starvation. Inside, you are not fine. You have been undernourished for so long that you do not know what healthy feels like."

If there was an argument to be found for that statement, I would supply it. But I can't seem to convince her, or even myself, that I am still right.

The doctor abandons her chair and collects her things. "When you are ready to participate in your recovery, then we can move forward. Until then, I suggest you get used to the bed."

ON THE TENTH day of my incarceration, Nikolai finally makes an appearance. His face is drawn, and the shadows under his eyes darker than I remember, but even so, his presence has a way of commanding my attention, regardless of how much I hate him. When I look at him the way he is right now, quiet and pensive, he does not look like the monster who did this to me. He does not look like the man who commandeered my life and trussed me up with puppet strings.

Today, he is just a man with tousled hair and enough stubble on his jaw to appear edgy. If I saw him on the street, I might even—for a fleeting moment—think he was recklessly handsome. He doesn't seem to have any trouble in that department, so I suppose women do consider him handsome. But I shouldn't.

I've had over a week to prepare my case against him. Shouting and carrying on like a child will get me nowhere. My emotions controlled me before, but now it is time to utilize the knowledge I have learned over the years. I'm a skilled manipulator. An even better liar. And maybe I'm overconfident, but I believe this hardened criminal can be convinced of my good intentions if he gives me the chance.

"Nakya." He nods in my direction. "How are you feeling?"

"Much better."

The words taste like acid, even if they are true. The things that the doctor told me only a few short days ago have been rolling around my mind like a wrecking ball, destroying everything I thought I knew.

Perhaps, I was slightly undernourished. It's hard to argue otherwise when the changes in my body become apparent with each passing day. The fog has lifted, and my energy levels have too, which is not ideal considering my current position. What is the point of being healthy if I'm unable to move?

I look up at Nikolai. My captor and my savior, depending on the day. Today, I need him to be my savior. His ocean eyes wash over me, and a rush of warmth floods my veins. His eyes are loud, electric, and undeniably captivating. Always evolving like the clouds in the sky, they never look the same from one moment to the next.

"The doctor reports that your health is improving," he says.

"It is. I did not realize . . ." The words don't come easily, and it's not an act. "I was not aware of how bad my health was."

Nikolai settles into the adjacent chair and reclines with his legs spread wide, thumbs toying with a cigarette he is yet to light.

"*Zvezda*, I am not an ignorant man. Do you think you can win me over with your honeyed eyes and sugary sweet lies?"

My chest squeezes, and bitterness takes a stranglehold on my vulnerability. I wasn't lying. It was perhaps the first honest admission I've made in years, and he doesn't believe me. But what does it matter? I'd be a fool to expect anything else from a monster.

"I wouldn't be forced to lie if you'd just let me out of this prison," I snap. "I'm human, and I don't deserve to be treated like this."

"I don't like to see you treated this way." His words are soft and deceptively genuine, but I can't believe them. I can't believe anything he says.

"When can I call my father? When will he come for me?"

His jaw settles into an unforgiving line, and a sinking feeling expands in my stomach.

"He will come for me," I assure him.

My certainty is a lie, though not for his benefit, but mine. I'm not ready to accept that my life is over, even if logic dictates it is. Nikolai's possession of me has changed the entire trajectory of my destiny. I was supposed to marry Dante. I had been saved for him. I'd been brought up with the understanding that I would marry him and follow the rules like an obedient daughter.

But with one command, Nikolai changed everything. If I were to return to my father's, Dante would no longer want me. I'd be considered damaged goods. Impure and tainted. And the question that stays hidden in the darkest recesses of my mind is what would become of me then.

Nikolai removes a lighter from his pocket, the unlit cigarette dangling from his lips. "I think you know if you went home, things would not be the same."

He throws out his careless observation while he lights his cigarette, and there isn't a sympathetic bone in his body for the plight he has caused. "Dante will not marry you after you've been with me."

His words ignite a storm of images in my mind. Naked. Groaning. *Inside me.* My thighs clench, and a flush creeps over my skin.

"I haven't been with you."

"Not yet," Nikolai concedes. "But Dante doesn't know that. And would he ever believe you anyway?"

Not yet. That seems to be the only part of his statement I focus on. It should disgust me. Nikolai is a casual lover who desecrates the idea of intimacy between partners. The act means nothing to him. And even though I am too jaded to believe in love, I always thought that Dante would at the very least be an attentive lover. In the fantasy my mind had conjured up, I liked to believe he would only want me once we married. But with Nikolai, I would be nothing more than a few fleeting moments of entertainment he would soon forget.

"You will never take my body," I tell him. "I am engaged to Dante. Nothing has changed."

"Except you aren't." He flashes a cold smile. "You never were. But don't trouble yourself with half-hearted lies, princess. You are too bony for me. I like my women soft. Feminine. So, for now, you are safe from my affections."

Heat rises up the base of my neck and burns my face while my lips spew venom. "And I wouldn't want your filthy, well-used cock.

So don't trouble yourself, Mr. Kozlov, you are safe from my seductions as well."

Nikolai's lips tilt at the corners, but flames blaze in his eyes. I find it difficult not to react to his verbal jousting, and I don't know why. My upbringing trained me to be docile, and I know when to pick my battles, but with him, I simply can't control it.

He releases a deep exhalation from his lungs, clouding the air with the scent of cloves from his black cigarette. "Do you believe Dante would treat you like a princess?"

"Italian men treasure their women. Dante is no different."

"And when he chose his mistresses over you, it would not bother you?"

My fingernails bite into my palms, but I make every effort not to let the irritation seep into my voice. "I am not delusional. Men have needs. He might sate them outside of the home on occasion, but he would always come back to me."

"And such behavior in your mind is not filthy?"

I don't answer. He's made his point, and I can't argue it, as much as I'd like to.

"What you can't seem to grasp, *zvezda*, is that your judgments have clouded your own vision. I may wet my cock as I please because I am unwed. But I can assure you that there is nothing more sacred to a Vor than his wife. Our code forbids adultery while yours simply expect it."

"You know nothing of my family or the values we uphold."

"No?" He laughs. "I know that your father took many mistresses outside of the home. He dipped his cock in whatever filth would have him. All while he kept your mother under lock and key, disfigured from his jealous rages."

"Do not speak of my mother!" I snarl. "You know nothing of her."

It's a rare display of emotion for me to get so choked up, but it seems to be the reaction Nikolai wanted.

"My father will come for me," I repeat. "He loves me. He will find a way to pay his debt and collect me."

Neither of us are convinced, but Nikolai's silence allows the subject to stay dead for now. Resolving to move on from our sparring and focus on the future, I meet his eyes.

"I would like to make a phone call to the director of my company."

"The doctor believes it in your best interest to see a therapist," he replies. "She also recommended a nutritionist."

And we are back to this again.

"I don't need those things. The company has a nutritionist I can speak to if I want. And therapy is a waste of time."

Nikolai shrugs, stubbing out his cigarette before he rises to his full height of well over six feet. "Dr. Shtein tells me that you would like to be free of this bed. Of this tube. Perhaps, she was mistaken?"

It isn't fair, this game he's playing. But when has life ever been fair? "Of course, I do."

"Then prove to me you are trying," Nikolai says. "And I will consider it."

CHAPTER 8
NIKOLAI

"Kolyan."

Mischa's voice diverts my attention from the monitor on my desk. He's propped against the doorframe wearing a wolfish grin. I'm not certain how long he's been there observing my distractions, but it's obvious he has.

In the Vory brotherhood, Mischa is a *bratok*. A soldier. But he is also a close friend, and after ten years by my side, I have little chance of being rid of him.

"What is it?" I grunt.

He gestures to the screen in front of me. "What are you looking at?"

I press the button on the monitor and watch it fade to black. "Nothing."

Mischa laughs. He knows it was not nothing. It is the girl. For two weeks, I have scrutinized her therapy sessions, watching the way she peels back a layer at a time, revealing herself like a lotus flower. The temptation to know her secrets was too much to resist, but lately, I have decided her thoughts are better left to the professionals, and my screen is better left on mute.

Mischa makes himself comfortable in the empty seat across my desk, volunteering his own theory. "Porn. It must be, considering the girls at Kosmos tell me they haven't seen you in nearly a month. Surely, your hand must be getting tired."

"The selection at Kosmos has gone downhill," I lie.

In truth, the girls are all very pretty. How much better can it get than a Russian owned space themed strip club? But lately, I have found my time better spent at home. A statement I don't want to analyze too closely.

"A pussy is a pussy." Mischa shrugs. "What difference does it make? Take your pick and enjoy. Though if you want a bit of advice, stay away from the redheads. They bite."

A drawn-out sigh sags from my chest. "What do you want, Misch?"

"You mean besides the pleasantness of your company?" He chuckles. "I came to give you a heads-up."

"About?"

"Mr. Buchanan's expert will be here shortly to inspect the painting."

I lean back in the chair and snort. Nine times out of ten, these so-called experts the clients send are scarcely more knowledgeable of art than a museum guide on his best day.

"No need to warn me. The piece is ready, and I have little doubt it will live up to his scrutiny."

"I never doubted his satisfaction," Mischa replies. "But my warning is only that Sergei will be escorting him today."

"I see."

My throat itches for a drink. The least appealing of all the items on my agenda is dealing with my father. It will be the first genuine conversation we've had since I cut his ear off and surpassed him in rank. Tensions will undoubtedly be high.

I have a hankering to suggest we crack into a fifty-year-old scotch when Nonna enters and alerts us to the visitors. Hardly a heads-up, I glare at Mischa, and he shrugs.

"I came as soon as I knew."

"Offer them a drink, Nonna. In ten minutes, see them up to the vault. I'll be ready then."

She nods and leaves the room.

"Find a way to entertain yourself until I'm done," I instruct Mischa. "But stay out of my shit."

He smirks, and I leave him to his own amusements as I trudge up the stairs to the vault. It's the most secure area of my home, and it takes no less than five minutes to navigate the security measures. Logic dictates that these operations are not to be carried out in the presence of even my most trusted men. In my world, you never know who may turn on you.

For all the trouble, the vault is considerably cozy inside. The steel reinforced concrete walls utilize the majority of the space, while the remains are left to the madness that infects my mind.

On any given day, the room may house a genuine artifact worth more than the average lifetime salary. Some of the items are authentic—either stolen or recovered artwork—but in instances like today, there is a forgery waiting inside.

For this occasion, the solicited work is *Five Dancing Women* by Edgar Degas. If I were a man who believed in serendipity, I might have given a second thought to the timing of the request. It was just after my most difficult acquisition to date.

One dancing Tanaka Valentini.

Even in the criminal underworld, there is a place for beautiful art. In most syndicates, it's negotiated for value, not beauty. It isn't uncommon to see priceless paintings used as collateral for drugs or weapons. As such, the works are often damaged as they are passed around and left to suffer at the hands of those with no true appreciation. Art collectors would be horrified if they knew what really became of some long-lost treasures.

There are a variety of reasons I might receive a request for a forgery. Sometimes, collectors want to lay claim to history's lost or stolen artworks. But more often than not, it's a black-market dealer who makes the request. In turn, he will pawn the work off on some unsuspecting fool with too much money to burn and not enough sense to know the difference. When they want to up the ante, I am tasked with acquiring valuable works from authentic sources. Whether it is by brushstroke or by force, there are no two ways about it. I am a thief at heart.

While I may not have affection for all the works I replicate, the Degas piece has commanded my attention. The original *Five Dancing Women* was stolen from a Jewish-Hungarian collector during World War II. While the other works from this collection are pending return to the heirs of the original owner, this piece remains lost. Looking at my replica, it is easy to understand why.

"She's really something special to look at, isn't she?"

I turn to greet the expert Mr. Buchanan sent, and as fate would have it, he is a familiar face.

"Christophe?"

He tosses his hands up. "Guilty as charged. How are you, old... I'm not sure how to address you. Is it friend or foe?"

Sergei, who is standing beside him, watches us indignantly, his eyes bouncing back and forth as he tries to interpret our connection.

"I studied under Christophe at Brandeis before he abandoned us for the real Ivy Leagues."

"Ah, yes," Christophe answers. "And as I recall you were one of the worst students I ever had. Lazy. Smart mouthed. Utterly unappreciative of the masters."

"We can't all be Picasso." I shrug.

Christophe turns to Sergei. "Truth be told, he has more talent in his little finger than most of us could ever dream to possess."

"Not a fair comparison," I argue. "Considering I don't have a photographic memory."

"An artist doesn't need it," he says. "He uses his imagination. Which is why I am no artist myself."

Sergei doesn't add to the conversation, and there's a pause of awkward silence before he checks his watch. "I'll wait downstairs."

I am relieved when he leaves, and Christophe seems to be of a like mind. "Pleasant fellow."

"Indeed," I answer. "Just be grateful you don't have to call him father."

Christophe laughs, and I gesture him into the room.

"I don't suppose there's any chance this isn't going to take all day, is there?"

"Five or six hours ought to do it," he jests.

Ice broken, he sets about the task of removing his instruments from the bag he carries. Magnifying glass, black light, time dated materials, and beetle-infested wood being just a few of the items at his disposal.

He gets down to business, examining the piece from every angle. While he seeks out imperfections, I bide my time with the ten-thousand-dollar bottle of whiskey I swiped from a collector at an art show in Zurich. The guy was a prick, but he had fine taste in whiskey.

At one point, Christophe takes a break and gestures for the bottle before thinking better of it.

"I suppose I shouldn't drink on the job."

I make it a point to savor the next drink while he watches. "When did you take up your time with freelancing? The golden campus not pan out for you?"

"I'm still a scholar," he answers. "My credentials are quite impressive, really. Mum and Dad are pleased as punch and seem determined to throw every half eligible English lass my way in a wickedly devised ruse to tempt me back home permanently."

"I don't think English women would put up with your shit."

"You're quite right about that." He chuckles. "Try telling that to Mum, though."

Christophe returns to his work, talking while he examines the pastel. "Honestly, the pay for freelance work is better, particularly in this business. It was all very romantic to be a starving artist when I was younger, but I've decided I'd like to retire early. Buy a yacht. Sail around the world and sleep with exotic women in every port."

"Don't tell your mother that," I advise.

"Dear god no." He snorts. "The old bird would have a heart attack."

He pauses on one piece of the dancer's shoe. A ballet shoe, to be exact. After several moments of tense scrutiny, he shakes his head.

"I don't know how you do it," he says. "Magnificent. You are a wasted talent."

"So you say. For all you know, I could be the real Banksy."

"No, no, definitely not. Haven't you heard? There's a different name in the papers every other week. Last one was some sort of famous singing duo."

"Keep the people guessing," I answer.

"What about you?" He trades the magnifying glass for his black light. "How's the Russian bakery business treating you?"

We both have a good laugh at the ridiculous notion. During my time at the university, I told him I would run my father's Russian bakery business when I left school. It was a flimsily crafted cover I invented when I was too bored or drunk to come up with something more creative.

"It does well enough." I gesture to the house. "As you can see for yourself."

"Indeed, it's a nice place you have here out in the middle of bumfuck nowhere."

"Just how I prefer it."

He pauses to look up at me. "And a pretty little peach secreted away down the hall."

"You saw the girl?"

"I presume it must be her, this girl with no name. She was apologetic when she bumped into us in the hallway. Tall like a willow and soft like the sea. Her pretty amber eyes will long haunt me."

"You should have been a poet," I deflect.

Christophe sniffles and murmurs something in response, but I don't hear it. It never occurred to me that Tanaka's appointment with the therapist would be ending around the time of their arrival. I had grown accustomed to her being locked in her room, but now that she's permitted to roam the house under the doctor's supervision, Sergei has seen her, and it's a development I dread. He will have questions. He will have many questions.

"All done." Christophe snaps off his gloves and glances back at me curiously. "She's beautiful."

"The piece?"

"The girl. But the piece is remarkable too. If I were able to compare the original, you might give me a run for my money."

"With certainty, I would."

He smiles and snatches the bottle from my hands, helping himself to a drink while we examine the dancing girls in the picture. "Degas said that art is not what you see, but what you make others see."

"And what do you see?" I ask.

"It's a beautiful, bloody sport. Unappreciated. They make something impossible appear effortless."

I nod in agreement. "It wasn't until recently that I came to understand the gruesome labor of a dancer."

Christophe whistles and shakes his head. "You were holding back on this piece. This is the problem with reproductions. You are forced to color in the lines. But that one—" He points to a stray canvas in the back of the room. "That one is a force of nature."

In my rush to prepare the piece for him, I forgot about my other works lying out. Most notably, the one he is currently gravitating toward. It feels intimate, and I want to stop him. But it would only serve to fuel his curiosity.

"She's a beauty," he repeats. "You have captured every emotion on her face. The toil, the agony, the pain. *Fall from Grace*. It's an apt title. Color me captivated."

There is no denying the muse for my piece. The night Nakya fell from grace, I was as shocked as the rest of the audience. While most of the onlookers politely chose to look away from her shame and focus on the show, I was not one of them. Her struggle to get back up again held me hostage, and at that moment, the heartbroken beauty enchanted me.

"It's a pity," Christophe muses. "The greatest love stories always end in tragedy."

A throat clears from the doorway, and I turn to find Sergei waiting there, half blitzed already. The rims of his eyes are red and glassy, and the broken capillaries around his nose seem more obvious than usual.

"Are you finished?" he asks brusquely.

"Yes, I'm afraid so," Christophe answers. "Though I could stay here and thumb through the inner workings of your mind all day, I have a real job waiting for me in the city."

I shake his hand and offer him a smile. "We can't all live a life of luxury, running Russian bakeries."

He removes a card from his wallet. "Well, if you ever get tired of peddling pastries, I think you'd do well selling your own pieces."

My eyes move to Sergei, who seems amused by the idea. To him, my pieces have never amounted to more than chicken scratch on paper. It was Viktor who decided that I should attend college to nurture my skills. Now common practice in the modern Vory world, a well-educated Vor is a valuable asset.

Christophe gathers his bag and offers me one last goodbye before Sergei tells him a car is waiting downstairs. With his departure, I am left with only the company of my father. His eyes move around the room, cataloging my things into order of nonsense. I know what comes next, but I only wish I had more alcohol in my system.

"What is with the girl?" he asks.

As *avtoritet*, it is now my right to tell him that it's none of his concern. But as my father, I am still inclined to show him respect. When it comes to Tanaka, I am not worried that he will connect the dots. Even if he were to discover the name of her father, it would make little difference to him. As far as he believes, my mother has been dead to me since he told me she ran off with an Italian man. He

THIEF

would have no reason to suspect I'd been searching my whole life for answers.

I edge toward the door of the vault, and Sergei follows suit. "The girl is just collateral."

"Pretty little thing." He scratches at his chin. "She has a tight ass. I wouldn't mind borrowing her—"

My fist collides with his jaw so fast that I have little time to understand what has come over me. Sergei reels back in astonishment, his teeth bloody and his eyes furious. I offer an apology in Russian while I try to come to terms with my actions. It would be in my best interest to smooth it over, but all I can think of is that I've just given him cause to poke his nose where it doesn't belong.

"She is mine," I declare. And this was not the thing I should have said because now he's laughing.

"Yours? And Viktor has approved of this?"

"It's nothing more than entertainment," I correct. "A temporary distraction. But I don't care to share her."

Sergei strikes out at me like a snake, his fingers wrapping around my throat. "You might be Viktor's little pet now, but don't forget where you came from, *syn*. If you ever disrespect me again, I will take this news to Viktor and watch him destroy your plaything after she has been passed around to all of the brothers."

As the spittle flies from his mouth, so do Sergei's true colors. This is not the father who boasts endlessly of my accomplishments in false showmanship. This is the competitor. The man who sets the bar to impossible standards. The man who will offer his hand to save you, only to rip your throat out. And with a face so similar to mine, I wonder if he is truly capable of the horrors I have always questioned.

He had no reservations about ousting Alexei and his mother from the family home after tragedy reaped his hearing. It's hard to conceive that a man who hates his firstborn so much could possibly harbor any love for his second. These things I know to be true, but I still hesitate to believe he sent my mother away.

It would be easier to accept if she left on her own. If she abandoned me to a year's worth of tears, I could justify whatever fate befell her. But Sergei is not the type of man who would allow a woman to embarrass him by walking away. When I search his lifeless eyes, I conclude he is not the type of man I can respect at all. And when I pry his fingers from my throat, it's with a new resolve.

I must find my answers, and I must do it fast.

CHAPTER 9
NIKOLAI

"Nika, the doctor would like to have a word with you."

I hold up a finger to signal the interruption, and Alexei nods from the small video screen on my phone. Nonna is at the door with the therapist in tow. This is not what I want to deal with right now. It's not what I want to deal with at all. I pay her good money to help Nakya, and she should not be bothering me with it when I have made it a point to avoid the situation altogether.

"I have some business that needs my attention," I tell Alexei. "Will you come by tomorrow evening?"

He hesitates, but after a moment, he agrees. When I disconnect the call, I am left to wonder if it's merely out of Vory obligation or familial.

My eyes move to the door again. "What is the problem?"

The therapist nods at Nonna, who shuts the door behind her as she steps inside and takes a seat across from my desk. "I would like to discuss Tanaka's progress with you."

"That is your concern," I say. "Not mine."

"You are paying me to give her the best possible treatment. Are you not interested to know if it's working?"

I drum my fingers across the desk. Truthfully, I am better left in the dark. The girl means nothing to me, and in the end, she is simply leverage. The only leverage I have. I shouldn't even be wasting my time or resources to fix the issues her father no doubt caused. It doesn't make any sense, considering I told myself from the beginning I might end her life.

But the problem does weigh heavy on my mind. More than it should. I wonder if she's eating on her own. I wonder about the current state of her health. I have been careful to avoid her, and I have kept myself busy so that the cameras don't tempt me. All for nothing because now the doctor wants to discuss it with me.

I lean back in the chair and examine the therapist. Her name is Sarah, and though she was recommended as a trustworthy source by Dr. Shtein, she seems like too much of a greenhorn to me. Her face is young and hopeful, and I think she'd do better working with college students than criminal organizations.

"Do you need more money?"

She sighs. "The rate hasn't changed. That isn't the issue."

"Then what is it? I am a busy man."

"Tanaka is progressing well." She fidgets with the hem of her blazer while she repeats the speech she's prepared for me. "There have been setbacks, of course, which is only natural, but she's doing much better. She is fully invested in the nutritional aspect of her meals and has been interested in learning the new program the nutritionist has set up for her."

"So what is the problem?" I repeat.

"We can only do so much," Sarah says. "Tanaka needs a support system outside of her medical professionals. If you truly want her to recover, I think it will give her the best chance."

My foot beats an anxious tempo beneath the desk. "What would you suggest?"

"Tanaka has lived under a unique set of circumstances for the duration of her life. Essentially, she has never experienced basic human rights of passage. She has never dated a boy or gone to the movies or walked through a park on her own. Her schooling further isolated her, and even in her ballet company, she was kept separate from the other dancers. There is a deep sorrow inside her that she hides well, but it's there. Every aspect of her life has been outside her control. Everything but her food and her dancing. It's no surprise that she has taken them to the extreme."

I lean forward, propping my elbows against the desk. "So she is starving herself to prove that she can?"

"It's not really that black and white." Sarah frowns. "But yes. Her ability to control something in her own way is a huge thing for her. The root of her issue is fear. In her mind, she thinks if she gains weight, she will lose what's most important to her, which is dancing."

"Her dancing career is over," I say. "The doctors have told her as much. She is finished."

"Then she will need to accept that in her own time. It's too much for her to grasp right now. But in time, I am confident she will understand her limitations. The brace has been removed, and she is very excited about the prospect of exercising again."

"Limited exercise," I amend.

"Of course," Sarah agrees. "Within reason. She understands she is being granted small freedoms but could lose them should she step out of bounds. Which brings me to my point. She needs something else to occupy her time. She mentioned she feels isolated here, and I believe it's contributing to her obsessive state."

"I told her to find another hobby."

"Hobbies are good." Sarah nods. "But making her feel useful, making her feel human, that's important too. Perhaps what would be beneficial is for her to socialize more with you and your staff."

I blink at her, still trying to wrap my head around how it came to this. Tanaka is not on holiday here. She is a prisoner. The doctor is well aware of her circumstances, and she freely accepted the payment for her services, but now she is trying to change the rules.

"It isn't the way we do things. You could spend more time with her. I'll pay you extra."

"I'm afraid my schedule won't allow it," she says.

Well, fuck. What makes her think mine does?

"I'll consider it," I say, mostly to appease her.

She looks skeptical. "Just a suggestion … Tanaka longs for a taste of the real world, but she also fears it. Perhaps you could take her on the occasional outing if you find the time. Having a safety net to fall back on will help her."

Safety net? I am the furthest thing from Tanaka's safety net. Now this crackpot of a doctor is adding outings to the agenda. I grunt a response and tell her I have work to do.

Sarah leaves, and I stare at the monitor. I've been careful to avoid it because I don't need to know the details of her sessions.

But now I want to.

CHAPTER 10
TANAKA

"Are you busy?"

The rumble of Nikolai's voice startles me. I was so absorbed in my stretches that I didn't hear him enter the gym. With only an hour per day to exercise, I'm forced to make the most of it. His interruption is a hindrance, but I'm also curious about the sudden appearance, considering he hasn't been to see me in weeks.

He's dressed like he just came in from outside, wearing his black leather jacket and flat cap. The slight tint of pink on his cheeks betrays cold weather, but I can only imagine it myself. The seasons have changed since my arrival, but I have not left the walls of the fortress since.

"I'm stretching," I tell him. "I still have thirty minutes."

"I have no intention of cutting your time short, Nakya." He bends down to dispose of the shopping bags in his hands. "But I brought something that might be of use to you."

The gesture is out of left field, and I'm not sure what to do. So I say a simple thank you.

He nods. "I thought that perhaps this afternoon you could help Nonna in the kitchen. After your appointments, of course."

"The kitchen?"

"Yes." He rubs a hand over the scruff on his jaw. "We are having a guest for dinner tomorrow evening, and she will be doing some baking if you'd like to join her."

It seems like an odd suggestion, but it's not like I have anything better to do. "Okay."

Silence is an ocean between us, and I don't know what else to say. Neither does Nikolai, apparently. His eyes are hostage to my new figure, and I'm self-conscious of his attention. Before, he said I was too bony, but perhaps now he thinks the opposite to be true.

"You look much better," he says roughly. "Healthy. Your skin is glowing."

It isn't what I expected to hear, and my answer is as awkward as I presently feel.

"Thanks. It's all the fish. The doctor said it's good for the skin ... so yeah."

This conversation is going nowhere fast. I'm out of sorts, and I don't know why, but my cheeks heat when Nikolai's eyes trace over my hips. I'm in the least flattering outfit I could imagine wearing—a pair of baggy shorts and a tee shirt—but it's all I have left apart from the one leotard he didn't destroy.

"Keep eating the fish," he says. "It does you good."

And with those words of wisdom, he departs abruptly, leaving me dazed and disoriented.

I'm tempted to check the bags now, but I wait until I've finished my practice. When the timer goes off downstairs, Nonna will be in to collect me and lock up the gym for the day. Since my release from the bed, I've been grateful to return to my practice. I was also surprised to find that Nikolai had a barre installed. Something I forgot to mention or thank him for while he was here.

It seems like an odd gesture of kindness from someone who has no interest in my returning to the stage. But I will take whatever small scrap he offers as far as my ballet is concerned.

"Time is up." Nonna enters the room in keeping with her schedule.

"Okay."

I finish my last set of pliés at the barre and collect my things, including the bags Nikolai left for me. Nonna locks the gym behind us but doesn't bother to escort me upstairs. I'm free to roam as I like unless I break the rules again.

"The doctor will be here in thirty minutes," she reminds me.

"Thank you. I'll be ready."

I trudge up the stairs to my room and set the bags down on the bed. The mystery of what's inside gets the best of me, and when I peek, my breath falters.

Ballet clothes.

He bought me ballet clothes. Tights, leotards, wraps, leg warmers. Everything I could possibly need to return to my practice with renewed vigilance. Something thaws inside my chest, and I realize when a wave of emotion crashes over me that this is the kindest thing anyone has ever done for me.

It seems paradoxical when he was the one to ruin my clothes in the first place, but my father never bought me clothes. Dante never bought me clothes. I was given an allowance to shop online, and every item I owned was chosen by me personally. Nothing was ever gifted. It's a new experience trying on clothing that someone else chose for me. I'm left to wonder what went through his mind when he picked each piece out. If he imagined the way they would look on my body. If he felt anything at all when he contemplated colors or sizes or fabrics.

The clothing is beautiful. Every piece is expensive and well made. But my favorite is the pale pink chiffon leotard dress. It's light and flowy and pretty. When I try it on, I don't want to take it off.

Inside another bag, I find a pair of pointe shoes with a note taped to them.

For later.

My heart squeezes, and I have to take a moment to process this turn of events. I'm not naïve enough to believe that Nikolai cares one way or the other if I ever dance professionally again, but this feels like hope. It feels like someone believes in me, and I haven't had that for a very long time.

I don't know how he determined my sizes, but it seems like he went through a lot of trouble to do this for me, so the least I can do is thank him properly. I sit down on the vanity bench and slip the pointes on to get a feel for them before I start my work. Every pair needs to be modified to fit perfectly, but not every pair needs the same adjustments. I can only ever tell by walking in them, which is what I intend to do now.

Traveling the length of the hall, I throw in a *petit jeté* along the way. My ankle is weak, and even though the brace is gone, it still hurts to land on it. But I am feeling much more like myself again, if only for having the impediment gone.

Nikolai is absent from his office, so I use the opportunity to float around the hallway, tossing in small movements as I go. The shoes need work, but so do I. When I reach the end of the carpeted rug, it occurs to me that I've landed on the threshold of his bedroom. It should come as no surprise when I find him there watching me, but it does.

"You were supposed to go slow." There is a hint of a smile on his face.

"I was just testing them. The shoes will need to be molded to my feet. I have no intention of going too fast."

"I should hope not," he says. "Another injury—"

"Thank you for the clothing," I blurt.

His eyes move over the pink fabric before pausing to linger on my breasts. They have swollen over the past month, and I'm suddenly aware of the way they tug at my leotard. The house is always cold, and it's always obvious. I should have worn a wrap, but I was so eager to test out my shoes that it didn't occur to me until now.

"You forgot to remove the tag," Nikolai informs me with a gruff voice. "Turn around, and I will do it."

I obey, even though it would be easy enough to do it myself. A small part of me wants to feel his fingers against the fabric. To experience a man's touch. It's not something I thought I could ever want for, but sometimes, I wonder what it would feel like to be touched by a man. As men go, Nikolai falls in the top percent of his red-blooded class. From his Herculean build to his wild hair and sharp cheekbones, he is a deity among the male species. A mortal casted in the image of a Greek god.

And that would make me his concubine.

The idea makes me shudder as his strong, calloused fingers skim the hem of the fabric against my shoulder blade before dipping to remove the tag. I don't feel a tug, but there's an audible snap. Aware that he is using a knife against the sensitive flesh of my back, I should be wary, but I find that I'm not.

The deed is done, but he's in no hurry to tell me so. Goose bumps skitter over my arms when he sweeps my long hair over my shoulder and traces along one of the shoulder straps.

"You should not have come here like this." His breath tickles the base of my neck, bathing me in warmth and cinnamon.

I can't find my words. Not when he's behind me, close enough to touch. Close enough that his body brushes against mine and his scent stirs between us. Traces of warm leather and cloves soak the air ... and something else I can't quite identify. Acrylic paint maybe?

His fingers graze the length of my arm, and it's not an accident. It's no accident when he draws me closer, molding me to his body. He buries his nose against my throat, inhaling me, and it opens a flood of warmth between my thighs. I sag into him, a drunken awareness hijacking my senses. I'm comatose, strung out in his arms, and for the first time in my life, I don't care. I want more.

I want to live before I die.

He will be the one to lure me to my quietus. Lulling me to an eternal sleep with his languid kisses against the space where my blood runs warm. For now, I am a slave to his touch. A servant to his commands. Another doll for his collection. Pretty and untainted by anyone but him.

Rough fingers bunch the fabric against my stomach, and blinding electricity hammers my synapses. His gypsy hands roam free, squeezing the flesh of my hips and strumming the tender flesh of my ribcage. But the beast in me isn't satisfied. She keeps screaming for more, and my captor is so willing to oblige. He takes possession of my swollen, heavy breasts by dipping his hand inside the fabric to scrape over my nipples. My chest arches, and I cry out as I've just been shocked back to life.

"*Zvezda.*" He kisses behind my ear. "You are so lovely. So soft and sweet and pure. I want to ruin you."

His feverish cock looms ominously against my spine, a cautionary threat to his quietly spoken words. I want him to ruin me too. I want him to crucify me. And it makes me a liar because I'm the one who's dirty and filthy and wrong. When his hand comes to rest between my thighs, the word is already on my lips. Poisonous and intoxicating, I want to tell him yes.

But yes isn't a fantasy. Yes is forever. The consequences of a decision made in a moment of weakness would mean nothing for him and everything for me. If he sends me back home a ruined woman, he may as well provide a coffin too.

"I can't." The words rush from my lips as I break from his spell and his arms. "I'm engaged to Dante."

There isn't another word spoken between us. Solitude is his answer.

Solitude is my life.

CHAPTER 11
TANAKA

Nonna is a quiet, efficient worker. She does her job without complaint or emotion, and I expect that she will hand down orders as she sees fit. But when I report to the kitchen to help her as I promised, she gestures to a pile of ingredients on the center island.

"There is fruit. Butter. Eggs. Dry ingredients in the cupboard."

"What am I making?"

"Whatever you choose," she answers. "It's a dinner party. So something nice."

With these vague instructions, I'm left to transform the ingredients on the counter. Off the top of my head, I can think of a few traditional Italian desserts, but in the end, I settle on a simple tart.

The nutritionist that Nikolai hired has devoted many hours to fine tuning my food belief system. Her approach is a positive one. Nothing is off limits, but balance is key. While I rarely ate fruit before due to the sugar content, I've discovered recently that adding it to my meals with a small amount of protein seems to be okay. Understanding the way my body utilizes food has helped to ease some of the anxiety I faced with expanding my food selection overall.

But I am not cured, and I'm doubtful that I ever will be. Every choice is still a struggle. At every meal, I go to war with my body, fighting the urge to cave in to my demons. I'm closely monitored, and right now, it's probably the only thing keeping me on track. Accepting that I must gain weight to be healthy is a never-ending battle. I feel better, but I hate the way I look.

When I look in the mirror now, I see a more feminine shape. Rounder hips. A fuller bust. A waist not as defined. It terrifies me. And in the back of my mind, I wonder what the director will say when he sees me. I've heard his comments toward other girls before, and in my fragile mental state, I don't think I could handle his criticism.

To distract myself from toxic thoughts, I focus on my hands. Rolling crust. Chopping fruit. Baking. Cleaning. Nonna glances over her shoulder on occasion to watch me, probably wary of me having a knife at all.

"You have baked before?" she asks.

I spread jam into the pastry shell. "Yes. I cooked often at home for my father."

She nods. We are silent again while I dump the fruit into the prepared tart and sprinkle it with icing sugar. Only when I present the finished product does she give me a hint of a smile.

"Very good. Nika will enjoy. Figs are his favorite."

I smile too, but it's weak. I doubt Nikolai will care what I've made after what happened this afternoon.

"Do you need my help with anything else?"

"No, that is all," she says. "Perhaps go upstairs and rest now."

I thank her and leave the kitchen. But upon entering the main room, I stop short. There is a woman at the front door. She is tall, blonde, and beautiful with legs for days and confidence I could only dream of possessing. Nikolai comes to greet her in the entryway, and she kisses him. She kisses the man who had his hands all over my body, and it feels as though someone's just anchored a cement block around my chest.

I'm immobile. Background noise. They don't see me as they shuffle up the stairs, but even if he did, it wouldn't matter. I pushed him away, and now he's giving me my just desserts. A Vor at heart, he is determined to give the final blow. His message has been received, loud and agonizingly clear.

I am not special.

I am replaceable.

The fool in me wants to believe it isn't true. He wouldn't do that. Not when he had his hands on my body today. Not when he whispered his confessions in my ear.

He wanted *me*.

Not her.

My body jerks up the stairs like a zombie. The third door on the right is my room. I should go inside and close the door and put on my headphones and think about when I get back onstage again. Only, my feet keep moving of their own accord, down the hall to his office. Cold fingers rest on the door handle, and I choke down the sour taste in my mouth.

I have no right to open this door. I have no right to care what he's doing, and I shouldn't want to see. Nikolai is nothing to me, and I am nothing to him. But he changed that when he touched me, and he should never have touched me at all. Because I'm turning the knob and I'm holding my breath and I don't want to see, but my brain demands the visual for what I can already hear.

The door swings open, and it's not better or worse than I imagined. It just is. A brutal punch to the chest would be more favorable than witnessing him this way. Legs spread wide, his dick is in her mouth while his eyes find mine.

She gets his pleasure, and I get the pain.

I was wrong to think I could protect myself from him. He doesn't need to take my body to ruin me.

Because he just did.

CHAPTER 12
NIKOLAI

When I arrive back from the city, I'm greeted by the smell of roast and vegetables, a reminder that soon my brother will be joining us for dinner. This meeting is important, but I find myself regretting that I made it for this evening. I'm still hungover from last night's activities, and entertaining is the last thing on my mind.

Nonna catches me in the entryway, gesturing for my coat and hat.

"Is Nakya ready?" I ask.

She nods. "I helped her dress earlier, now she is resting."

"Thank you." I move for the stairs. A hot shower is in order, and perhaps a small hair of the dog. But Nonna isn't prepared to let me have either.

"The doctor wanted me to pass along a message."

I pause. "What is the message?"

"The girl had a setback today. She refused to take her breakfast, vomited what she ate at lunch, and would not speak at all during her therapy session."

Each statement is a blade to my gut, but Nonna doesn't seem to notice as she delivers her words with deliberate efficiency. She goes on to tell me that Tanaka did not go to the gym today either, which she found rather odd.

"I will address it."

Nonna nods and leaves the room, and I take the stairs. She told me Nakya was sleeping, and I'm tempted to see for myself. But my palm hesitates on the door while I listen for a sound inside. There isn't one, and like a coward, I'm satisfied enough to open the door.

I find the broken angel lying in the center of her oversized bed. She is curled into herself, hands tucked against her chest, and even in sleep, she appears tormented. I should leave her alone—it's for the best—but I can't bring myself to shut the door. Not when I notice the goose bumps on her exposed arms. According to her doctor, it's a symptom of her condition. She is always cold because she does not have enough body fat.

Retrieving the throw blanket from the end of the bed, I am careful to drape it over her without waking her. And then I am careful to watch her for no good reason, regretting every decision I've ever made.

It would be foolish of me to wonder if my actions had any effect on her. I wouldn't say it's the first time I've hurt a woman's feelings, but it's the first time I've had to see their face again. This is unchartered territory. Nakya is stuck here with me, and I knew that she would see. I wanted her to see. I wanted her to hear.

Petty, perhaps, but after her cold dismissal in my bedroom, I wanted to be petty. From the beginning, she has been open with her feelings about me. She believes me to be filthy. She believes I am not worthy of someone like her.

Who could ever want you?

Maybe she is right. But it didn't stop me from wanting her when she came to me, wearing the clothes that I bought her. Floating like an angel, only to sting like a bee when her senses caught up with her.

Since her arrival, I have struggled to maintain my distance. Women are a valuable commodity in my world, and I rarely make an effort to get what I want from them. It takes little more than a look. A touch. A smile. It has always been easy for me, and it would be falsely humble to say otherwise.

But it hasn't been common practice for me to bring my conquests here. That is something new. Something I started for the sake of my own amusement. I like to watch Tanaka squirm. I like to get my dick sucked knowing she's just down the hall, hearing every second of it.

At times, I have caught myself wondering if she spares a second thought about my activities. If she wishes even for a second that she were the girl on her knees, taking what I offer her. I have imagined it more than I should. The thoughts ravage me even while I resort to choking my dick with my own fist like I'm a teenager again.

She didn't pull away from me last night. Not at first. I felt the fire in her skin. The strain of her nipples against my fingers. The soaked pussy between her thighs when I rubbed her virgin panties. For a fleeting moment, she wanted me too. And now, she will only ever see me as filthy again.

Her dark lashes flutter open, and I'm caught staring. The warmth in her honey eyes fractures, and she visibly recoils at the narrow distance between us. She can hardly look at me, and I don't blame her.

"Have I overslept?" Her voice is dead, her beautiful face plagued with sorrow.

"No. We still have an hour."

She is quiet, and I am too. I have no explanation for my being here. I only know that I need to leave before I get any closer. She doesn't need to smell the alcohol or perfume on my clothes.

She doesn't need another reason to hate me.

"If you come to my office now, you can make your phone call."

She sits up in bed.

And just like that, everything else is forgotten.

CHAPTER 13
TANAKA

Nikolai lumbers down the hallway, leaving a faint wake of smoke and perfume in his path. His shirt is wrinkled, and his eyes are bloodshot, and I don't want to consider what's kept him occupied in his absence, but I can't seem to stop anyway.

He gestures me into his office and points at the chair opposite his desk. I do as I'm prompted and sit down while he slides a landline across the deep expanse of cherry stained wood.

"Five minutes," he tells me. "Then Nonna will come for you."

An unnatural stillness settles over me when I nod. He's giving me five minutes with the phone.

Alone.

My fingers tremble when I pick up the handset. He wants me to dial the numbers before he goes. The numbers for the director of my company, who I told him I wanted to call. Maybe he knows the number, or maybe he doesn't.

It's a chance I'm willing to take.

I dial the number with false confidence. Outwardly, I know I'm holding it together. But inwardly, my heart is in my throat.

He can't know.

He can't.

I have to pull this off.

"Hello?" Gianni answers.

"Hello, Jean Claude. It's Tanaka."

A beat of silence follows, and I know it's up to me to steer the conversation. Even when Nikolai leaves, my responses will likely be recorded on camera for later dissection. We must tread carefully.

"I was just calling to check in," I say lightly. "If you have time, I'd like to fill you in on my rehabilitation."

"I see," Gianni answers.

From the doorway, Nikolai's eyes meet mine, and for a split second, I think he knows. He knows, and he's going to slaughter me right here in his office. But instead, he taps his watch and issues a final reminder.

"Five minutes."

And then he is gone, taking my breath with him.

"Are you recovering well then?" Gianni asks from the other line.

What he's really asking is if I'm all right.

"I'm fully focused on my health," I answer. "And hoping to return to the company very soon, should there still be a spot for me."

Gianni is quiet for too long, and I don't like the sound of that silence. He knows what I'm asking. *Has my position been held for me? Has he spoken with the director? What can he tell me?*

"At this time, we believe it would be best for you to focus on your recovery. We can discuss your position with the company when you are ready to dance again."

I swallow, and it hurts. Everything hurts. I don't want to accept what he's telling me. Even though I knew it would come to this, I don't want to believe it.

"The company sends their love," Gianni adds. "They all wish you a full recovery."

I think he's trying to tell me that he wants to help me, but his hands are tied. I can't be certain, but it must be what he came to warn me about that night. He knew Nikolai was coming for me. He knew my life was about to be obliterated.

"Have you had any luck on the investigation into my shoes?" I ask.

"Very little," he replies. "But there is a rumor it was an outside job. Someone by the name of *il demone*."

My stomach twists. He must be confused. Or I am. Something is getting lost in translation.

"I don't know who that is," I answer. And I wish it were true. I wish I didn't know that *il demone* is the name my father is known as on the streets.

"Where are you staying during your recovery?" Gianni asks.

It's a bold question. And I can only hope my answer doesn't get me killed.

"I'm at home. In Massachusetts."

He needs to know I'm still in the same state, so he can come for me. So he can take me away from this place and Nikolai.

"I hope to pay you a visit soon," he says.

Nonna enters the room, and I close my eyes. "I hope so too. Speak to you soon, Jean Claude."

"Soon," he echoes.

SHORTLY AFTER THE arrival of the guest downstairs, Nikolai comes to collect me from my room. Clean from a long shower, his hair is still damp, and he smells like himself again. Cloves and smoke, and maybe a bit of spicy aftershave. He made an effort to look presentable, but his face still looks like he spent a night in hell. In black trousers and a starched white button-down, he seems torn between light and darkness. Sinner or saint, it's hard to tell from one minute to the next.

His eyes make a quick pass over the red dress hugging my figure. "Nonna dressed you well."

It's the same dress I was wearing earlier, but either he failed to notice or he's providing obligatory compliments in hopes I will behave this evening. I'm not certain who he's expecting for dinner, but it seems strange he'd want to include me. For all Nikolai knows, I could spoil everything. But I suppose he's counting on me to be the well-heeled girl trained to be respectful of men and their business.

"Our guest is waiting." He gestures for me to come closer, and I do, but not close enough for him to touch.

After last night, I want nothing more to do with him. I want only his suffering, and I have secretly vowed that I will do everything in my power to ensure it, though I don't know how yet. I only know that I was a fool to be swayed by him for even a minute.

He is a thief. A liar. And I will never forget that image of him again.

We walk side by side, greeted at the bottom of the stairs by Nonna, who readily provides us each with a drink. Vodka cranberry for me, and a whiskey for Nikolai.

"He is in the main room," she announces.

Nikolai nods and downs the amber liquid in his glass with one long swallow. Nonna leaves with the promise to return with another, and then we are off again. He guides me into the main room where our guest is waiting. And once I set eyes on him, I recognize him.

Alexei.

Like Nikolai, he has an overbearing presence. Tall, lean, and muscular with ice blue eyes. He rises to greet me, and his eyes never leave my face as I say a quiet hello.

"Nakya, you remember Lyoshka."

I nod.

"Thank you for coming," Nikolai tells him.

"I can't stay long."

Both men are rigid with equally cool features. The civility between them is forced, though I don't know why. But when Nonna directs us to the dining table, Nikolai offers the head seat to his guest of honor.

THIEF

Perhaps he is trying to win him over, but more than likely, it's a matter of respect. There is always a pecking order in the mafia, and in this particular scenario, it would appear Alexei outranks Nikolai.

We take our seats, and for some length of time, they discuss business in Russian while I poke at the first course. Under any other circumstances, I'd love minestrone, but I find it an odd choice to be served this evening. I'm not hungry anyway, and my thoughts are far away when Nikolai barks my name. I look up from my plate.

"Eat," he demands.

I make a point to disregard him, informing Nonna that I'm finished when she comes for the dishes. She frowns but removes the bowl regardless.

The conversation continues across the table, but it seems to be increasingly one-sided. When I look up from my salad, I find it's because Alexei's attention has diverted to me. He seems unaware that Nikolai is still speaking when he interrupts.

"Who are you?"

I have no reason to be rude to him. There is, in truth, a small part of me that basks in the power he holds over my captor. Nikolai is watching our exchange closely, his eyes challenging me to speak out of turn.

"My name is Tanaka Valentini." I offer Alexei a warm smile. "I'm here as collateral for a debt my father owes."

If Alexei reacts to my honesty, I don't see it. My eyes are locked on Nikolai, taking a small victory in the way his fingers stiffen around his glass as he brings it to his lips.

I turn my attention back to Alexei. "And may I ask who you are?"

"I am of little importance," he answers. "In fact, it puzzles me exceedingly what honor has bestowed a bastard like me the presence of your captor this evening."

Nikolai's eyes flash. "I do not trouble myself with the relations you speak of. It seems you have mistaken me for Sergei."

Alexei shrugs. "It is hard, sometimes, to tell the difference between you two."

A crimson flush edges up the pulsing ridge of Nikolai's throat, and my stomach flips in response. I know I probably pushed him too far, but Alexei is unconcerned about his role, even when Nikolai excuses himself from the room.

When he's gone, and the room is silent, I blurt something that would be better kept to myself. "Are you really his brother?"

Alexei pierces me with his eyes. "How did you know?"

My eyes wander over his features, and while it isn't blatant, there are some similarities. It's mostly their mannerisms, though, that I have seemed to connect. "You look alike. And you also hinted at it. *Bastard. Relations.* I think the only missing ingredient is brotherly affection."

His eyes study me curiously while he sips from his cognac. "It's hard to warm to a man like Nikolai."

I think maybe he's trying to tell me that Nikolai is not a good man. He doesn't need to say so. My heart still hurts from the memory of last night.

"Does he treat you well?" Alexei asks.

I find myself nodding on autopilot, though I'm not sure why. It's probably not wise to say anything else. Their hatred runs deep, but guaranteed, their loyalty runs deeper. It's the mafia way.

"Why did you come to dinner tonight?" I ask. "If you don't get along with him?"

Alexei responds with a flippant gesture of his hand. "I'm not sure. We still have business to discuss."

Nonna returns with another course of roast and vegetables. While Nikolai is absent, I decide to eat a little because it smells good.

"If you stay here long, perhaps you can come visit my wife sometime," Alexei suggests. "She could use a friend."

My fork halts, and I look up at him.

A friend.

I've never had a friend. I wouldn't even know what that relationship entails, but the opportunity sounds too good to pass up.

"I would like that very much," I answer. "What is her name?"

For the first time since his arrival, there is a sign of life in Alexei's eyes. "Her name is Talia."

"Talia," I repeat. "It's a beautiful name."

"She's a beautiful woman." He smiles. "But she is not yet familiar with this world, and I fear that it makes her an easy target."

I nod in understanding. Growing up in this life, I'm intimately acquainted with the baggage that comes with it. But for an outsider, it can be disorienting, I'm sure.

Alexei retrieves the phone from his pocket and wakes the screen. "I have a photo of her. Let me show you."

It's probably not appropriate of me, but I stand and move to the other side of the table. I'm eager for the opportunity to leave this house, even if only temporarily. The idea of having a friend fills my heart with hope.

Alexei hands me the phone, and I stare at the photo, cataloging the details of the woman on the screen. She is beautiful, but there is also something heartbreaking about her. The gray eyes staring back at me are haunted and sad, and I'm left to wonder if she's happy with her husband. And then I wonder why I would even question it.

What mafia wife is ever happy?

I want to assure him that she's beautiful, which is probably what he wants to hear, but instead, I tell Alexei that she looks like she could use a friend. He nods, and it takes him some time to drag his eyes away from the photo.

"She has not had an easy life," he admits. "And I don't know that I make her happy, but I try."

The profound level of sorrow in his voice provokes me to do something I probably shouldn't. But I reach out and touch his hand, if only to let him know there is always hope.

"Will you tell me about her?"

For the remainder of the meal, we get lost in conversation. He opens up about his wife's background, giving me intimate details about someone I've yet to meet. But I can see that it's what he needed, and when I hear her heart-wrenching story, I feel like we are friends already.

After such a deep subject, the natural progression is to move on to lighter topics. Alexei explains his position within the Vory, their hierarchy, and some of their customs. The things he tells me are not so different from my own family's codes, and I'm surprised to learn that I even find some of their practices more agreeable.

It's when we are on the matter of children that Nikolai chooses to return. The timing isn't ideal, considering he left us as strangers and returns to find me leaning in to study more of the photos on Alexei's phone. The flash in his eyes as he examines the narrow distance between us warns me that his mood has only darkened, but for the first time in as long as I can remember, I'm enjoying myself, and I know he's about to ruin it.

"You are dismissed, Nakya," he thunders. "Go to your room."

Not about to argue with his tone, I move to get up, but Alexei halts me with his hand on my arm. "She can stay."

A silent war rages between the two brothers while I remain in my seat, hands clutched in my lap. The game of trying to provoke Nikolai is no longer fun, and at the end of the day, it is him I must answer to.

"Perhaps I should go to my room," I volunteer.

"I think perhaps you should stay here," Alexei argues. "It's not a problem, is it, *bratan*? You trust me, yes?"

Nikolai's nostrils flare, and I can't be sure, but I'm beginning to think I have become the proverbial stick between the two.

"With my life," Nikolai answers. "As blood should."

Sticky silence descends over us before Nonna suggests we all move to the sitting room for drinks. She is quick to follow our movements, already prepared with fresh beverages. It's my third vodka cranberry of the night, and I am feeling it more than I should.

I don't drink often. Only on a few occasions did I steal a sip from my father's liquor cabinet or nurse a beverage during a dinner party, but in general, I don't make it a habit of imbibing. In the past, it was partly because my father had high expectations for

THIEF

my behavior, but mostly, it was because there were too many calories.

Tonight, however, I am not thinking of the caloric content. I am only thinking of the impending doom that awaits me if this tension does not dissipate before Alexei takes his leave.

Watching Nikolai as he speaks to his brother in Russian, I'm cursed to wonder what made him this way. Volatile one minute, and placid the next. His emotions do not ebb and flow like a ripple in the sea. They are either a tidal wave or the eerily calm silence before disaster strikes. I have known him to be kind, and I have known him to be cruel. But it's apparent I am not the only recipient of his mercurial mood swings.

He is self-destructive in his own right. For someone constantly surrounded by people, his relationships are shallow and meaningless. He seems to have sabotaged the only ones that stand a chance at a deeper connection. I have an intense desire to understand what caused the rift between these two brothers, and more importantly, why their shared DNA needs to be kept a secret.

While I'm attempting to sort through these thoughts, Alexei's attention drifts back to me, much to Nikolai's vexation. It's deliberate at this point. Alexei wants to provoke his brother, and it might be amusing if I wasn't the one who will bear the brunt of it.

"Enough." Nikolai moves in front of me, obscuring Alexei's view. "I thought we could be civilized, but it's obvious that you can't let go of the past."

"Perhaps when I am dead," Alexei answers. "I will let go of it then."

Nikolai curses his displeasure in Russian. "You never listen. You would not listen when I told you she was a whore. You would not listen when I told you she was servicing your Vory brothers. You needed to see it for yourself."

"And you needed to take what was mine," Alexei sneers. "Because you couldn't allow me to have anything. You are just like Sergei."

Before I can comprehend what's happening, the two men are grappling with each other on the floor. Rage-soaked insults are hurled between punches as I watch on in horror. Drink glasses shatter, and the coffee table splinters across the room as I take shelter behind the sofa. I am not immune to violence, but this is pitiful.

"Stop it!" I scream.

Nikolai is the one to turn and look at me. His eyes lance right through me, piercing me with blame.

"Come." Nonna tugs on my arm, and I'm not even sure when she entered the room. "Leave the men to their business."

CHAPTER 14
TANAKA

Any hope that a hot shower would dissolve some of the tension in my body is lost when I climb beneath the sheets. My muscles are fatigued, my eyes are heavy, and soreness has taken a stronghold over me.

The house is quiet now, and I'm left to wonder how the evening ended. It should make little difference to me, but I'm curious how Nikolai fared in the gladiator sports downstairs. Reason dictates I care only because he's my captor and he's in charge of my fate. But if I'm honest with myself, I know it's more complicated than that.

I'm not left to wonder for long. When I'm on the verge of sleep, the bedroom door thunders open, and Nikolai emerges from the shadows. The light from the hallway creates a halo of orange around him, illuminating a swollen jaw and blackened eye. But it isn't his face I'm worried about.

When I meet his gaze, an edgy, twitchy feeling crawls over me. I need to get away. Far, far away.

He stalks toward the bed, and I scramble to the other side. I've got one foot on the floor when his arm comes around my waist and captures me from behind. His lips ghost over my ear, breathing fire into my skin.

"Where are you going, little doll?"

I squeeze my eyes shut, desperately seeking shelter from the storm in his. The strength I need to endure has abandoned me, and I won't survive him this time. He's going to wreck me.

He drags me back to the middle of the bed, immobilizing me with the weight of his body. His skin is feverish, and his breath is laced with whiskey. But it's the tension rippling through his muscles that scares me the most.

"Perhaps you would rather go home with my brother. Is that it, pet?"

"No," I whisper.

"You spent the evening flirting with him." His booming voice vibrates against my chest. "So why shouldn't I send you home with him?"

"Please." I cling to his arms. "That isn't what I want."

"Guess what, kitten?" His words blow over my throat. "I don't care what you want."

A tear falls down my cheek, and Nikolai collects it with his tongue. His fingers take ownership of my face, and he forces intimacy by staring into my eyes.

"Tell me that you want me."

"No." It's a faint protest, drowned out by his mouth crashing into mine. The first thing I taste is his blood, and the second is his whiskey.

My first kiss. He's taken my first kiss. The shock anchors me to the bed, rendering me a prisoner to his lips. Swollen and rough, fiery and insatiable. He has the will of a fighter and the artistry of a lover. Right now, he's both. And I'm a slave to my weakness. A slave to him. He squeezes my jaw open, and his tongue clashes with mine. It's intimate. It's a violation. Yet I thirst for it.

"You are my angel," he murmurs. "And if I want, my whore too."

My body arches against him, and my fingers tangle in his hair, wishing for the strength I don't possess. "I hate you."

"I think you wish that you did." He forces his leg between my thighs.

I'm not wearing any panties, and my nightdress has migrated up over my hips during the struggle. A flush sweeps up the back of my neck and over my face as I endeavor to put myself back together again. The thought of him seeing me spread open is terrifying. Humiliating. But Nikolai doesn't care about my modesty.

His lips are lazing over my throat now, his angry cock straining against his trousers. I'm supposed to remain pure. There was a reason, I'm certain, but I can't think of it now. Not when he's pawing at me, licking and biting and kissing my flesh. My nails sink into the rigid angles of his back, searching for my sanity. My breath comes in waves as I wonder if this is it. If this will be my damnation. His mouth reaches the swells of my breasts, and I stop breathing altogether.

"Fuck these tits," he grunts as he squeezes them together between his fleshy palms. "Fuck you and your pretty little tits."

The lashing of his tongue softens the harshness of his words when he lowers his head to suck my nipples through the silky fabric. A thousand jolts of lightning arc through me. I don't want to want him, but he is manipulating me with his touch, his sounds, and the drugging scent of his body.

The same way he manipulated all the other women before me.

"Nikolai." I shove him. "We can't. I can't. You were with her. You chose her."

My protests stall when his fingers move between my legs and drag against my bare sex. The place no man has ever touched before. The place only my husband is supposed to touch. Logically, I know this, but I'm so wet for him that it doesn't matter what my mind knows is best for me. My body doesn't want what's best for me. My body wants to lay down and sacrifice for him.

"You are mine to play with." He pulls down the nightdress and kisses each of my breasts. "Mine to toy with. And fuck. And use. And degrade. You belong to me now, *zvezda*, and I'm going to let you know it."

My head rattles against the pillow, but my protests have dried up. He's right, and I know he's right. He can do anything he wants to me.

To further prove his point, his hands grip the back of my thighs, pushing them up until my knees kiss my chest. Cool air passes over the most intimate part of me, and embarrassment colors my cheeks as his eyes drink me in like this. I'm on display, just like the doll he says I am. It's lewd, and it's dirty, and I try to squeeze my thighs back together, but they don't budge.

"Nikolai."

"You can call me Nikolasha," he tells me. "Whenever I eat your pussy."

His mouth comes down on me, and I yelp. But when I feel him bury his tongue inside me, spasms rock my body. I squirm against him, fighting for each ragged breath as he laps at me without restraint. My knees buckle, and I feel like I'm falling. I'm out of control, and I'm falling, and there's nothing to save me.

My fingers coil in his hair, twisting with the intent of pushing him away, but instead, I pull him closer like a deviant. He kneads the flesh of my ass cheeks in his hands and drinks from my body like I'm the sweetest nectar he's ever tasted. I'm hypnotized. Strung out. Drunk on a pleasure I never realized existed. But I know it's a lie. I'm not the sweetest nectar he's ever tasted. Every time my eyes fall shut, I see him with her. I see him with all the others who came before me. And I hate it. I hate him.

I tell him so.

He grunts. "You won't hate me when your pussy is raw from my lips."

Sharp teeth pinch the most sensitive part of my flesh, and I reflexively yank on his hair. His grip dominates me, and I am left to thrash against him as he schools me in the art of control. I claw at his arms. His shoulders. Even the back of his neck. I tell him in one breath that I hate him and beg him not to stop in the next.

None of it matters. Nikolai has his own agenda.

"You are going to come on my face," he murmurs. "And you'll be filthy just like me."

I don't want it to be true. But it is. The onslaught is sudden and explosive. With the tug of his puppet strings, the master fractures the good girl inside me. All that's left in the wake of his devastation is a broken doll who wrings out every ounce of pleasure from his mouth before she deflates.

I'm bankrupt. Devoid of contrition as he kisses my thigh and smears the arousal from his face into my skin. Tomorrow I'll repent, but for now, the devil's got his grasp on me.

Nikolai unzips his pants, and my tongue darts out to wet my lips as his cock springs free. It's a violent pulsing monstrosity. I watch his face as he strokes it in his fist. Eyes half-drunk, he soaks in the sight before him. I'm still spread wide, my sex wet and swollen and tender from him.

He edges his body between my parted thighs, and I try to squeeze them shut, but he just pries them back open. I think this is it. This is where he will ruin me. This is the moment that my life will be over.

He drags my body closer to the giant throbbing dick, and I shiver. It's going to hurt. I might cry. I don't know how my body will ever accommodate him. The piercing heat thrusts against my sensitive flesh, dousing his cock with my arousal. I take a breath, and the world doesn't end.

He doesn't violate the sacred barrier, even if I secretly wish he would. Instead, he reaches for my hand and guides it down between my legs, wrapping it around his heavy flesh. He shows me the way, teaching me how to touch him. How to grip him. How to force the sounds of agony that rip from his throat. Lusting for that power, the student quickly surpasses the teacher. The tides have changed, and now it is this savage of a man who is a slave to me.

He collapses forward, his palms coming to rest on my knees as his head falls back in a drugged daze. His hips move disjointedly, jarring his cock into the tiny opening of my fingers. He's fucking my hand, and not my body. But it doesn't matter. It doesn't matter because I'm in control, and he can't stop himself.

I watch his face, cataloging every detail. The tension pulling at his drooping eyes. The five-o clock shadow feathering over his sharp cheekbones. The tousled hair that I attacked. He didn't look this way with her. He didn't look this way with anyone.

I've left my mark on him.

And now, he's determined to leave his on me. His cock pulses, and he yanks it from my grasp, jets of hot cum spraying against my sex. I wrench at the unexpected sensation, and he offers me a lazy smile as he smears the fluid inside me with his fingers.

"What are you doing?" I demand. "You can't do that."

He isn't reactive to my protests, and I'm not even sure he heard them. His eyes are dazed and heavy as he squeezes the head of his cock into my opening, seating just the tip inside.

I jolt at the foreign intrusion before falling eerily still. His skin is on my skin. His cum is inside me, and if I even breathe, he could push past the point of no return.

Murmurs of his approval rumble from his chest as he glides back and forth with the slightest of movements. It seems to go on until my lungs are about to burst, and only when his dick is soft does he pull out and tuck himself away.

"Next time, *zvezda*, I will empty myself inside you."

CHAPTER 15
NIKOLAI

"Why don't you tell me what you think your future looks like," Sarah suggests.

Nakya gazes out the window, rapping her fingers against the bottle of water in her hands. She is curled into herself, so small the chair swallows her whole. After last week's tantrum, I feared she might need to be placed on the tube again. But her doctors assure me she is back on track.

The shadows darkening her eyes don't inspire confidence, but I'm not privy to her current mental state. The last I saw of her was the night I stole into her room and sampled her virgin pussy. I can still taste it on my lips, and against my better judgment, I still want more.

"I don't know what the future looks like," Nakya says finally. Her voice is bleak, and I fear that the little dancer has lost her light for good.

"Do you see yourself back onstage? Or perhaps in love? Married? Children? What does the future look like for you?"

She takes too long to answer, and I should not feel so desperate to hear the words spoken from her lips. But more and more, I find that I want to know her. I want to tame the chaos in her mind, and that is a problem.

"I was supposed to marry a man who works for my father." Nakya tugs at the corner of the wrapper on her bottle. "But now I don't think I will."

"Does that upset you?" Sarah asks.

It's the question I would have asked myself, had I believed she'd give me an honest answer. Nakya is not naïve to the surveillance at my disposal, but regardless, she has been forthcoming during her sessions. She probably assumes that I have better things to do than watch her, which would be correct. Yet here I am.

"The decision was made for me already," Nakya says. "But I do not love Dante as a wife should love her husband."

Her answer leaves me to question her authenticity when so many times, she has chosen to use Dante as her invisible shield. At every opportunity, she has thrown him in my face. If she does not love him, I can only draw one conclusion from her actions. She will do anything to keep me away.

"And how do you think a wife should love her husband?" Sarah asks.

"In my world, love doesn't exist," Nakya answers softly. "Marriage is a duty, and little more. It means remaining devout to your husband while turning a blind eye to his extracurricular activities. Dedicating your life to being small and insignificant, while he reigns supreme. How can love ever be nurtured in such an environment?"

Sarah is quiet for a moment, tapping her pen against her notepad. She knows she must tread carefully here. Being on my payroll, she is aware of all that implies. She can help Tanaka talk through her emotions, but she must avoid making suggestions.

"Do you think perhaps you would like to marry someone else in the future? Someone who is loyal to you?"

"No." My little dancer jerks her chin reflexively. "I don't want to get married at all."

Her answer is that of a silly girl who doesn't want to accept her fate. She is a mafia princess, and as such, she has no choice but to marry.

"Okay." Sarah takes a sip of her own water, probably trying to determine which direction to steer the conversation.

"I don't like my life." The words burst forcefully from Nakya without warning, spearing me right in the gut. "I never wanted any of this. I didn't choose to live like a prisoner. I didn't choose to lose my mother. There is no silver lining, and there is no future. My future is out of my control, so it's a stupid question. The only thing I ever wanted to do was dance, but now that's been taken from me too."

Ever hopeful, Sarah tries to remain positive. "You are still dancing. I'm told that your recovery is going quite well. Even if it's not what it used to be, you are still a dancer."

Nakya's hair falls into her face, her shoulders trembling as she shakes her head. "It's over for me. My career is finished. My ankle can't sustain the pressures of professional dancing, even if I did manage to attain another position. And it's all his fault. He did this to me."

"Who?" Sarah asks.

"My father," Nakya whispers. "It was my own father."

The truth no longer evades her, but it doesn't bring any peace to know she no longer blames me. Her world has been ripped apart by the man who was supposed to protect her. If he was any kind of father at all, he would have protected her from me too.

I ache to comfort her. I ache to confess that I understand her pain. But that isn't why I brought her here. And everything about this situation is wrong. She wasn't supposed to hate her father. She was supposed to be precious to him. That was how I would kill him slowly. His Achilles' heel.

I just didn't expect that his weakness wasn't her.

AFTER THE DISASTROUS attempt at dinner with my brother, I've been forced to choose another avenue for information. While Mischa is by no means Alexei, he is very good with computers, and I trust him more than I trust most.

At this evening's Vory gathering, I'm not surprised to find him lurking near the bar. Viktor's middle daughter has just turned eighteen, and all my brothers have come together to celebrate the milestone.

"I need you to do something for me," I tell him.

Mischa doesn't look at me. He's distracted by a brunette with huge tits hanging off the arm of an *avtoritet* who outranks him by several decades.

"She looks familiar," he says.

"Hey, *zadrota*, did you hear me?"

He reluctantly drags his attention to me and nods. "Sure, *Kolyan*. Whatever you need."

For a moment, I doubt myself. Admitting my intentions to anyone is a risk, even Mischa. A Vor should never appear vulnerable, and without solid proof against my father, this could backfire spectacularly if he discovers what I'm doing.

"What is it, *bratan*?" Mischa slaps me on the shoulder. "You can trust me, yes?"

When I meet his eyes, I know that I can. He is my oldest friend, and I trust him with my life.

"I need you to do some digging around," I say. "Quietly. And by quietly, I mean if anyone ever finds out, I will cut your nuts off."

Mischa smiles. "You know I'm rather fond of my nuts. Wouldn't do a thing to jeopardize them."

"At least we can rely on that."

"So what is it?" he asks.

I'm not prepared to say her name aloud. I have made a point not to utter it since the day she walked out on us. To do so now would feel like a betrayal to my father, myself, and the Vory brotherhood. If what I've been told is true, she abandoned us. She deserves no more of my time or my thoughts. But regardless, she has them.

I remove the scrap of paper from my shirt pocket and hand it to Mischa. One glance at the name, and it's evident he knows.

"What would you like me to look for?" he asks quietly.

"I want to know who she ran off with. Names. Addresses. Dates. I want to know what she ate for breakfast last week."

He nods. "I'll see what I can do."

We both drain our glasses, and I gesture to the bartender for a refill.

"Does this have something to do with Manuel Valentini's daughter?" Mischa asks.

I reach for a smoke and meet his gaze. He never saw Nakya at my house, and I don't like that he knows about her at all. "How did you hear about her?"

"Word is getting around." He shrugs. "Manuel has sent his men to hit our clubs, and Viktor is not happy."

This is news to me. I wouldn't have expected such foolish behavior from Manuel when his daughter is in our possession. He should know that Viktor won't tolerate it, and his carelessness presents a new problem. In the wake of these new developments, Viktor could easily decide Nakya is no longer worth the hassle. In the grand scheme of things, my agenda is unimportant when compared to the greater good of the Vory. And Viktor will always do what he deems best for the brotherhood.

"You might want to consider alternative options," Mischa says, "before Viktor suggests them himself. A man in your shoes, I am certain he would expect you to take the initiative."

In any other circumstance, what he's suggesting would make sense. Tanaka is more of a headache to the brotherhood than she's worth. Manuel's debt could be taken from his own flesh and blood, and the problem would be solved. But I didn't take the girl just to kill her and be done with it. I had grand intentions of making her suffer the same way I suspect my mother suffered at the hands of her father. But the thought of doing so now makes me sick. I have tasted her. I still hunger for her. And whether I want to admit it or not, she's inside me, infecting me with her poison.

"I'll consider it," I tell Mischa. A lie, probably, but an effective end to the conversation.

"Kosmos." He has his attention on the brunette again. "That's where I know her from. I fucked her in the ass while I ate out her sister."

"You would be wise not to say that too loud," I suggest. "The *avtoritet* appears to be quite fond of her."

Mischa shrugs. "That's what happens when you fall in love with a stripper. She has been sampled by everyone else before you."

"What difference does it make?" I ask. "It wouldn't hurt you to keep your dick in your pants from time to time."

He laughs. "You are one to talk. Before you took the Valentini girl, I recall you visiting the club quite often."

His implication is not lost on me, but I choose not to acknowledge it. The *pakhan* is heading our way with his daughter in tow, and this is not the sort of conversation he would want her to hear.

"Kol'ka," Viktor greets me. "I would like a word with you in private."

Mischa nods and gives the birthday girl his well wishes before making a quick exit. Once he's gone, I turn to Ana myself. Viktor's daughter is a pretty girl. Young and wide-eyed and unblemished by the outside dangers of this world. Much like Tanaka, she has been sheltered to preserve our culture and her safety. But now that she is blossoming into a young woman, and her appearances at social events are becoming more commonplace, she is sought after by many of the Vory. I can think of at least ten men who would like to secure her hand in marriage, along with the inevitable rise in rank that would come with it. It's good to be in the *pakhan's* favor.

"Happy Birthday, Anastasiya." I nod in her direction.

A blush steals over her cheeks, and she bows her head submissively. Ana has been raised to be respectful of male authority. It's a trait that Vory men covet in a woman, and one I thought I admired too. But that was before I met the little dancer who challenged my every word.

"I thought that Ana might accompany me to dinner at your house this week," Viktor says.

I force a smile, but meanwhile, I'm dissecting the meaning behind this. "Of course. Name the day, and I will have Nonna prepare a feast fit for a queen."

Viktor nods and looks at his daughter. "Run along to your sisters, Ana. I have some business to discuss."

Ana hesitates for a moment too long, her eyes moving over my face in what can only be admiration. I bring my glass to my lips, but it's still empty. Viktor clears his throat in warning, and she totters away as she's been instructed.

The *pakhan* directs the bartender's attention to us, and this time, he doesn't delay our drink preparations. "My Ana is a beautiful girl, is she not?"

"Very beautiful," I acknowledge. To say anything else would be a death wish. "She will make one lucky Vor a very happy man someday."

"He will be a lucky man," Viktor agrees, "to have a wife like Ana."

The bartender delivers my whiskey, and I swipe it from the bar, downing it in two long swallows. Viktor is watching me too closely, and I don't have to guess where this conversation's heading. It's far past time to marry off his eligible daughters. Already, an arranged marriage with one of the Irish has fallen through. If Viktor waits too long, he risks rumors of the girls being impure.

"Sergei suggested that perhaps you would be a good match for her."

Of course, he did. It should come as no surprise, given our last encounter. He wanted to make Nakya his plaything, and this is his way of proving he's still in control, regardless of rank.

I clear my throat and bite down too hard on a piece of ice. "And what do you make of his suggestion?"

"I tend to agree that you would be a good match," Viktor muses. "And Ana seems to like you well enough."

"She is still very young," I observe carefully. "Are you certain she's ready for marriage?"

"She's a year older than my own wife was when I married her."

Unsettling silence falls between us while I contemplate my next move. To refuse Viktor's suggestion would be considered nothing less than the ultimate insult. I'd be lucky to walk away with my life after such a remark. It's not uncommon to marry for the sake of duty. That Viktor would even deem me worthy of his daughter is an honor I don't deserve. I should be proud, and I should be grateful. But instead, I can only think of my captive back at home.

Viktor seems to read my thoughts, and he responds in kind. "It's time for you to stop playing with the Valentini girl. With your promotion comes responsibilities. You need to set an example for your brothers. Settle down and start a family. Show them the way that a Vor conducts himself in matters of the home."

Every word feels like another nail in my coffin, but there is little I can do but nod.

"I understand that Manuel has been causing trouble, and for that, I apologize. I was unaware he would be so foolish."

Viktor shrugs. "He is merely a fly. A nuisance. One that I assume you will be handling soon?"

"It will be done," I assure him. "But I must ask for one favor."

Viktor adjusts his tie and takes a sip of his drink. "What is it?"

"You were right to assume I had other motives for taking the girl," I confess. "But I have yet to discover the truth about my mother. I'm asking that you grant me more time so that when the answers are revealed, I will have vengeance for the crimes committed against her."

Viktor's brows knit together, betraying his doubt. "You are so certain that such crimes were committed, but how can I be certain that you aren't falling for the girl?"

"My word is all I have," I answer. "And my assurances that when the truth is revealed, justice will be served."

Perhaps it is a lie, but I'm too deep in to see my way out. I am a Vor, and as such, I should have it within me to do what's necessary. To admit otherwise would earn a dishonorable trip to my own grave.

"It's far past time to start taking flesh," Viktor says. "Had it been anyone else, she would have been delivered to her father in pieces already."

His words reek of truth, but it doesn't quell the urge inside me to slit his throat for speaking of Nakya that way. I have the highest respect for my *pakhan*. He has always given me a fair deal, and he has always done right by me. To feel such hostility toward him is troubling, and it proves that he is right. Nakya has made me weak, and if I don't get my affairs in order, the life lost will be my own.

"I will agree to your request, on one condition," Viktor decides. "The girl is still a virgin, yes?"

I choke out an affirmative.

"If you want to prove your word," he says, "then allow Mischa to bed her. I want the sheets hand delivered to Manuel. It will be his last chance to fall into line before we start hacking her into pieces."

My vision turns black, but I feel myself nod. "It will be done."

CHAPTER 16
TANAKA

"Nika says you can bake something for this evening," Nonna informs me as she sets up breakfast on the table in my room. "It will need to be done soon. Perhaps after you eat."

"What's happening this evening?" I ask.

"Dinner party."

She gives no further explanation and leaves the room. It doesn't seem likely that Alexei would return for dinner after the last fiasco, so I'm banking on another Vory associate. By giving me meaningless tasks like baking, I'm certain Nikolai thinks he can keep me out of trouble. But given that he's been avoiding me, I wouldn't know for certain. His orders are handed down through Nonna because he is too much of a coward to face me himself.

I intend to demand my time in the gym as usual, but as it turns out, Nikolai has other plans. When Nonna returns after breakfast, she insists I accompany her to the kitchen before I've even had my shower. And unlike last time, she hands me a long list of specific items she wants me to make.

"This will take all day," I protest.

THIEF

"Then you better start now," she says. "Dinner is at seven."

She turns away and prepares to work on her own list. As frustrating as it may be, I know she's also just doing what she's told, so there's no further point in arguing. We work together in silence, and I was not mistaken in my estimate. It does take all day.

My feet ache, and I'm covered in flour when I finally pull the last item out of the oven. Baked apples with sweet filling. It is only one of the four desserts we prepared for this evening, in addition to the breads and salads and meat dishes. I have no idea who could possibly be so important to deserve the amount of food we have prepared, but I hope they appreciate it.

"Nakya."

I turn to find Nikolai watching me from the doorway, and my heart slows. His face is expressionless, and the ocean in his eyes has turned to ice. I have seen that look on a man's face before. I had seen that look when my father handed down orders to his own men. That same numbness came over them when a job needed to be done, but it wasn't something they were particularly fond of doing.

And right now, it looks like Nikolai is about to do a job he doesn't much care for either.

"It's time to go upstairs and get dressed," he says. "Come."

He doesn't wait for me to answer. I follow him through the house and up the stairs, exhausted and weary of another formal dinner. He is already dressed for the occasion, and it isn't his usual jeans or motorcycle boots. Tonight, he is wearing all black, from his slacks to his button up to his oxfords. A dangerous style for a dangerous man.

Meanwhile, I am unshowered and messy from the labor of the day. Luckily, he seems to be too distracted by his own thoughts to notice.

"There." He points to a dress already laid out on my bed. It isn't one I've seen before, but I'm almost certain it might be one of Nonna's. It's beige, and it's ugly. "Put this on, quickly."

"I have to shower," I protest. "I haven't had time to do my hair or makeup—"

"No." His tone is unyielding, and I'm confused. I went to all the trouble of cooking a feast fit for royalty, yet he believes my appearance is not of importance. My father would have never allowed me to attend a dinner in my current state.

I cross my arms and hold my head high, determined to take a stand. "I'm not going to dinner without cleaning myself up first."

"Put the dress on," Nikolai says through gritted teeth. "Or I will do it for you."

I hold my ground, mostly because I don't want to believe him. I'm not wearing that dress, and I'm not going to meet guests in this state. But my captor has other plans, and he stalks toward me with tension rippling through every visible muscle. Instinct makes me cower when he grabs my arm, and I try to turn away from him.

"Enough," he barks. "I would not hit you. I have never hit you."

The storm is back, and I'm afraid to meet his eyes for fear of what I'll find there. But when I do, shock punches the breath from my lungs. It's a storm of a different color. Sorrow so deep and violent, it chokes every bit of blue in his irises, turning them to gray.

Just gray.

I fall limp in his arms when he pulls me toward him and begins to undress me. With the prospect of more bad weather ahead, the fight has gone out of me. Something bad is coming. I can feel it.

Nikolai drapes the beige fabric over my head and zips it in the back. But it does little to conform to the shape of my body. It's merely a loose, shapeless sack he's dressed me in. Ugly and unflattering, the way he must see me.

"Shoes."

The shoes dangling from his fingers are flats. Cheap and plain to match the dress. And just as before, he is the one to put them on. Kneeling before me, he shoves each foot into the uncomfortable canvas.

He resurrects himself, and his eyes stare through me. "Now we go downstairs."

"Please don't make me, Nikolai. Not like this."

THIEF

I don't have a scrap of makeup on. My hair isn't even brushed. Shame is welling up inside me, and I am horrified that he would want to present me to anybody in this state. But his only response is to wrench me by the arm and drag me from the room.

My resistance has returned, and I battle him every step of the way, desperate to avoid whatever's coming. Halfway down the stairs, he pauses, arresting my face with uncompromising fingers.

"Understand this, Nakya. If you step out of bounds tonight, you will only have yourself to blame for what happens next. Should the *pakhan* decide you are better off passed around as amusement for the brothers, there won't be a thing I can do to save you."

Fear paralyzes my throat, and I can't breathe. I can't even move. Because this time, he is not a liar. The leader of his mafiya is coming here tonight. The man who Nikolai answers to. The man who might, in fact, decide my fate.

I wanted to believe I was safe here. I even foolishly fell for the notion that I might be able to trust this man. But that trust was misplaced. As powerful as Nikolai might be, he is not in control. Yet he is the only hope I have. I must do what he tells me, and I must believe that there is still humanity inside him. He won't let those animals take me. He will fight on my behalf to keep me alive.

Once he sees the acceptance on my face, he lurches me forward again. Already, I can hear the voices of our guests. But before we reach them, we are met by another man at the bottom of the stairs. He is young, perhaps younger than me. And even though he bears the Vory tattoos, his features are not as harsh as my captor's.

"Nakya, this is Mischa," Nikolai introduces us. "You will go with him and do whatever he says."

I'm passed off without a second thought, and Nikolai abandons me to the stranger as he walks down the hall.

"Come with me," Mischa says. "We'll go into the sitting room."

I follow him on wooden legs. It doesn't feel right. I think I might be sick, but then it occurs to me I haven't eaten lunch today. That alone should have alerted me to the dangers lurking ahead this evening. Since the removal of the tube, Nikolai has been regimental about my meals. Every day without fail, they are delivered at the same time, and I'm not permitted to do anything else until my meal is finished.

But today he forgot. Just as he has forgotten about me.

A thought that's only compounded when he parades another woman into the main room. Only woman isn't really accurate. She is still a girl. Barely out of her teens, judging by her baby-faced features. Regardless of her age, there's no mistaking her superiority. Nikolai refuses to divert his attention from her or the man at his side for even a second. Intuition dictates that this is the *pakhan*.

The men speak in their mother tongue, and the girl takes too much liberty allowing her starry eyes to roam Nikolai's face. Her cheeks are pale and pink, her face hopeful and naïve as she hangs on every word. Nikolai says something that makes her laugh, and he smiles at her. I can't recall him ever smiling at me. I can't look away from the horror show, even though I know I should. She is too innocent to hate, but I do. I hate her almost as much as I hate him.

"His fiancée," Mischa says. "Anastaysia."

Acid burns the back of my throat, and another wave of nausea rolls over me. It can't be true.

"They are engaged?"

Mischa nods. "Soon, it will be official. Nika is lucky, it's an honor many men would kill for. She's a beautiful girl, isn't she?"

I can't say a word in her favor. I'm sure she is beautiful, but all I see is the vile creature stealing what doesn't belong to her. It doesn't make sense for me to feel this way. Not when he continues to throw me away at every opportunity.

Mischa watches me too closely, and I fear I've revealed myself. But when he leans in to whisper in my ear, it's much worse than that. "It's better you forget him now. In the end, it will save you pain. For tonight, you have me, and I promise you could do much worse with my brothers."

Pressure weighs on my shoulders, and as if on cue, Viktor's gaze moves to me. He asks Nikolai in Russian if the deed is done, and Nikolai assures him tonight.

Blue eyes collide with mine, but they won't save me. Not tonight, and not ever.

"Mischa," Viktor calls out. "Take the girl upstairs."

CHAPTER 17
NIKOLAI

Nakya's face fractures under Viktor's command, and I grow unnaturally still as Mischa drags her dead weight from the couch and up the stairs.

Red threatens my vision, and I desperately try to focus on Ana's narrative about her end of year studies. The events of this evening are not happenstance. Mischa will take her while we dine, and I'll be forced to endure the dinner without a show of emotion.

My best friend will be the one to ruin her.

Viktor's methods are brutal but effective. It could be worse. I know it could be worse. But anyone who isn't me is not an option. Even now, I can only think of how I will murder him when it's over. But logically, it will still not change anything.

Nakya will never be able to look at me again. And that's a murder of a different kind.

Viktor makes a toast, and I nod absently. I check my watch. It's been two minutes. Ana won't stop staring at me. She is desperate for my attention, and she should have it. There should be nothing else that exists outside her. She is the *pakhan's* daughter.

Someone else approaches, and through my blurry vision, I make out Alexei's face. He wasn't invited, and even Viktor can't seem to understand his sudden appearance.

"Lyoshenka. What are you doing here?"

"I've been assisting Nika with the acquisition of the piece you requested, and I'm aware this is not an ideal time, but a time-sensitive lead has just come through. Would you mind if I steal him away for a short while?"

It's a lie, and it's not well executed. Alexei is referring to the Rembrandt. Something he knows Viktor won't say no to. Though I'm not certain he ever denies Alexei of anything he requests.

"Business is business," Viktor says. "Ana understands that it always comes first. I will have a drink with Franco while we wait."

Alexei nods, and I follow him wordlessly as he leads me upstairs. He is here for a reason, but whatever it may be, it's not my primary concern right now. My concern is the closed door of Nakya's room. The one where Mischa will take her and make her his before I rip his throat out for obeying orders.

Alexei turns to me, and I'm aware he requires my attention, but I can only focus on the door, listening for the slightest of sounds.

"Don't you want to know why I'm here?" Alexei asks.

"You mean besides instilling hope that I will find Viktor's impossible Rembrandt?"

"I heard of Viktor's intentions this evening," he answers. "And I know what you're doing with the Valentini girl. I know your motivations for taking her, and why you requested those files from me."

I drag my attention to him, determined to uncover the purpose of his statement.

"You want the truth about your mother," he says. "And I can assist you. But I will not allow you to punish an innocent girl for the sins of her father."

My awareness drifts back to the door. I still can't hear anything, and I know if I breach that barrier, it will ruin everything I have worked for. If Viktor discovers that I've interfered with his orders, he will have my head. But I also know that I can't stop myself.

"Go," Alexei tells me. "I'll wait in the office."

He isn't doing it for me. He doesn't believe me capable of anything selfless, and perhaps he is right. I watched without protest as Mischa brought Nakya up here with one intention. But my intentions have changed when I turn the knob to find him holding my sobbing, broken doll. She is hyperventilating in his arms while he attempts to comfort her. But even worse, she is naked.

My eyes cut through Mischa. He is clothed, and he has not yet taken her, but it makes no difference. I'm out for blood when I snatch him by the collar and drag him from the bed. My fist crashes into his face three times before he shoves me away.

"You knew this would happen, Kolyan. You said it was okay."

"It isn't okay," I snarl. "You made her cry."

He glares up at me and shakes his head. "You made her cry. She's attached to you, and she doesn't want me."

I look at Nakya, collapsed on the bed, curling into herself like a child. Mischa is right. I have broken her with my actions.

"I'm sorry," I whisper.

I want to go to her. I want to comfort her. But Mischa stops me.

"It needs to be done," he says. "You have no choice. It's her body or her life."

His words settle over me, and I can't deny the truth. There is no other option. Either I take the girl and provide proof, or Viktor will demand her actual flesh. She will hate me for ruining her. She will never see that I'm trying to save her too.

"Misch—"

"We can speak later," he says.

He leaves the room, and I am left alone with my little dancer. She is still sobbing when I collect her in my arms. I shelter her with my body, desperate to convey the depth of my despair in seeing her this way.

"Forgive me, Nakya," I whisper into her hair. "Forgive me."

"You were going to let him ... touch me," she utters between broken sobs.

I reach for her face and force her gaze to mine, so there can be no further misunderstandings between us.

"I will be the only one to touch you, *zvezda*. The only one to take you. And once I do, I'm afraid you will have no say in the matter. You will be mine."

ALEXEI IS WAITING in my office as he promised, tapping out a message on his phone. Undoubtedly, it would be to his wife. While I have only ever known my brother to be a reserved man, he cannot hide his devotion to the pretty blonde who has somehow managed to thaw his frozen heart.

I reach for the bottle of cognac I keep near my desk, extending it to him in offer as I sit down. He declines the hospitality with a shake of his head.

"Thank you," I say.

"I didn't do it for you."

"I know," I answer. "But still, thank you."

If he hadn't come, there is no telling how this evening might have ended. I open the cognac and indulge myself with two long pulls.

"It's messier than I thought it would be."

Alexei scrutinizes me with unforgiving eyes. I think it's easy for him to believe I am cut from the same cloth as Sergei. As far as I can tell, he's only ever painted me in that light.

"I know you think I'm like him," I say. "But I have doubts. Perhaps I don't know him as you do. Perhaps he has been a different father to me than he ever was to you. It's why I set out on this journey to begin with. To discover his true nature. To discover the truth."

"Perhaps he has been a different father to me?" Alexei scoffs. "He was never a father to me at all."

The irony is that he doesn't see how alike we are. He has always longed for Sergei's approval, and I have always longed for his freedom from Sergei's overbearing presence. We are both envious of what the other man has, but too proud to admit it.

"I can't take responsibility for what he did to you, Lyoshenka."

"I didn't ask you to," he answers.

"But you hold it against me. You let it come between us. What happened between you and Sergei is not right, but it should not poison our relationship as well."

"You did that all on your own."

I rub the back of my neck and listen for the voices downstairs. I will need to get back soon. Viktor will not wait long, despite his cheerful mood tonight.

"What do you plan to do with her?" Alexei asks.

The image of Nakya's tear-smudged face haunts me still. There will be little choice in the matter, and it weighs heavy on me already. "I will return her to her father."

"That was not your intention when you began. In what shape do you plan to return her to her father?"

He wants confirmation that he's right about me. That I'm a monster like Sergei. My honesty will not sway him, but I offer it to him anyway.

"My intentions were different when I began. In that regard, you are correct. But time and circumstances have changed my position. Whatever happened in the past, her father will be the one to pay."

Alexei looks doubtful. "So even if you learn that Manuel was the one to cause your mother's most brutal and violent death, you have no plans to harm her?"

I resist the urge to punch him in the face again because technically, I owe him. "Are you telling me that Manuel was responsible for my mother's death?"

"No," he answers. "I want your word that you won't hurt her."

"I already said I wouldn't," I snarl.

"But you intended to when you took her?"

"What is the point of this?" I demand. "What would you like

from me, Lyoshenka? Must I get down on my knees and grovel before you?"

"A Vor would never get down on his knees for any man."

"And I'm not offering. I am merely asking what it is that you would like for me to say."

"Do you care for her?"

His words provoke a heavy, sinking feeling in my stomach. I can't bring myself to acknowledge the question either way.

"You could take a page from my book," Alexei suggests. "If you want to keep her, then marry her. Viktor will not be able to interfere with the sanctity of those vows."

"I am not you," I mock. "If I married the girl, he would just kill me. He wants me to marry Ana."

Alexei stands up and shrugs into his jacket, apparently finished with this conversation.

"So marry Ana," he says. "And send the girl back to her father as a ruined woman. I'm sure he will forgive her."

He's a bastard for saying so. Alexei knows just as well as I do that Manuel will never forgive her.

CHAPTER 18
TANAKA

I wipe the steam from the mirror in the bathroom, hesitant to see the girl staring back at me. My face is puffy from crying. The whites of my eyes bloodshot. My skin is red from the scalding water of the bath and the subsequent scrubbing of the towel. It falls from my hand, and I stare at my naked form in the reflection.

The therapist Nikolai hired to fix me told me I should find something I love about myself every time I look in the mirror. But tonight, there is only hate. I hate every filthy thing about me. My hips are too big. The stomach that used to be concave is flat and squishy, and my ribs are suffocated beneath a layer of flesh that wasn't there before. I'm soft in too many places, and I want to punish myself for allowing him to control me this way.

He made me ugly, so he wouldn't want me, but it doesn't stop me from wanting him. Mischa was right. There's something wrong with me. There must be to want someone who is so bad for me. Someone who would throw me to the wolves without a second thought.

I did not think I had another tear to shed, but still they streak down my face. I have never cried so much in my life. My father would never have allowed me to be so weak. But I can feel it happening, and it's out of my control. I'm splintering. Shattering. Fracturing. He's taken away my power and left me only with pain.

I lock my hands into fists and yank on my hair. The hurt sometimes helps, but not this time. It only reminds me that I'm alive, and I am defenseless.

I walk from the bathroom, still naked, and listen for the sounds downstairs. I can't hear anything, but I can imagine it well enough. The dinner party lives on, and Nikolai sits beside his soon-to-be beloved fiancée while I suffer in silence.

Fatigue seeps into my bones, and the divide in my heart grows with every passing day. I'm tired of fighting. I'm tired of hoping for a brighter future when there is none to be found. He can have his Russian wife. And when he tires of this game, I can finally have the only peace this world has to offer me.

Death.

Without bothering to dress, I open the bedroom door and walk down the hall to his office. This is the only place to find the cure for what ails me now. A bottle of cognac beckons from his desk. Probably expensive.

I swipe it and drift back to my room like an apparition. Unnoticed and unfelt. Laughter floats up from down below, and I cannot mistake that timbre. Nikolai is enjoying himself, and I think I should enjoy myself too.

The cognac opens with a satisfying pop, and I drink straight from the bottle. It burns my throat and eyes, and eventually my stomach too. But it's a good burn. A burn that makes everything else fade away.

My party is cut disappointingly short when the door opens, and Mischa is standing there. His eyes move to the bottle in my hand, and then over my naked body.

In the back of my mind, there's a small distant voice that tells me

I should care. I'm supposed to be a good girl. I'm supposed to be proper and modest and reserved at all times. But tonight, Nikolai decided to make me filthy instead.

"Nakya." Mischa frowns. "Don't you know you should never drink alone?"

I collapse back against the pillows, the alcohol flooding my brain and my system. I don't care anymore. And that's what I tell him when I cross my legs and make a flippant gesture with my hand.

"Are you here to take me?"

He rubs a hand over the back of his neck and sighs. "If not me, then someone else will. It has been ordered, and it must be done."

"Because of my father," I say.

"Because of your father," he agrees.

He isn't the worst looking guy in the world. In fact, right now, he is superior to Nikolai in every way. Because he is here, and Nikolai is not. Even if he doesn't have the same imposing build or the electric blue eyes, he is a man. And I suppose if I'm to be ruined, I should be able to choose which man will do the job.

Anyone but Nikolai.

Anyone but the traitor downstairs.

"I want you to do it," I tell Mischa. "I'm ready now."

He sighs as though he's already tired of this game but comes to sit beside me on the bed regardless. Admittedly, I feel like I'm going to throw up all over again. But maybe if I close my eyes, it will be over quickly, and I will have the last word.

The bottle is still clutched in my hands when I implore him to do it. Mischa's eyes rake over me, and I think that he wants to. But for some reason, he still hesitates.

"I should speak to Nikolai first."

"I don't care what Nikolai says," I insist. "I want you to do it."

Mischa is still conflicted, but he disrobes anyway. He pries the cognac from my fingers, and my heart pulses in my throat. I have nothing else to do with my hands when he kneels on the bed before me.

He's naked, and I can't bring myself to really look at him.

"I'm just going to rest my eyes," I whisper. "But it's okay. I want you to do it."

I hope that if I keep repeating the lie, it will be easier. But it doesn't get easier when he leans down and tries to kiss my neck.

His scent is all wrong. His body is all wrong. And I can't keep pretending that I want this when I don't. So I disconnect and try to go to another place.

Nothing can hurt me if I'm not present.

It seems to work for a while. I can't feel Mischa. I can't feel anything. But my mental sanctuary is not as impenetrable as I had hoped. The sudden commotion ruins everything, and when I blink, he's there in my vision. *The devil.* A monster who thinks he can take Mischa away from me.

"Give him back!" I demand.

Nikolai turns, his eyes flaying me open. "What did you just say?"

"Give him back," I repeat. "I want it to be him."

His hands lock into fists at his sides, and his nostrils flare as he stalks toward me. A voice tells me to run. Maybe it's Mischa. Maybe it's my own sanity, unraveling. But I run. Around the bed and straight past Mischa, down the hall. Nikolai gives chase.

There are only two places for me to go. His bedroom, or his office. Fear, not logic, is dictating my direction, so I choose his office. Locking the door behind me, I dart beneath his desk and try to catch control of my breath.

The lock turns, and hope abandons me.

I'm curled into myself, gasping for breath when he bends down to meet my eyes. His are cold and possessive. Cruel and mocking.

"What now, *zvezda*? Where will you run to now?"

I don't answer him, so he snatches me by the wrist and yanks me away from my hiding place.

"Please," I whisper.

He drags me back down the hall without mercy. "Save your begging for all the men who will come after me."

A sob heaves from my chest at the viciousness of his words. He can't mean them. I don't want to believe he means them. He is angry with me for choosing Mischa. I know that's what it is.

"I never wanted him. I swear it. I just wanted to get it over with."

"Tell him that," Nikolai demands as he tosses me back onto the bed.

Mischa is almost fully dressed when he meets my gaze, and I implore him to forgive me. "I'm sorry. I didn't mean it."

"I know."

He leaves the room, abandoning me to my monster and his rage. I try to curl into myself, but Nikolai is not done. He flips me onto my stomach and utilizes the restraints from the bed to secure my hands above my head.

I shake my head frantically, pleading into the pillow. "Please, not like this. I didn't mean it."

The metal clank of his belt buckle is all I hear, followed by the zipper of his jeans. He's undressing. And I'm in this position because he's going to take me face down, so he doesn't have to look at me.

He moves behind me, prying my legs apart and pressing his fingers against my sex. Everything stills behind me, and the only sound in the room is that of his heavy breath.

"You aren't wet," he murmurs.

I strain my neck to look back at him, but his response is to push my hair into my face, obscuring my vision. His cock nudges against me, and I sob harder.

"Please," I cry out. "Not like this, Nika."

He freezes. I've never used such an intimate endearment with him, but I'm using it now. Time is suspended as I listen to his labored breaths, waiting to see what path he will take.

When his hands find the back of my thighs, they are unexpectedly soft and overwhelmingly large. He could easily pry me apart and never put me back together again, if he wanted to. But instead, his calloused thumbs press against my flesh in slow, shallow circles. A shiver charges up my spine, and Nikolai cups the globes of my ass in his hands, emitting a low, throaty groan.

"You are too obstinate for your own good," he says. "You don't deserve kindness from me."

"I never wanted him," I whisper again.

"So who then?" he demands. "If not Mischa. Or would you still insist on saving yourself for your precious Dante?"

When I don't answer, his fingers move between my thighs, and there is no mistaking his effect on me. I am slick, and I am wanting. Wanting things I've never had. Things that are no good for me.

Nikolai slides over the moisture gathering between my parted thighs and dips a finger inside me, making me clamp around him.

"Answer me." He squeezes my ass cheek with his other palm.

But I can't. Because now his fingers are on my clit, massaging me in a slow, circular pattern. My hips are tilting back toward him, opening without shame. I want more.

I need more.

He grabs a fistful of my hair and tugs, inflicting pain while he gifts me pleasure. "I'm not going to ask you again, *zvezda*. Tell me now, or I will bury my cock inside you without consideration of your fragile virtue."

I moan into the pillow and thrash against him. This isn't right. None of this is right. I hate him. His body has no right to take my virtue. He doesn't have the right to bring me pleasure when he takes no value in the sanctity of what I'm giving him. But it would be weak to deny the truth when he can so clearly see, or feel, it for himself.

"It should have been you," I say. "But you are a hedonistic coward who thinks only of himself."

In the next breath, I'm flipped onto my back, Nikolai's hand wrapped around my throat as he breathes into my face.

"Say it again," he challenges. "Tell me to my face."

"You are a coward," I spit at him. "Go and marry your Russian bride and set me free. You have no need for me now."

His eyes move back and forth between mine, and I am a fool for revealing the jealous undercurrent in my voice. I'm a fool to let him believe for a second that it bothers me. More importantly, I'm a fool for reacting the way I do when his lips crash down onto mine as if he owns me.

I breathe him in and part my lips for his, allowing his tongue to sweep through my protests and lay claim to my mouth. His body is naked and hard against my stomach, and his flesh is on fire.

My legs curl around him as he drinks from my lips, and I plead between breaths for freedom. His answer is to unleash my hands from the restraints and drag them over his body. I curl my fingers into his hair and twist, encouraging the pain I want him to feel. But it makes little difference. He is a thrusting, pulsing, grunting machine.

"Tell me you want me," he demands.

"You disgust me." My nails sink into his back while my words lay into his ego. "You don't deserve to take me when this means nothing to you."

He groans and shoves his throbbing cock against my wetness. "You are a little liar and a stuck-up bitch," he answers. "And I will take pleasure in stripping you of your crown."

"Then do it," I challenge.

He kisses me to shut me up while he fingers me to make me pliable. I claw at him. I inhale him. We binge on each other, and I feel him everywhere. But mostly, I feel my willpower careening out of control as pressure builds deep inside me.

"Come on my fingers," he coaxes. "Show me what a princess looks like when she has fallen from grace, *zvezda*."

Explosions of light burst against my eyelids as white-hot lava melts between my legs. I unravel for him, spinning and spinning until I collapse, wrung out and useless. Everything comes back slowly. The awareness of him. The image of his face so close to mine. His ocean eyes are calm and serene, absent of the lies he likes to weave.

His honesty is brutal, even in silence. And the reverie on his face terrifies me more than any of his words ever have.

"Ruin me," I whisper. "And never let anyone else touch me again."

He closes his eyes and wrestles his cock against me. This trip is a one-way ticket, and there are no refunds or returns. He's going to take my virginity. He's going to ruin me for all other men. I don't feel sorry for it. I only feel impatient.

He squeezes the head inside me as he did before, giving me tiny micro thrusts. His eyes fall shut, and he looks intoxicated before he's even all the way in. It's hard to fathom that it's because of me.

I did that.

"Breathe, little doll," he whispers.

And I do. His body collapses forward, and as he does, his cock takes root inside my body, fracturing my virginity and possibly my sanity too.

He shudders, and I shiver, and together, we breathe. It hurts, as I expected it to, but mostly, I just feel full. Full of Nikolai. And he is raw. There's nothing between us, and I've never felt so exposed.

He buries his face in my hair, inhaling me. The muscles in his forearms shake. He's holding back until I'm ready. And I have the suffocating realization that I need him. I need him on my side until I can find my way out. This is what I tell myself. This is what I try to focus on so that my heart remains caged.

"I'm ready," I whisper.

His pelvis rolls back, and it drags his cock away, leaving me impoverished until it fills me all over again on the return. I touch his hair and smell his skin and watch his face while he fucks me. I watch the way his eyes open and close while he murmurs how good I feel around him.

He squeezes my face and kisses me again. He kisses my throat and my jaw and my hair.

"So sweet." He hums. "Why must you be so sweet?"

It's the last spoken thought before his body pulls tight and he buries himself deep, shuddering out his release. Bare. He is bare, and he's filling me with his cum. His eyes are sated and heavy when he pets my face, his cock softening inside me.

"It does mean something to me," he says. "This gift you have given means more than you could ever know."

CHAPTER 19
NIKOLAI

In the sober light of morning, the little star is no longer under my spell. Cool amber eyes find mine in the reflection of her mirror, disinterested in my presence. I left her in the darkness of night, stealing away to the sanctuary of my own room. And now she is wearing her armor, but she should know it won't do her any good. I will blow it up or burn it down. Whatever I have to do to show her that she is mine.

Freshly bathed, she prepares herself for the day. It's the same ritual I've watched her execute from the monitor in my office more times than I can count. She brushes her hair. Applies her makeup. And then she castigates herself in the mirror for twenty minutes, a slave to her disease.

I don't know if she wishes she was perfect, or if it's only her obsession. But either way, she is perfect to me.

This morning, a black silk robe hangs loosely off her shoulders. And despite the cold reception on her face, her nipples are hard for me. I hope she is sore. I hope that every time she moves today, she feels my cock inside her. I want her to crave it. I want more than anything to demand she never thinks of any other man but me.

"Where are my sheets?" she asks.

"Gone."

Her eyes pinch together. "To my father?"

I don't answer. If she expects remorse, she should know I have none. I don't regret taking her, nor am I sorry for the evidence delivered to her father. It's the way things are done, and she knows this.

She cinches the belt around her robe and crosses her arms. "It's a disgusting tradition."

I want to do all manner of disgusting things to her. For example, right now, I'd like nothing better than to shove my cock into her mouth to shut her up. I could easily spend the day buried inside her, brutalizing her tender pussy to remind her of her place. However, I have other pressing matters to attend to. With this in mind, I toss the morning-after pill onto her vanity, along with the birth control pills the doctor provided.

She picks them up and examines them, relief flooding her eyes when she sees the first package, only to be washed away with panic at the second.

Her eyes shoot up to mine. "I can't go on the pill."

"Why?"

"It causes weight gain."

"So does a baby." I walk toward the door.

"You've fulfilled your duty," she says. "You ruined me. I see no further need for protection—"

"You can either take the pills or take a baby inside you, but either way, you will be taking my cock, *zvezda*. Don't fool yourself by pretending otherwise."

I FIND MISCHA AT KOSMOS, half-drunk with a stripper grinding on his lap. It's not even ten a.m., and I'd be hard pressed to determine whether he's been at it all night or he's just getting started.

He lives the life of a perpetual bachelor, enjoying all the perks the brotherhood has to offer. Unlimited booze and women have satisfied many a Vor, myself included. But when I look at him this morning, it is not envy or amusement I feel. There is only pity.

Over the past few years, I have indulged my baser desires often and with whomever I please. But it has been a fleeting satisfaction. This morning, I am a changed man. I have tasted honey, and I can't ever imagine settling for anything less again. Knowing that Nakya waits for me back at my home is a privilege unlike any other.

Considering the facts, it's a foolish notion. Soon, I will be engaged to Ana, and Nakya will be returned to her father. It's the only way this can work. The only way I can save her. Our paths were not meant to parallel forever. Logically, I know I'll be forced to give her up, but it doesn't make the decision easier to accept.

Like many of the Vor, marriage is a natural step for me. I have thought about it from time to time, believing it would happen on its own schedule. But I never imagined the face of my wife or my unborn children because there wasn't an instinctive fit. The molds were empty, something yet to be determined. But now the pressure to fill them is bearing down on me, and it isn't Ana's face that I see as my wife or even the mother of my children.

The face that I see is sharper. High cheekbones and honeyed eyes. After this morning, how could I not imagine Nakya swollen with my children? They would have her tenacity and my strong Russian genes. They would be unstoppable.

If it was meant to be.

Mischa opens his eyes at half-mast, a Cheshire grin spreading across his face. "Kolyan." He makes a sloppy gesture with his hand. "Come and join us, won't you?"

I look at the stripper. Bare tits bounce around as she grinds on Mischa's lap, her tiny red thong swallowed up by her ass cheeks. She does nothing for me. In fact, when I look around at the variety of naked women ready and willing to please, none of them do anything for me. Brunettes, redheads, blondes. Women of all flavors and shapes. Natural or perfectly sculpted silicone. There isn't a club in this city that boasts a better selection, yet not a single one of them inspires an erection. It only fuels my frustration as I snap my fingers at the stripper.

"Go away. We have business."

She pouts but does as she's told. Mischa grunts and pulls out his cigarettes, extending one in offer. I light up and allow the much-needed nicotine to soak into my lungs.

"You said you wanted to show me something."

Mischa takes a long drag and nods, exhaling through his nose. "You still pissed at me?"

"I never was."

He laughs, and I want to punch him. Of course, it's a lie, but it's better than the truth.

"You told me to have a go," he says. "You said we needed to follow Viktor's orders."

"I know what I fucking said."

"She's trouble, Kolyan," he slurs. "You should cut and run now while you still can. Before you get any more invested."

"I'm not invested."

Another lie, and a pointless one at that. Mischa can read me better than most.

"Have you spoken to Viktor?" I ask.

Mischa stubs out his cigarette and stands up, zipping up his jeans. "I need a fucking burger or something."

I gesture to the back door, and we walk to my car in silence. I'm anxious to hear his response, and after last night, I wouldn't be surprised if he sold me out. It's what I deserve.

"I told him I got the job done," Mischa says.

I look over at him, and I'm lost for words. He lied to the *pakhan* for me. If I go down, he's going down with me, and the pressure I feel to protect him only adds to my current mental state.

"Thank you, Misch. I know I don't deserve your loyalty, but I am grateful regardless."

"It's a loose end," he answers. "The story might work for now … until he sees the girl and her feelings for you all over her face."

If Nakya has any obvious feelings for me, I'm unable to see them myself. She is locked down tighter than a crypt, and like any thief worth his salt, I want to pry her open and uncover all her secrets.

"He won't see her," I assure him.

"I wouldn't count on it," Mischa says. "Considering he told me to give you a message."

"What's the message?"

"He wants her at the Christmas party."

My fingers tighten around the steering wheel. "Why the Christmas party?"

Mischa shrugs. "I don't know the reason."

Viktor is still testing me. It could be the only reason. He wants to ensure my loyalty to Ana, and I dread what this party might entail.

I pull up to a drive-thru, and Mischa orders between drags of his cigarette, and then we park while he eats. He said he had something for me, and I want to get on with it, but I also need him sober for the impending conversation.

The car is quiet, so I turn on the radio and smoke another cigarette. Mischa polishes off two burgers and a large fry before leaning back in the seat and patting his belly. "Much better."

"I don't have all day, Mischa."

"I know," he says. "But don't get pissed. It isn't really about your mother."

"Then what the fuck is it?"

"As it turns out, Manuel and one of his guards have the same taste in women. Or more specifically, one woman. They've both been banging the same chick. My new friend Eduardo is highly motivated to keep his job and his dick."

"So we have an in?"

"We have an in." Mischa nods. "But the guy is a nobody, really. He wasn't able to get me much, just some old surveillance videos from the basement. Which, for the record, your mother wasn't on any of them."

"So what is on them?" I ask.

He tosses me his phone, and I unlock the screen. An endless number of files are ready to view, and I'm not even certain where to begin.

The first video I open contains a haunting image of Nakya's mother in bed late at night. I fast forward through hours of nothingness until Manuel comes stumbling into the room, obviously drunk. There isn't audio but isn't necessary. The image is enough, and one I won't soon forget. He beats her and fucks her unconscious body, leaving her in a puddle of filth when he climbs into bed.

The next video is of a similar nature, only this one takes place in the kitchen. He burns her hand on the stove and shoves her face into a sink full of dishwater. When she comes up gasping for breath, a sickening need motivates me to freeze the frame on her face. Without her veil, she looks so much like Nakya. And it occurs to me that this is what will become of her if I send her back to Manuel. An empty shell with dead, soulless eyes.

"When was this taken?"

"Five years before her death," Mischa answers.

Manuel's wife died long before she ever made it to the grave. She was a victim too, and if he could do this to his own wife, there's no telling what became of his mistresses.

A heaviness settles into my chest as I scroll through the images. There are hundreds of video stills. Thousands of hours of his abuse.

"Eduardo tells me that he revisits the videos often when he is drunk," Mischa says.

He saved them because he is sick. He saved them because he is a vile waste of energy who doesn't deserve to live another day on this earth.

I'm tempted to end him now and be done with it. But those thoughts come to an abrupt halt when another still catches my attention. One that isn't Manuel's wife, but his daughter. Acid boils my gut before I even open it. I shouldn't. It has no business being a part of my decision. What happened in Nakya's past can't be changed, but my finger hovers over the play button, regardless. If I watch this video, it will change things. It will change me. Mischa knows it, and I can't understand his motives for doing this.

"Why are you showing me these?"

"You wanted to know Manuel's character."

"I knew from the moment I met him that Manuel Valentini wasn't worth the breath it took to speak his name." I scoff. "So don't bullshit me."

"I got curious about the girl." He shrugs. "She seems fucked up."

"She isn't," I snarl.

It's a lie, and it doesn't take a team of psychiatrists to determine that much. But I don't want him speaking about her that way. I don't want anyone speaking about her that way. It's my secret to keep. She is my broken doll to repair, and mine alone.

"Just watch it," Mischa urges.

I click play, and my stomach lurches at the grainy images on the screen. My suspicions were right, and this is the confirmation. Manuel wasn't just violent with his wife. He was violent with Nakya too. She spills a glass of water on the carpet, and without a second thought, he backhands her so viciously she falls limply into the coffee table.

I know I should stop. This can't matter to me because it won't change her circumstances. But nothing is as intimate as experiencing her pain, and I can't bring myself to look away from the horrors she endured. I need to understand them. I need to know her darkest shame.

The first video blends into the next until it is an endless stream of savagery that only gets worse. Manuel pulling her hair. Pushing her. Slapping her. Biting her. The abuse progresses over time as she grows, and eventually, she becomes the recipient of his fists and even his feet when he kicks her.

My fists are trembling with a gluttonous compulsion to bathe them in Manuel's blood. I want to drain him of his life force. I want to beat his face until there is nothing left. Mischa sees it, and wisely chooses not to tell me that he was right. This video has only solidified what I already knew to be true.

Nakya is inside me. She has bested the thief by stealing something that doesn't belong to her. And when I kill Manuel, it won't be for my mother.

It will be for her.

CHAPTER 20
TANAKA

I hesitate at the end of the bed, wary of the clothing laid out for me. The clothing I picked out. They are nice clothes. Beautiful clothes. The same that I have worn many times over.

Something my father taught me was that I should always dress modestly. Modesty translated into skirts and blouses and feminine dresses. The only pants I could get away with were the leggings I wore to class. But for as long as I can remember, I wondered what it would be like to wear whatever I wanted.

I used to collect magazines, admiring the glossy photos of women in their bold attire. Jeans and ripped shirts and trendy new fashion pieces that my father would never approve. I dreamed of a day I could wear something like that, even though I doubted it would come. My clothing has always been insistent on one unbending truth.

I'm a good girl who does as she's told.

But right now, the neutral tones on the bed are suffocating me with their lies. Because I'm not a good girl anymore. I would be a fraud if I wore these now. And I'm surprised to find how little I care.

Something broke inside me when Nikolai took me. The pressure I felt to be perfect deflated like a balloon. I've been carrying it around for so long that I didn't think I could ever be liberated. But I am. The only torment I feel is that I lost my virtue to someone who cares so little. A man like Nikolai thinks nothing of taking me in the middle of the night, only to steal away before the light of morning.

In some ways, I wish I could be like him. I wish I could just not care. He will come back for me, and he will take me again. Something I equally long for and dread. My armor must remain intact. And in the interim, I must learn how to navigate this world as the kind of woman I've always wanted to be.

Gathering the clothes from the bed, I return to the closet, tossing the worthless garments onto the floor. The ritual continues as I tear through the racks of mind-numbing colors, adding to the pile of what I no longer want in my life. In the end, all that remains are my ballet clothes and a few small shoe boxes at the end of the closet.

In one of those boxes, I find what I'm looking for. A pair of jeans. They still have the tag on them, purchased more for symbolism than for usefulness. I bought them online when I was feeling brave, and I've held onto them for two years. Often, I would take them out and try them on, walking around my bedroom the same way that fashion models do.

Today, I will wear them as a regular woman. A woman with the freedom to choose.

I pair the jeans with a white leotard and leave them rolled at the ankle. They are a loose fit. *Boyfriend cut*, the tag reads. And when I look in the mirror, I don't recognize myself, but it feels good. And I decide that I might not be able to control my numbered days, but while I'm alive, I am going to live.

Down the hall, Nikolai's office is still open. He rarely locks it, I've discovered, but probably because he doesn't have anything to hide in there. It's just a desk, computer, a phone, and his whiskey.

Inside the desk drawers are a few essential office tools, but unfortunately, I don't find a pair of scissors. There is, however, a letter opener. It's heavy and sharp, so I think it will do the job well enough.

To my satisfaction, when I return to my closet, I discover that it does. It shreds through the blouses and dresses quite easily, up until the point when it begins to dull. Regardless, I don't stop until every last piece is ruined. And when I'm finished, I look up to find Nikolai in the doorway, watching me curiously.

"What are you doing?" he asks.

"I want new clothes," I tell him. "You can add it to my father's bill, right?"

I expect a fight out of him. What I don't expect is the booming laughter and an easy smile that transforms his face. It's the first time I've ever seen him so unguarded, and it knocks me off balance.

"Yes, we can add it to his bill," he says. "Now come here."

I rock back off my knees and stand, moving toward him with an acute awareness of his every breath. He looks tired but calm. Sky blue eyes warm me like the sun, and strong, steady hands wrap me in comfort as he draws me closer.

"I like you like this," he murmurs.

"Like what?"

His eyes carve a path over my body. The body I have only ever hated. And even if I feel at home in his arms, I can't feel comfortable. I have so many doubts about what he sees when he looks at me this way. Is he delusional or am I?

He tips my chin up with his fingers, his voice firm but gentle. "Stop."

"Stop what?"

"Stop thinking, *zvezda*," he implores. "For once, believe me when I tell you that you are beautiful in every way. Yes?"

"Okay," I lie.

His breath blows over my neck, and he kisses the place where my pulse beats for him. "It would be easier if you hated me."

I let my face rest against his warm chest, feeling his heart beat too. "You're going to ruin me, aren't you?"

"I thought I already had."

We are both quiet then. He chooses not to relieve my fears, and I choose not to acknowledge them. He is right that it would be easier if I hated him. I should hate him for everything he's done. He can't let me go, and I can't make him.

His lips find the hollow of my throat, and when he kisses me, fire licks along my skin. I return the favor by rising on my toes to taste the flesh that's most forbidden. The one where I might leave a mark, and I hope I do when my teeth graze his skin.

He grunts when he feels it, and things take a swift turn in his favor. Pinning me to the wall, he grabs my ass and lifts me against his crotch, throbbing heat stabbing into my belly. The straps of my leotard come down, baring my breasts as if he owns them. His hand rubs between my legs, and his clothes rub against my sensitive nipples. I jump at every touch, clinging to his shoulders and squeezing my thighs around his hips.

And I learn something new but not unsurprising about my captor. He bites back. First my throat, and then my collarbone, and finally my aching nipples. The game of who can leave their mark on who is sure to be won by him because I feel him everywhere. Red, mottled blotches cover my skin where he's tasted me. My flesh is swollen and tender, a testament to his ownership over me.

My fingers twist and pull at his hair, trying to bring him closer so I can do the same. I want to bite him. I want to mark him. And more importantly, I want to own him. He groans and nips at my ear, his breath hot on my skin.

"You are turning into a very bad girl," he hums. "Someday, I will let you mark me, pet."

Someday.

The ever-present reminder that this is temporary. I try to shove him away, and he captures me by the wrists, shaking his head.

"Don't pout, my sweet. It will be your body that I take every night."

To prove it, he yanks my zipper down and removes my jeans.

Next comes my leotard, and in a blink, I'm naked. It isn't fair that he doesn't give me the same courtesy, only reaching down to unzip his jeans and retrieve his cock. But when I see the tan, heavy flesh, my trials are soon forgotten.

"Are you sore, *zvezda*?" he asks as he rubs the fat head against my small opening.

"Yes," I answer.

He groans and thrusts his hips forward, stabbing inside me. I cry out, and he rumbles his approval against my chest.

"You should always be sore from my cock," he declares. "You should always remember who owns you."

He squeezes my hips, tilting them to meet his needs, and my head falls back against the wall.

"Put your hands up," he says. "And hold onto me with your legs."

I put my hands up, and he pins them to the wall with his. My legs squeeze around him, and it's the only thing holding me up as he rocks his hips forward. He tortures my nipples with his tongue while he fucks me, and there's nothing I can do but endure it.

"These tits belong to me." His words are punctuated by his thrusts. "So does this ass. And this pussy. If you understand nothing else, *zvezda*, then understand this. You are mine."

His momentum builds with every hushed declaration, and I confirm that he's right when pleasure rockets through my body. Spasms arc through me, forcing me to bow and contract around him. We are panting. High. Hungry for each other. And I can't deny how much I like this. He's inside me, and for now, he is mine too.

He stops and starts drunkenly, confusion marring his brows.

"Stop, stop," he urges, but I'm not doing anything. I can't do anything with the way he has me pinned. Still, his hips grind a to a halt, and his fingers kiss my face. "I'm going to blow if you keep doing that, *zvezda*."

"I'm not doing anything," I protest.

"You are," he insists. "You are ruining me. What the fuck are you doing?"

Even in my doped-up state of mind, I'm cognizant enough to recognize it's a rhetorical question. It's a question I don't have the answer for. So I stay quiet, watching him as he alternates between fucking me and cursing me out.

"Tell me that you belong to me," he says.

I shake my head and squeeze my eyes shut, exhausted.

"Tell me that you belong to me, and I will make you come every day."

His lies pour salt into the bitter wound between us. He has no right to say such things.

"I won't be your mistress," I tell him. "I would rather die."

Hard fingers squeeze my face. "Look at me."

I open my eyes, and his are flame blue. He thrusts harder, faster, determined to prove he's still in control when he comes inside me. And on his last sputtered breath, he confirms my deepest fear.

"You will be whatever I want you to be."

CHAPTER 21
NIKOLAI

"Kol'ka," Viktor's voice greets me from the other end of the line.

"How are you?" I ask.

It's not unusual for him to call me, but I find myself dreading it more every day. The longer I lie to him, the closer I am to coming unraveled. He will start making demands soon. Demands I have no choice but to obey. This is the life I wanted—the one I was born into—yet it feels suffocating.

"I am well," he answers. "But Ana has been asking after you. She is eager to see you at the Christmas party this evening."

I close my eyes and lean back, grateful he is not here to witness the tension on my face. "I look forward to seeing her as well."

The words feel like a betrayal to Nakya, and it's unsettling, to say the least. I owe her nothing. My duty is what's important.

"Ana requested that you wear a blue tie this evening," Viktor says. "She will be in blue as well."

"Then I will have Mischa pick one up."

"I trust he will be bringing the girl along?"

His statement catches me off guard, and it seems Mischa forgot to mention that detail.

"He will," I assure him. "We are traveling together."

"Very good," he says. "I know she is not Russian, but perhaps she will make a suitable companion for him in the interim. A nice plaything, anyway."

My teeth come together so violently, the force reverberates through my jaw.

The line is silent, and I know it's up to me to fill it. Courtesy dictates that I should ask pleasantries about his daughters and snuff out any suspicions he may have about Nakya. But I can't force the words, try as I might.

Viktor takes it upon himself to fill the gap. "I suppose I should tell you that Manuel was not happy with the package delivered to his doorstep."

"I don't imagine he was."

"If nothing else, it will motivate him to pay off his debt. Or perhaps I only imagine the best in him. I suppose it could also provoke him to write off his daughter altogether."

"I don't know what he will do," I admit. But neither of those options are what's best for Nakya.

"How are you coming along with your quest for answers?" Viktor inquires.

"I will have them soon," I lie.

Another silence. He doesn't believe me, and he shouldn't. It's not like me to be dishonest with him. It's not like me to betray my brotherhood for my own selfish desires. But it's the bed I have made for myself.

"I hope so, Kol'ka," he says. "You are running out of time."

"Did you pick up my tie?"

Mischa nods, tossing a shopping bag onto the bed. He's wearing new trousers and a black dress shirt, and I haven't failed to notice that his hair is freshly cut and groomed too. While it might be custom to wear our best for the annual Christmas party, it doesn't suppress the urge to wallop him in the face.

I tear into the bag and retrieve my new tie.

"I told you to get blue, you *doorak*."

"You specifically told me to get red," he answers.

I utter a few more insults about his intelligence under my breath while I put it on. I did specifically tell him to get red, but I'll never admit it.

It isn't Mischa's fault that he's been put in this situation. It's nobody's fault but my own. But that doesn't mean I can be civilized about it.

The only solace I have is that while Nakya is on his arm tonight, it is my cum dripping down her legs. She had no time to question my reasons when I burst into her room this afternoon and bent her over the bed, fucking her twice to prove a point.

She belongs to me. And soon, she will come to acknowledge it with her own lips.

"You know, if this bothers you," Mischa says, "I could be needed elsewhere tonight. An unavoidable situation comes up, and we could avoid this problem altogether."

"What problem?" I shrug into my jacket, avoiding his eyes. "There isn't a problem."

"If you want my opinion—"

"Which I don't."

"As your friend, I think it needs to be said," he persists. "If you don't get a handle on this situation now, it's going to end badly for all of us."

"What is there to handle, Mischa?"

"It's written on your face, Kolyan. And if I can see your obsession with this girl, do you think it will be long before others recognize it too? Already, Viktor has his doubts."

"Christ." I rub my tired eyes. "I need a fucking cigarette."

Mischa finally makes himself useful by providing me with one. I walk to the window, resting on the ledge while I blow smoke out into the black void of night.

"If it makes any difference, you should know that I would never touch her."

I meet his gaze and smile. "I know. Because I would kill you if you did."

CHAPTER 22
TANAKA

As part of my exercise in liberation, I make an executive decision to go bold with my makeup tonight. Gold has always paired well with my skin tone, but my father thought it was trashy. Tonight, I apply it in layers, each one a little more daring than the former. I've done cat eyes for ballet performances before, so it doesn't take me long to add a perfect liquid line. The last and final touch is a dauntless shade of red lipstick, which I end up applying and removing several times before finding the courage to leave it.

It shouldn't matter, but I took Nikolai's directives to heart. After he fucked me like a savage this afternoon, he gifted me a red dress and left me with one instruction for tonight. Simply that I must be the most beautiful woman in the room. A tall order, and an impossible one at that. But when I think of the alternative, it's worth every effort.

The door to my room opens, and for the second time today, Nikolai barges inside. This time, he also has Mischa in tow. I look up from my vanity and suck in a breath. The pair of them really are a sight to behold, but it's Nikolai who steals the show.

The fitted black suit is his magnum opus, and I pity any man who stands beside him this evening. But worse, I already envy the woman who will.

My heart squeezes, and I smile through the pain, rising from my seat to greet the two men. Nikolai's possession is felt on every inch of my skin as his eyes sweep over me, but the satisfaction is short lived.

"You are to stay close to Mischa's side tonight."

His words cut me to the quick, and I look at Mischa, who seems as appeased by the notion as I am.

I don't know what's better or worse. Being front and center to witness Nikolai's date with Ana or being left behind at home. Regardless, the decision is not mine to make.

"Okay."

"You have five more minutes." Nikolai glances at his watch. "Meet us downstairs when you finish."

He leaves, and I spend every second of the next five minutes thinking of reasons to hate him.

The car ride is quiet. Mischa and Nikolai are up front, and I'm in the back. They barely speak to each other along the way, and the trepidation simmering between all of us is so sticky it's hard to breathe.

When we finally arrive at the compound, I leap from the car and take mouthfuls of fresh air at the first opportunity. Nikolai turns to look at me briefly before guiding me closer to Mischa. It's time to go inside, but none of us move. Nikolai's hand is still on my arm, and he isn't letting go.

"Kolyan," Mischa whispers under his breath.

His tone is a warning. Nikolai's actions are garnering unwanted attention from the men at the door, and he's playing a dangerous game of chicken. But he doesn't seem to be aware of the consequences, or even aware of what's happening around us. His eyes are on me, dazed and uncertain.

THIEF

I take it upon myself to remove myself from his grasp, opting for Mischa's arm instead. My motivations are unclear, even to myself. Maybe it's spite. Maybe it's jealousy. Or maybe I just don't want to endanger him in any way. If it's true, it's a fool's errand. I should know by now the only one in danger is me.

The distance between us seems to shake Nikolai back to his senses, and he walks ahead of us, leaving Mischa and me to trail behind. Mischa doesn't look at me, and for that, I am grateful. I would do well to burn from my memory the night I offered him my virtue. But the shame is not only mine to bear. I'm certain Mischa will most likely remember it for eternity.

The men at the door stop us and exchange greetings, once again reminding me of my insignificance in this Vory world. I am not a wife or even a girlfriend, and therefore, I'm fair game for their wandering eyes.

Inside, Viktor and his daughter are quick to greet us. He seems to be in a jovial mood, but Ana's face is quick to fall, and her father is quick to notice.

"You are wearing red," Viktor notes, his eyes observing Nikolai's tie.

Nikolai answers in Russian, blaming Mischa for the mix-up, but it does little to soothe Ana's unhappiness. I didn't notice it before, or perhaps I just assumed it was themed. Mischa and Nikolai are both wearing red ties, and I am wearing a red dress. Viktor does not seem to think it's a coincidence as his eyes move from Nikolai to me, his lip curling in disgust. He says he would like to speak to Nikolai in private, and they disappear down the hall.

When we are called to dinner minutes later, it seems the issue has been settled for the time being. Viktor returns as his celebratory self, one arm around Ana and the other around Nikolai.

Mischa and I sit farther down the table, away from the soon-to-be newlyweds. I focus on the food served and busy myself with trying to identify each dish. It's a feast consisting of Russian traditional foods and delicacies. A few of which I've come to know in my time at Nikolai's, but most of which I'm yet to learn.

The meal is not as appealing as it should be. I spend most of the time pushing food around on my plate and trying to divert my attention from the other end of the table. On more than one occasion, I feel Nikolai's eyes on me, but I don't dare look up. With certainty, he will want to punish me for not eating, but with certainty, I don't care.

When the plates are cleared, the group is ushered into another room for drinks and conversation. Mischa and I remain at each other's side, wordless. But it isn't long before Nikolai is making a fly by, issuing an order.

We are to meet him near the bathrooms in five minutes.

My limbs are stiff, and I get the distinct feeling that I'm walking the plank as we travel down the hall. Mischa, too, seems nervous, and when Nikolai arrives to meet us, words are exchanged between them.

I can only catch some of the conversation in their native language since they are speaking so fast. But from the gist of it, I understand two things. One is that Mischa thinks Nikolai is being an idiot, and the second is that Nikolai is in charge, so it doesn't matter what Mischa thinks.

Nikolai issues him another order to stand guard outside the door, and then he is manhandling me inside. The lock clicks behind us, and I try to move away. I make it two steps before he has me trapped in his grip again.

"Why are you making this harder than it has to be?" he demands.

"I haven't done anything," I snap. "You are just angry because you can't control this situation—"

His lips swallow the rest of my words. The kiss is violent and possessive, and his hold on me is brutal. In seconds, he wrecks the style I spent an hour perfecting when his fingers tangle in my hair. I should care that he's acting like a child, but relief is all I feel.

He wants me and not her.

"Tell me you belong to me," he whispers. "And I'll fuck you sweet."

I close my eyes and breathe him in. Cloves and smoke and danger. He has taken so much from me already, but it isn't enough. He wants everything, and he won't settle until he has my soul too. But I refuse to cave on this. I refuse to give him everything when I'm the one who loses in the end.

When he recognizes the rejection on my face, his eyes flash, and he forces me to my knees.

"Have it your way, then. I'll fuck you dirty, pet."

He unzips his pants and tugs me forward by his hold on my hair, rubbing my face against the bulge in his briefs. He is brick hard already, and there is a small damp spot where his pre-cum has leaked out. Evidence that he's been thinking about this since dinner.

"Suck me," he demands. "Show me how pretty a ballerina looks with a cock in her throat."

I couldn't move if I tried. His hold on me is unyielding, and regardless, his briefs are still in the way. He doesn't seem to be in a hurry to remove them as he rubs himself against my face. Instead, he unties the top of my halter dress, letting the straps of silk fall away so my breasts are open and available to him. They are tender already, and I jump when his fingers brush over my nipple.

Nikolai seems to consider this a victory as he offers a cruel smile. "See, little star? It's not so bad being a toy. I will fuck you whenever I want, and you will like it because you are filthy just like me."

I try to shake my head because I want to deny it, but he makes his words true when he yanks down his briefs and shoves his cock in my face. I can smell his arousal, and it arouses me. I don't want him to be right, but I need this dirty, depraved act with him. I need him to fuck me in this bathroom to prove I'm all he requires. And he's going to make it a lesson I won't forget when he forces his cock into my mouth, all the way to the back of my throat.

I gag, and he pets my face.

"My dirty little doll," he praises with a ragged breath. "You like this cock in your mouth?"

It's a question I can't answer because my mouth is full. He isn't looking for an answer anyway. He's only looking to fuck me.

And he does.

It's rough, and it's sloppy. This isn't for any other purpose than bringing him immediate relief. His hips buck and roll while he drags himself in and out of my mouth. He's too long to fit inside, but it makes no difference. It's enough for him.

He inhales sharply and curses with every pass. I may be the one kneeling at his feet, but right now, he's a slave to me. I want to suspend this moment in time. I want to keep him hanging on the edge of agony forever. But ultimately, the control always comes back to him.

Long, dark lashes sweep over his cheeks as he lurches forward, holding me in place as his dick shudders in my mouth. There is no conversation about pulling out. He doesn't want to, and after my rejection, he's determined to prove he owns me.

I'm not willing to give in so easily, and when he pulls from my mouth, I spit it on the floor. In the face of my defiance, he offers me a lazy smile.

"I should make you lick that up."

"You could try," I challenge.

"I think you would like it too much," he says.

Using my hair as an anchor, he wipes his softening cock on my cheek, anointing the last of his cum into my skin. I glare up at him, and he offers me his hand. He leads me to the sink, and I catch a glimpse of myself in the mirror, shocked by what I see. Lipstick smeared and mascara running down my face. Tangled hair and blotchy skin.

Whatever satisfaction I took in this turn of events is fading quickly. In just a few moments, Nikolai will return to his duties as Ana's future husband, forgetting what happened here. And I am left to wonder if soon he will forget me too. When Ana wears his ring and his star, he will take her as he pleases. It leaves a bitter taste on my lips, and I hate him for it already.

"You look pretty like this," Nikolai tells me as he wets a paper cloth. "Dirty and used by me. I like it very much, *zvezda*."

"I suppose your wife won't ever look this way," I answer. "You will probably treat her differently, considering she's Viktor's daughter."

He rubs the back of his neck, his tension returning. "Do not speak of things that you don't know."

"I know more than you give me credit for. You will marry her, and there is no point in denying it. The longer you keep me, the closer you come to risking your future and mine. So I am pleading with you now, Nika. Let me go before you tire of me. Let me find my own happiness and remember you this way before everything sours."

"You are a brave girl." He leans in so that his words brush my lips. "But you know I can't let you go, Nakya. I stole you, and I will keep you until I am ready to say goodbye."

It isn't an admission of his feelings. In all fairness, those words could mean anything. He likes to break me so he can put me back together again.

The proof is in his actions, weakening me blow by blow. A gentle caress of the cloth, the smoothing of my hair. The tying of my dress, and the soft, tender kiss he leaves on my lips. Maybe they are sweet.

Or maybe he's just wiping away the evidence.

CHAPTER 23
TANAKA

Nikolai leaves the bathroom first, giving me time to collect my thoughts and reinforce my emotional armor. When I do step outside, Mischa is waiting for me in the hall, his face devoid of emotion. Like Nikolai, he has strong Slavic features. Pale eyes and the facial structure of a Viking. He has all the attributes that would make him considerably handsome to a wide audience of women, but I am not one of them. It appears the feeling is mutual because, as it stands, he can barely look at me.

"I'm sorry," I tell him. "About that night—"

"You have nothing to be sorry about," he answers. "And it's probably best if we never speak of it again."

I nod, and we are both quiet again. Down the hall, it appears the dancing has commenced. I don't know that I'll ever be ready for what the rest of this evening holds, but I'd rather get it over with than hide in this hall. Mischa, however, has other intentions. Just when I thought the conversation was dead in the water, he touches my arm to get my attention.

"Are your feelings for him genuine?" he asks. "Or are you just doing what you think is best for your own situation?"

THIEF

His implication rattles me. To think he has any right to question my motives is beyond laughable.

"You are asking me if I love him or hate him?" I glare. "Then it depends on the day. The hour. Sometimes, the minute."

Mischa scrutinizes my face. It wasn't my intent to utter that awful word. *Love.* His accusation unsettled me, and I wasn't thinking straight. But of course, Mischa doesn't see it that way.

"He can't be with you, Nakya," he says. "You have to know this. Whatever is happening between you two doesn't matter. He can never be with you."

I swallow the bitterness in my throat and straighten my spine. "I know."

"If you truly care about him, then do what's best for him. Get out while you still can. Go somewhere far away and forget your name. Forget your old life and your family and any world that ever existed for you."

"That's an easy solution for you," I answer. "Are you going to help me?"

He lowers his head. "I can't."

"Then don't tell me to escape. I have nowhere to go. No money, no resources—"

"Find a way," he insists. "You are the daughter of a criminal. It should not be that difficult for you to figure it out. You've been raised tough, and you are a survivor. If you want to live, then leave."

The hard truths hurt, and this time is no exception. I know that Mischa is right. Nikolai is too blinded by his own confliction to do what's necessary in this situation, and soon, it will be too late. Already, I crave him. I miss him when he's gone, and I anticipate the smallest interaction we might have. It isn't healthy. I have clung to the illusion that my captor can be my savior too, but it isn't possible.

I have to be the one to walk away. But something is still holding me back. I'm not ready to let him go, and I can't admit that to Mischa right now.

"I'll try to find a way," I croak.

Mischa nods. For the sake of his friend, he wants to believe my assurances. For the sake of my sanity, I want to believe them too.

We walk down the corridor together, edging into the fray. Laughter and music assault my ears, and around us, the merriment is in full swing. Between the drinking and toasting and conversations and dancing, I try to find my bearings. I don't belong here. This is an occasion for celebration, and I have nothing to celebrate. Everyone is blissfully intoxicated, sparkling in their finery, and the most shocking thing of all is that love is present too. There are so many couples in love. I would never have believed it if I didn't see it for myself, but maybe what Nikolai said is true. *There is no other man who holds his wife in higher regard than a Vor.* And at the epicenter of all that love is the man who can never love me, dancing with his future wife.

To see him with her after he just left me makes me flinch. I expected it. I thought I was prepared for it, but it only nurtures the disease inside me. The belief that I will never be *enough*. My arms hang limply at my sides, and I feel too weak to move.

The torment shocks me back to reality. This was the reminder I needed that it's time to be strong. Maybe what I told Mischa wasn't a lie after all. Maybe soon, I will be strong on my own. Away from this world and away from the mafia.

"Don't look," Mischa says. "It will only make it worse."

I pull my gaze away from Nikolai, grateful that Mischa is here to keep me from making a fool of myself.

"Dance with me?" I ask.

He chews on his lip while he contemplates an answer. It's a dangerous question and probably not fair to him. But I want to do something to take my mind off Nikolai.

"He will probably kill me for it." He offers me his hand. "But it will be worth it to say that I danced with the most beautiful girl in the room."

"You are just trying to make me feel better."

"I wouldn't lie about that." He grins. "I've seen you naked, remember?"

"I think you were right when you said it would be best if we never spoke of that night again."

He laughs. And we dance. For a few minutes, I'm just a girl in a red dress. Not a prisoner. Not a ballerina. Not a mafia princess. Mischa makes me feel at ease, but he doesn't make my heart flutter. I wish he did. Things would be easier if it was him. But it isn't him, and when Nikolai's shadow falls over us, he makes that abundantly clear.

"Mischa," he barks. "There is business at Kosmos that requires your attention."

Mischa nods, relinquishing me. "Sure."

He doesn't ask what sort of business requires his immediate attention because there is none. Nikolai just wants him gone. And once Mischa takes his leave, I'm the next item on his agenda.

"Go sit with the women," he orders. "It's time for the men to do business."

I leave the caveman with a piercing glare and nothing else. He doesn't deserve my words or the breath it would require to utter them.

The women are gathered in an adjacent room littered with tables and chairs. Divided into small groups, they drink and gossip among themselves. I wade through the crowd and choose an empty area in the back where I can be alone with my thoughts.

On the opposite side of the floor, the men tend to their business, which really means drinking whiskey and smoking cigars. That, at least, is the same in every mafia culture.

"Tanaka."

It appears that my sanctuary is not safe from everyone because Alexei has found me. Beside him, a ghostly woman clings to his arm. In person, his wife looks more haunted than I imagined. Tragic is the only word I can think of to describe her. She is beautiful and pale, but empty.

I give her a reserved smile, and Alexei smooths his palms over her shoulders. "You will be just fine, Solnyshko. You have your star, yes?"

She touches the tattoo on her hand where her husband has left his mark on her, and a small fire of jealousy kindles inside me. I don't want to be owned. I don't want to be property. But by the way his eyes soften when they fall on her, it's obvious he loves her. He would do anything for her. And that is what his star signifies.

"I'll be just a few short steps away if you need anything," he says.

"Okay."

Alexei releases her reluctantly, and she comes to sit beside me. There's an awkward gap of silence in which I try to figure out the best approach for this situation. Alexei wanted me to befriend her. The girl has been through all nine circles of hell, and she needs an ally in this strange new world. She was not born into the mafia, and it's evident as her eyes dart around the room.

"I don't fit in here either."

"What do you mean?" Her reply is spoken in a soft and childlike voice.

I decide to take an honest approach with her. Someone who has been through as much trauma as she has will undoubtedly find it difficult to trust anyone. But if I level the playing field, she might open up.

"I am simply collateral," I explain. "My father owes a large debt, and I am in Nikolai's charge until he comes through with it."

"Oh. When do you think that will be?"

"Never," I answer. "He cannot pay."

Her eyes widen, and she looks stricken at the thought. "So what will happen to you?"

I glance around the room, subconsciously seeking out my captor, and it appears Ana isn't the only contender for his affections. There is yet another woman who I don't know making her way into his orbit. I force my attention back to Talia and clutch my hands in my lap. "Whatever Nikolai decides."

She is quiet for a pause, and I think that maybe I took the wrong approach after all.

"I was collateral too," she blurts.

I offer her a smile. "I know."

"You do?"

I don't want to taint our budding friendship, so I won't mention the things Alexei told me. It would be a fallacy to say his intentions are the only reason we find ourselves together this evening when I genuinely do want to be her friend. She would be the only real friend I ever had.

"I overheard Nikolai mention you," I say.

"Oh."

We fall into a natural silence, observing the chaos around us. But it's difficult to ignore the blatant staring of our feminine cohorts. Talia fidgets beside me, tension seeping into her features.

"Don't worry. You will get used to it. They don't like you because they will never be you."

Her brows pinch together. "I don't understand."

"Your husband." I nod to the other room. "He is the ah ... councilor to Viktor. He outranks their husbands in every way, which means that you do also."

"Oh."

"They are very traditional," I explain. "You will be starting a family soon, yes?"

"That is what Alexei says." She wrings her hands in her lap.

"He is handsome. You are lucky. Nikolai speaks very highly of him."

"He does?"

"He does," I assure her. "I do find it strange, though, how similar they look in some regards, don't you?"

I'm not sure why I even mentioned it. It's not my place, but I feel it might be important for her to know. The new friend in me wants to give her every possible advantage to survive in this world. And while the rivalry between Alexei and Nikolai still lives and breathes fire, Talia would do well to avoid poking the dragon.

She doesn't get a chance to answer my thought. An indomitable shadow falls over us, and before I even look, I know it could only be one man.

"Nakya."

Nikolai settles in front of me, contrite. The shadows beneath his eyes are more pronounced in this light, and I wonder if he's been sleeping well. But then I remember I'm not supposed to care. He tells me that we'll be leaving soon and then turns his attention to my new friend.

"Talia, I haven't had a chance to properly introduce myself."

She looks at me for approval, and I think she's confused by the gesture. After her experience with men, in general, it is of little wonder, but I am surprised by Nikolai's softness. Sensing her fear, he kneels on our level, attempting to put her at ease.

"I need to speak with you," he says in a hushed voice.

Her eyes are still on my face, and I do the best I can to assure her that it will be okay. Nikolai may be many things, but I know he won't hurt her, and I want Talia to know it too.

"Alexei will not listen to me," he begins. "But I know he will listen to you. Sergei is not going to let this go. Neither is Katya for that matter. You should both be careful."

I don't know what he's talking about, but Talia appears to. She doesn't get a chance to respond. From across the room, Alexei has spotted us, and now he's hell-bent on laying Nikolai out.

Nikolai rises, squaring off with his brother yet again. They proceed to argue in Russian, the same issue of contention between them. Somehow, it always comes back to Katya. My sympathies go out to Alexei. Such a betrayal by his brother would certainly leave a permanent scar, and I can't imagine for the life of me why Nikolai would hurt him that way.

Thinking better than to allow their tempers to ruin another evening, the argument fizzles out. But Nikolai is not to be the only recipient of Alexei's hostilities. When he turns to pull his wife from her chair, his words are harsh and unfair.

"Go to the washroom and compose yourself. And when you come back, perhaps you can make it through the evening with better judgment."

Talia shrinks in the face of his unprovoked outburst, and I feel the need to protect her.

"I will accompany her."

"You will not," Alexei answers. "She must learn how to conduct herself at these events."

Talia leaves, and I scowl at her husband. I thought him to be a respectable man, but just like Nikolai, he allows his stubborn pride to rule his life. He is a fool, and I'd like to tell him so, but if I want to see Talia again, my thoughts are better kept to myself.

Talia is gone longer than I anticipated, and when she finally does return, her face is streaked with tears, and she is visibly shaken. But when she seeks out her husband, it only gets worse. He's across the room with the same woman who was fawning over Nikolai earlier. Instinctively, I know it must be Katya.

Without warning, Talia collapses, and I rush to her side. Nikolai is not far behind, and before I can decide what to do, he hoists her into his arms and carries her down the hall. We find an empty chaise, and he makes her as comfortable as he can while I sit beside her, reaching for her hand.

It's the only support I have to offer. When we try to talk to her, she has gone to another place in her mind. Our questions remain unanswered, and she stares off into nothingness.

"Get Alexei," Nikolai instructs me.

I don't want to leave her, but I do as I'm told.

CHAPTER 24
NIKOLAI

Alexei's wife is despondent and obviously traumatized, but there is little I can do for her. I remain quiet at her side, a steady presence until Nakya returns with Alexei. Rather than seeing the situation for what it is, he flies off the handle as soon as he comes down the hall.

I rise to meet him, but he isn't in a state to hear what I have to say. He reacts with his fist first. I dodge the blow, but I'm not a man to back down. I'm prepared to set him in his place when Nakya inserts herself between us, palms raised and face stern.

In Russian, she calmly informs us that this is not the time or place, redirecting our focus to Talia. It takes a full minute to register that she's speaking my mother tongue. My little liar is quite at ease with the language, but articulates as most novices do, slowly and succinctly. She chose an inopportune time to pull her trick out of the hat, so for now, I leave it alone.

She was right to redirect our attention back to Talia, and I hope that Alexei will see it that way too. Like me, his temper often gets the best of him, and he finds it difficult to admit when he's wrong. Not wanting to further upset Talia, we opt to continue our conversation in a mishmash of Russian and English.

"I should kill you for even daring to look at my wife," Alexei says.

"Do what you must." I sigh. "I was comforting her as you should have been, instead of playing this game you continue to play."

Alexei looks at his wife, and still, his default reaction is to doubt her loyalty.

"If you wish to punish someone, Lyoshka, then it needs to be me. Not her. She has done nothing wrong, yet you treat her as if—"

"Do not tell me how to conduct myself. This is my marriage. My business."

"I am not telling you as a Vor," I say. "I am telling you as your brother. This is not the man I know."

Silence settles over us. Alexei appears bewildered by my open admission of our shared DNA. He believes it to be Sergei's greatest shame, but he should know it's not mine.

"It's time we put an end to this, *bratan*."

He thrusts out his chest, and his mouth twists into a scornful smile. "Yes, I believe it is."

There is no mistaking the words as a threat. He outranks me, and he has Viktor's favor. It would take very little from Alexei's mouth to turn Viktor's opinion of me. If he ever chose to disclose my indiscretion with Katya, the *pakhan* would order my death without a second thought.

"I am sorry for the way that I went about things with Katya," I say. "But I don't regret doing it, Lyoshka. She had you fooled."

"We are not discussing this," he answers.

"You have to know that if you married her, she would have ruined your reputation within the Vory."

"It's your reputation that should be ruined," Alexei sneers. "You may have Sergei's approval, but you are not a man of honor. You are undeserving of the stars you bear."

If the insult had come from any other man, I would have cut his throat. But this is my brother, and I am tired of this battle between us. I am tired of our wasted words.

"You have always been jealous of me, *bratan*."

Alexei is prepared to deliver another equally vicious blow with his tongue when I raise my hand. "And I have always been jealous of you."

He does not answer, and I doubt he believes me. The worst part of the cruel words Sergei gifted his first son is that Alexei believes them. If his father says he's defective, it must be true. If his father says he's worthless, how can he argue that? To compound the problem, Sergei's affection for me has only added to his troubles.

"I am deeply sorry for any pain I have caused you, Lyoshka. Whatever you choose to do, I will respect your decision as a man and a Vor. If you must send me to my death so that you can have peace, then I implore you to do it. But I am done with this war between us."

My appeal is genuine, and I hope that Alexei can recognize that. But he does not give me an answer, and we are left without a resolution entirely when Katya makes an appearance. As always, her timing is not ideal. But I refuse to give her one minute of my time or attention as I join Nakya at her side.

"Your wife looks ill," Katya observes. "You must allow my maid to watch over her so you can come back and enjoy the party, Lyoshka."

She is dangling the line, but Alexei does not bite.

He looks at Talia, and his eyes soften. "I am taking her home."

"But you can't," Katya insists. "There is still so much more to come. I have worked so hard on the planning—"

"My wife is more important than your party," he says. "She is the most important woman in my life."

THE CAR RIDE home with Nakya is about as pleasant as I expected it to be. She's either tired or angry, but if I had to venture a guess, it isn't difficult to decide where the dice fall.

THIEF

It was not my finest moment, using her in the bathroom, only to abandon her for Ana moments later. There are probably many things I should say in this situation, but there is only one thing I can do.

I can't afford to give her hope when none lives. I won't do her the dishonor of lying about our doomed relationship. But it doesn't change the fact that the thought of her with anyone else blinds me with jealous rage. She has every right to hate me. She has earned that right. But maybe just once, I would like to see honest affection in her eyes.

When we walk through the front door, she is prepared to go her own way. But I take her hand in mine, leading her up the stairs and down the hall.

"What are you doing?" she asks.

Her body is weary. I took her roughly today, and she is probably sore, but I suspect she's more likely suffering from her indifference at this moment.

"You will stay in my room tonight," I tell her.

"Why?"

I reach out to touch her face. The face of an enchantress with the eyes of an angel. I have never seen a beauty quite like hers before. Her eyes flutter closed as my fingers learn the line of her jaw, and when my thumb drags over her lips, her breath escapes her.

"If you were my wife, I would worship you every day."

"But I'm not your wife," she says. "And I never will be."

"For tonight, let us forget that it's true." I enclose her in my arms, and she does not argue.

Her resistance fades as the minutes pass and I kiss her purely for the sake of kissing her. When my fingers move to the knot of silk at the nape of her neck, she shivers. We've been through this already tonight, but this time is different.

I release the straps, and then her zipper. The silk falls around her feet, and I couldn't recreate this image with all the paint in the world. She looks beautiful in red. But she is a goddess divine when she's naked.

Her breasts are small and firm, and her ballet practice has given her no use for bras, which I like very much. A woman should be available to her man, and my Nakya is always available to me. Her legs are long and lean, strong enough to squeeze the life out of me when I'm fucking her. She is a canvas unlike any I've ever seen, and it pains that she doesn't know her value. Great pieces of art can be unappreciated, but such is not the case with her. I've stolen many priceless things in my life, but nothing as priceless as her.

"Come." I thread her fingers through mine and lead her to the bed.

Pulling back the covers, I gesture for her to get in, but she hesitates, seeking out the meaning of this. I would tell her, if I knew it myself.

"Stay with me tonight," I implore.

She does not give in easily. Her eyes are sharp, and her armor is still intact.

"How many women have you brought here?" she asks.

Her jealousy stirs my dick to life, even though I'm too spent to take her again. "You'll be the first."

She purses her lips, and I know she doesn't believe me.

"I do not bring women into this room, Nakya. The only women who have been in this room now total two. You and Nonna. But I'm afraid I must divulge that she does not warm my bed, she only makes it."

For a few long breaths, she is completely still. When she finally crawls into my bed, I'm tempted to tie her up and keep her here forever. But for now, tonight will have to do.

I undress while she watches, her face propped on her hand, the sheet pulled up just above her nipples. I remove everything but my briefs and lie down beside her.

For a moment, we don't touch. We don't move. I'm not even sure she's breathing, but I know I'm not. It's more intimate to bring a woman to my bed without the intention of having sex. I'm not even certain I know how to begin.

"I think it's good what you told your brother tonight." Her words fill up the cavernous space, and it's not what I want to discuss, but I suppose it's better than lying like a corpse next to her.

"We have a strained relationship. I doubt what I said will matter."

"I think he will forgive you."

I don't answer because I'm not as hopeful.

"What were you trying to warn Talia about?" she asks.

I look at her. She is my captive, and rightfully, she doesn't need to know these things, but I can't think of any good reason to keep them from her.

"You understand this world. You know that honor comes above all else, yes?"

"Yes."

"The *pakhan* did not believe my father was being an honorable man. He demanded that I cut off his ear, and I did. But my father is misguided in his anger, and instead of blaming himself or even me, he finds fault with Alexei."

"Oh." Nakya frowns. "Would he ever hurt Talia?"

"Sergei?"

She nods.

"I would like to say that I know for certain, but I don't. He is a skilled liar, and I have often questioned his true character."

"He hides it from you?"

"It's hard to tell sometimes."

The admission is an honest one, and more than I should give her. I can't trust that she isn't just fishing for information to use against me later, but I would like to believe that Nakya has more honor than that herself.

"And what about Katya?"

"What about her?"

"You also made a point to warn Talia about her."

"Only because she has her sights set on Alexei. She is rabid for a high-ranking Vory husband, and she is delusional enough to believe that she can destroy their marriage and take him for her own."

"It looked like he was not the only one she was after this evening."

Her words are tainted with possession, and it encourages me to lean over and kiss her again.

"She only wants me for my rank," I murmur against her lips. "But it makes no difference now."

Her eyes fall shut, and I said the wrong thing.

"No, I suppose it doesn't. Viktor won't let you marry her when Ana is up for offer."

Pillow talk extinguished, the room is quiet again. My eyes are heavy, and I can think of nothing else to do, so I pull her into my arms and bury my face against her neck, inhaling her.

"Go to sleep, *zvezda*. Tomorrow is a new day."

CHAPTER 25
TANAKA

I wake in Nikolai's arms. The only logical reason I can find for his desire to cuddle is that his judgment was impaired from too many drinks at the party last night. But when I look at his face, he is not asleep, and he's not under any illusions of what took place.

His eyes are soft and warm, traveling over my face as his fingers ghost over my arm.

"Good morning, *zvezda*."

I smell of him. Cloves and smoke and aftershave. Our bodies are at ease together, wrapped in warmth, and I think it's the best night's sleep I've had in forever.

"Why do you call me that?" I ask.

"*Zvezda*?"

I nod.

"Why wouldn't I? You are my star. My dancing ballerina. My northern light. I think you lead me to do good."

My heart skips a beat. It's probably the nicest thing he's ever said, and he follows it up in true Nikolai fashion by wrapping my hand around his hard cock. He guides my fingers up and down his shaft, and his ocean eyes roll back like the tide.

"I want you," he says. "Ride me. Allow me to see you."

Panic cripples my hand, and everything stills between us.

"Please, Nakya." He cups my face in his palm. "Do not go to that place in your mind. You must allow logic to win sometimes. I would not ask this of you if I did not think you were perfect in every way."

His words make sense, but I'm scared. My confession is barely audible, and I can't see his reaction because my eyes are closed. But I feel his breath on my lips. His body moving closer to mine.

Sometimes, it's better when he makes demands, and I don't have to think. Free will is the most fearsome thing of all to someone who has only known captivity. And perhaps Nikolai understands this. He pulls me on top of him with little effort, spreading my legs across his hips, and laying my head on his shoulder.

"Keep your hand here." He places it on his chest, against the cage where his heart lives. And I know now that he does have one because I can feel it.

"Don't move it," he says. "The heart doesn't lie. If you can't believe my words, then believe this."

Strong and steady, his pulse hammers against my skin.

Even his heart is a liar.

He grabs the flesh of my ass, dragging me down against his cock. We don't need to draw it out because everything we do is foreplay. My body is wet for him already. And when he grabs a fistful of my hair, forcing my lips to his, he enters me without frills. This is the prelude, the main act, and the encore all rolled into one.

My song is muffled by his lips, and this is not the kind of sex I ever imagined myself having. It's unholy, and it's righteous. Corrupt but blessed. Shamefully lewd and sinfully sweet. And now, I don't believe in heaven or hell. There is only purgatory.

He thrusts up inside me, stabbing me with his cock while he steers my ass with his hands. His sounds bleed into me, and I inhale them like crack. I could get off on getting him off. But Nikolai wants to push me to my breaking point, and then even further still. He makes me come. Once. Twice. And a third for good measure.

He marks me with his teeth, grunting indecipherable exclamations in between. Our last fuck was quick and dirty, but today, it lasts forever. Every part of me hurts, and I think that's what he likes best.

Maybe, I like it too.

"One more time for me," he insists. "Come on my cock one more time."

"I don't have anything left."

I'm exhausted, collapsing on top of him while he fucks me from below. He worships my skin with his hands and his mouth and begs me to come just one more time. I'm overly sensitive. Wrung out. My breasts are tender, and I'm raw from his large dick.

But inevitably, Nikolai always gets what he wants. The orgasm is as weak as I feel, but I come for him. Right before he stuffs himself as deep as I can take him and purges a long, torturous release of his own.

My spell in captivity has forced me to find new uses for my time. Before, my days were spent in the studio, persecuting my body and perfecting my routines. My calendar revolved around the company's schedule, and the occasional social event my father forced me to attend.

But when I look at the calendar today, I'm surprised to find that entire months have gone by, and I struggle to remember the exact date I arrived. The blank square on the wall does little to help me process my feelings. Though Gianni already hinted at it, I'm certain my name has been removed from the company as if I never existed. The ballet waits for no man or woman. Each of those positions is coveted. Prized.

And once, it was by me too.

But my practice has dwindled to little more than an hour a day.

I'm not as strong as I used to be. It would be easy to blame Nikolai for my lack of motivation, but the truth is that he's become a welcome distraction from the truth I have yet to face.

The chime on the alarm signals the therapist's arrival, and within moments, Sarah is in my room. She says something when she walks in, but my eyes are still on the calendar, and my thoughts are too loud to focus on her.

"Tanaka?"

I count off the days until the end of the month, wondering how many hours of dance I can squeeze in. There must be a way to get back on track. I count and add and plan, but it's all for nothing. Eventually, my finger falls away from the orderly squares. The squares that used to rule my life.

"You look upset," Sarah observes. "What's on your mind?"

I don't move from my seat at the desk, opting to face away from her. She doesn't deserve to know my every thought, but maybe it's time I finally say it aloud.

"I don't think I ever want to dance again."

There is a moment of silence, and it feels like a death. Grief has swallowed me whole, and in a time of mourning, silence is only appropriate. Maybe that's why Sarah isn't so bad. I talk to her, not because I should, but because she knows when to ask questions and she knows when to stay quiet.

Every week, she comes back here. She invests her time in me. She tells me she believes in me and tries to keep me healthy. We discuss body image and dancing and whatever else comes out of my mouth. But I'm under no illusion it's because she cares. Nikolai pays her to fix me.

As if she could.

"During our past few visits, I was under the impression that your practice was improving quite steadily," she says.

"I was lying."

Another bout of silence follows my admission, and I squeeze my eyes shut to keep from crying. I feel like a child again. This loss is as great to me as my own mother. I'm fragile and I'm broken, but I always have been. Maybe I'm okay with that, though, even if Sarah isn't.

"You started ballet at a very young age," she remarks. "I know that studies have shown it's not uncommon for dancers to suffer severe injuries under your circumstances."

"I don't care what the studies say," I tell her. "It's the only thing I ever wanted to do, and now I can't."

"Maybe instead of focusing on the loss of your professional career, you can adapt your expectations. You can still use that passion for good. You could teach—"

She stops herself midsentence, realizing her mistake. I'm a prisoner to the mafia, and teaching or finding another outlet for ballet is out of the question.

"Sometimes, we get so focused on what we can't do that we forget what we're still capable of," she amends.

I don't answer her. The power of positivity isn't going to work for me today. My grief is a process, and eventually I will tread water again, but I will do it in my own time.

"How are your eating habits this week?" she asks.

"They're fine."

"Nikolai tells me otherwise."

Betrayal pierces my thoughts, and I turn to look at her. I have been good. I've been doing mostly okay. But I know he's referring to the Christmas party. It isn't fair for him to count that against me.

"It was one time, and it was only because I was in an uncomfortable situation."

"Nonna also says that you haven't been clearing your plates, even though they are small portions. It's a very slippery slope, Tanaka. They only mention it because we all want you to succeed with your program."

"I'm fine," I reiterate. "If anything, I've been eating too much. I had to buy two sizes up in my clothes, and I don't like it."

"You are at a perfectly reasonable weight," she says. "The doctor mentioned that you've finally reached a healthy body mass index. Do you remember how we discussed changing the way you see yourself versus controlling your food to maintain your safety zone? Should we go over it again?"

"No," I answer.

"How do you feel right now?" she asks. "Do you feel healthy? Do you have more energy? Tell me something positive about your new eating plan."

I tap my fingers against the desk. I do feel like I have more energy, but I don't want to admit it to her because right now she feels like the enemy. I feel like she is conspiring with Nikolai and Nonna to make me miserable, and I am angry with all of them, no matter how illogical it might be. I decide that while I can't control my food, or my body, or my dancing anymore, there is still something else I can control.

"I'm done with therapy," I tell her. "I want you to leave now."

There isn't a response. I expect her to argue, and I'm preparing my mental arsenal. I will go to war with her if she makes me. But I'm done giving away my secrets like candy. She just needs to say one thing. One protest. One argument. And I will let her have it.

But she doesn't give in to my tactics.

Instead, she disappoints me by leaving the room without another word.

CHAPTER 26
NIKOLAI

I find Nakya in the gym, stretching her leg against the barre I provided. She is wearing only a pink leotard and leg warmers today. Since I gave her free rein with my credit card, there has been a dramatic change in her wardrobe. Lately, I've enjoyed seeing her in the high-waisted jeans and bodysuits she purchased. She's a different girl than the prim little dancer I first met. She is wilder, perhaps.

But she is also self-conscious of her healthier new body. I enjoy the way her thicker flesh feels against me. There is nothing like getting lost in the softness of a woman. It calms me. And I get lost in Nakya as often as I can now.

Seeing her healthy is important to me, and as long as she's in my care, I will do what's necessary to keep her that way.

"Sarah tells me that you think it's up to you to fire her."

She returns my gaze in the reflection of the mirror. "I don't need therapy anymore. I'm better now."

"I wouldn't go that far."

She releases her leg and turns to face me, meeting my eyes in challenge. "I don't have anything else to say to her. She's wasting my time."

"That is for me to determine. Besides, what else do you have to do?"

"You mean other than being your fuck toy?"

It's the most vulgar thing she's ever said, and it makes my dick hard. But I'm not about to let her get away with it.

"Watch your mouth, *zvezda*."

"Why should I?" she asks. "You wanted me to be filthy, didn't you? Your dirty little doll. So I'll say it as much as I like. Fuck toy, fuck toy, fuck—"

The last of her tirade is cut short when I close the distance between us and catch her by the hair. A faint sound of protest hums in her throat, but she has come to heel as she should.

I lean close to inhale her before my lips come to rest on her ear.

"If you really want to be my fuck toy, I will tie you to the bed for three days and use every orifice on your body for my own amusement. So be careful what you wish for, princess."

Her chest heaves, and fire spews from her amber eyes. She's itching to pick a fight today, and I'm not sure why. Sarah warned me to expect these tantrums on occasion. With progress, there is always some regression too.

"Why won't you just let me go?" she demands. "Send me back to my father."

And we are back to this again. I'm tired of her antics, and I want to let her know it. My palm dips to her breast, toying with the nipple beneath the thin material.

"You are not a very good liar," I tell her. "We both know you don't want to go back there."

She tries to smack my hand away from her breast, so I pinch her nipple, and she yelps.

"Stop!" she bellows. "I don't want you. I'm sick of being your whore while you make plans to marry your precious Ana."

"Is that what this is about?"

It seems that no matter how far we come, it always circles back to this. She can't let it go, and I can't give her the answers she wants.

"I just want to go home," she says. "I want to go home and … marry Dante."

She could have said anything. Anything but that. I make it known when I turn her around and force her to the floor.

"What are you doing?" she cries as I release the snaps between her legs, baring her pussy to me.

Despite her declaration to marry Dante, the shameful liar is wet for me. And I think she gets off on making me do this. She wants me to fuck her like an animal, but her prim little mouth won't admit it.

I unzip my jeans, and she tries to wiggle out of my grip. In the struggle, I yank down her leotard and slap her tits. She stills in shock, gasping for breath as she cranes her neck to look at me.

"You are a monster."

"And you are his whore."

I emphasize the point by yanking her back onto my cock until I'm balls deep. She shrieks and claws the mat beneath her, still making every effort to tell me how much she hates me between broken breaths.

I fuck her like a barbarian, punctuating my thrusts with the insults she is desperate to hear. I tell her she's my slut. My filthy doll. And she comes even though she doesn't deserve to.

After a promise to punish her for it, I pull out and release myself on her red, swollen tits. And when I step back to examine my masterpiece, I'm satisfied at the sight of my savagely fucked little toy, breathless, spent, and covered in my cum.

I don't bother to help her clean up. I have only one piece of advice for her before I go.

"You think of this," I tell her, "when you marry Dante. Think of the cock that took you first. The cock you'll wish you had when you're faking it for him."

"What do you have for me?"

For once, Mischa doesn't seem to notice the stripper trying to get his attention across the room. I hate meeting him here, but it's better than having him at my place. I don't want him seeing Nakya there, remembering the way he almost took her.

"You are my brother," Mischa says. "We bear the stars of the Vory, and for as long as I can remember, we have looked out for each other. Trusted each other. And we have never let anything come between us, small or large."

I listen to his impassioned speech with critical eyes. Whatever is coming, I know it can't be good.

"I'm asking you not to let anything come between us now, Kolyan. Not the girl. Not this news I have to deliver. I'm giving you what you asked for with little hope it will bring you peace. I worry this will set you on a course you can't return from, and I ask for your word that you will allow me to advise you as a friend and ally in whatever path you choose."

The brown paper folder in his hands commands my attention, and I know that this is it. He has the answers I have sought for a lifetime. Yet I can't bring myself to open it now.

"She's dead, isn't she?"

Mischa hesitates, then nods. "I don't suppose you will consider that as closure."

"No."

"Then I urge you to act now, Kolyan, before things get any more complicated than they already are. I think you should not put it off another day."

"How did you get this information?" I ask.

His eyes drift away from mine. "I had some help from Alexei."

I'm tempted to punch him square in the face, and Mischa knows it.

"He already knew," Mischa says. "And he was the one to

approach me. In fact, he was the one who did most of the work. I am only the delivery boy because he'd rather not deal with you himself."

I snatch the file from the table and stand. There is nothing left to say. Mischa can request my word as much as he'd like, but I won't give it. Not until I know what this means for me.

Or Nakya.

CHAPTER 27
TANAKA

Something I've learned about Nikolai is that he holds onto an insult with steel reinforced teeth. We've scarcely spoken a word in over two weeks, and I know it's because of my comment about Dante.

It shouldn't bother me, considering he marked me like a dog and left a proverbial arrow in my heart. I don't want Dante, but I like to throw him in Nikolai's face because it's the only weapon that seems to penetrate his invisible forcefield.

I really didn't have a good reason for doing it, but I was angry. Everything in my life is spinning out of control, and I can't find my balance. The longer I stay here, playing whatever role he sees fit, the more difficult it becomes to see myself in any other reality. I'm at his mercy, and he won't give me the lies I need to hear.

I want him to tell me that he won't marry Ana. I want him to say that I'm not broken anymore, and everything is going to be okay. But his truth is bitter and loving him is too. The thief stole my heart, only to hold it in the palm of his hand, extorting my affections when it suits him.

Too often, I have found myself wandering the house at night, awaiting his return. My restless soul won't let me sleep, and my mind won't give up wondering where he is. Tonight is no different. Anguish nags at me as I stare out the window and trace the constellations with my finger. He hasn't taken me in two weeks. I would be a fool to believe he hasn't been with anyone else. It's the mafia way, and this is the fate I'm cursed to live, whether it's with Nikolai or with Dante.

I close my eyes and wish for sleep, but it evades me in the same way the sun chases the moon. It's either dark, or it's light, and there is no eclipse on the horizon.

I take to wandering the house again. Nikolai's room is empty, and I indulge my habit by touching his things. His clothes, his jacket, his cap. They smell like him, and his bed does too. Sweet tobacco and cloves. I curl into his pillow and breathe him in. I wonder if he ever feels as tormented as I do. I wonder if he ever lays here at night and thinks about coming to my room to steal me away again.

In answer, a melancholy tune echoes from above like a soundtrack to my madness.

At first, I think it's my imagination. But the tune plays on, and when I look up at the ceiling, I can almost feel his energy luring me there.

I've never been up to the third floor. Nonna told me it was off limits, and I didn't care to find out why. But at this late hour, I can't think of a single reason to obey. I slip from the bed and walk quietly to the landing. I've only ever gone down the stairs before, and it feels dangerous to be climbing up instead.

When I encounter a door at the top, my adventure ends abruptly. It's a solid door. Different from the others in the house. It looks heavy and secure, and I know there's no way I'm getting through, but I also know this must be where Nikolai keeps his secrets. I want to collect his secrets like he has collected my tears. I want to dissect the intimate details of the man who haunts me day and night. But there's a barrier in the way.

My shoulders sag, and I'm prepared to take leave with my disappointment until I see the small sliver of light reflecting off the floor.

It's cracked. Just barely, but it's cracked.

I press my fingertips against the door, but it doesn't budge until I put my entire body's weight against it, creating a gap wide enough to slip through. My pulse jumps as my feet move forward. It could be the last bad decision I ever make, but desperation leaves me greedy for answers. And when I reach the threshold of what can only be described as a vault, I finally have them.

Two things hit me at once. The confounding realization and subsequent relief that Nikolai is not out with Ana or anyone else, and that he is, in fact, here. Shirtless and paint splattered in nothing more than a pair of well-worn jeans that hang loosely from his hips.

There is a suspended moment of time I'm gifted to soak it all in. He's humming along to the music, deep vibrations rumbling from his chest as his hand moves quickly and expertly over the canvas in front of him. At least a dozen others surround him, and I feel like I'm in a dream when I see them.

Dancers. They are all dancers.

And they are all me.

It's too much for my mind to process. What I'm witnessing isn't what I know him to be. He is mafiya. A thief. Not an artist. But my judgment can't argue with realism. I confined him to a box inside my mind, and he hasn't just stepped outside it, he's blown it entirely apart.

He created these pieces. He conceived and designed and toiled over these works.

I expected to find so many other things. Death. Torture chambers. Violence. Money and guns. But not art. I can't fathom it. Right now, I don't want to. I want to pretend I never saw it. It's the only way to protect myself. But the chance is lost when Nikolai turns and catches me watching him.

I'm prepared to flee, but one command from him halts me.

"Stop."

I freeze.

His eyes hold me hostage. "What do you mean to do by sneaking around?"

"I'm sorry."

"That's not an answer." He discards the brush in his hand against the easel. "Tell me what you were looking for."

His face and his heart are closed. Shielded. He does not trust me. I don't trust him either, but we don't need trust to destroy ourselves.

"I was looking for you." I tap my toes against the cold floor, wishing I could create a sinkhole to escape his scrutiny.

The music plays on, the only sound between us. The tune is classical and beautiful and not something I would expect from Nikolai. But then again, he has proven me to be a fool when it comes to my expectations.

He makes the first move, stalking me like a jungle cat.

"Why would you be looking for me?" He forces my chin up with his hand. "Have you come to make another declaration of your love for Dante? Or perhaps a worthless plea to return home to your loving father?"

His words are laced with undisguised bitterness, and a ray of hope shines brightly inside of me.

"I've come to do neither," I tell him. "I've come because ..."

I can't say the words. I'm not ready to admit how impoverished I feel without him. I'm definitely not ready to confess that I purged my depraved needs by thinking of him while I touch myself.

I cave into myself and look up at him. My values have taught me that it's not my place to be forward with a man. But right now, it's the only thing I want to do. When I reach up with an unsteady hand, he doesn't move. He's rigid and unresponsive, but the cold war fractures when my fingertips touch his face.

His eyes fall shut, and he narrows the distance between us by dragging me against his body. His engorged cock lays heavy against my belly, already ripe with want. My lips find his, and I'm ready to let myself be lost in his skin. But there is still one thought plaguing my mind.

"Have you been with others?"

Nikolai locks me in his arms to prevent me from pulling away. His eyes are softer than they were only a minute ago, but not any less beautiful.

"Would it matter?" He toys with the strap of my silk chemise. "I thought you were merely biding your time until your return home."

"It does matter." My heart pulses wildly. "I want your everything while I have it. Wait until I'm gone, and then you can—"

"Nakya." He sucks my bottom lip between his teeth, forcing my mouth open. The ensuing kiss is violent and possessive, but entirely too short.

"I don't want anyone else," he breathes. "Why would I when I have you?"

His words are genuine, but I still have my doubts. And I'm certain he is tired of giving me assurances he has no need to give. He could take me either way. He could do whatever he likes. His loyalty is not owed to me. But regardless, it's what I see in his eyes when he whispers his next words.

"You gave yourself to me, my sweet. And it is not a difficult task to give you my loyalty in return. I have no reason to lie when I tell you that you have poisoned me against any other woman."

"So keep me then," I plead. "Keep me and make me yours, Nika. Carve your star into my skin and never let me go."

He kisses me, and it isn't a promise, but an admission. He wants to keep me, but he won't make a promise he'll be forced to break. As much as I need those words right now, I need him more.

We come together in a slow burn. Hot, sticky hands undress each other and explore the canvases of our bodies. He cups me between my legs and kisses my throat. "Whose pussy is this?"

"Yours."

He groans and dips his fingers inside me, toying with me while he sucks on the flesh above my collarbone. "Tell me you're mine."

He wants it. Needs it. He's been begging for it. And I'm done playing games.

"I'm yours."

Our naked bodies collide and tumble to the floor. He enters me with a sigh, and I squeeze around him. He's on top of me and inside me, fucking me drunkenly as he struggles to maintain the connection between our eyes. But he isn't just fucking me this time.

He's making love.

I nurture his affections, peppering him with kisses. Whispering words meant only for his ears. I beg him never to stop. I beg him over and over to keep me. He begs me over and over to tell me again that I'm his.

We shatter, and we nap, and we wake up, only to do it all over again.

My fingers hover centimeters away from the painting, breath absent from my lungs. It's beautiful and horrific. A violation. An obsession. An open window to my psyche. And I can't look away.

Nikolai wipes away a tear I didn't even realize I'd shed before he sweeps my hair over my shoulder and kisses my neck from behind. "Tell me what you are thinking, *zvezda*."

"Why?" I whisper.

Why did he choose to paint the worst moment of my life? And how did he get inside my head? How did he know me so intimately at that moment? The shattering loss that rendered me immobile. The deep, violent despair. Every emotion is so tangible that it feels more like a memory than a painting. *Fall from Grace*, he calls it.

"How could I not?" he answers. "It's not every day that you witness the fall of an angel."

I sob, and he holds me. It's ridiculous that I'm so emotional over a piece of art, but it's so much more than that. It's the realization that, from the beginning, he has seen me. He has known me.

The truth is painted on as many canvases as I can see. Each one is different, but in many ways, they are the same. They are all me.

"I can't believe you made these," I say. "I can't believe your talent."

"It's not so difficult when you have a beautiful muse."

He allows me time to process each piece. Until every detail has soaked into my brain and become a part of me. And then we find ourselves on the floor again, touching and kissing, but too spent to take it any further than that.

Side by side, we stare up at the ceiling, his palm skating the curve of my hip as he lights a cigarette.

"You should quit," I tell him.

"I will." He exhales. "Eventually."

I smile and shake my head. "Isn't it bad for the art?"

"Very," he answers. "But now there will be a small part of me in your paintings. A signature, if you will."

My paintings. He says it as if they belong to me, but I know they won't be coming with me when I go. I imagine them a hundred years from now, gathering dust in a collection somewhere. What will people think when they look at them? Will they know that girl even existed, or believe her to be a figment of the artist's imagination?

"What else do you paint?" I ask.

"Forgeries, mostly," Nikolai answers casually. "But they are not all paint. Some are other mediums."

"So that's why this room is so heavily locked down?"

He smiles. "I am a thief, *zvezda*. As such, I've been known to steal a few valuable pieces now and then."

I'm surprised to find how much I don't care about his admission. He is honest about himself, at least. And in my mind, I like the idea of being bad with him. I reach for the cigarette and swipe it from his hand. He turns to me, curious, watching as I bring it to my lips.

His lips tilt at the corners when I inhale just a tiny bit and start to cough. "That's really good," I sputter.

He laughs, and his eyes are the lightest I've ever seen them when they move over my face. "My little doll wants to be wild?"

I nod.

"First of all, you're holding it like a joint." He repositions the cigarette between my fingers. "Now inhale, but only a little bit. Let it cool before you inhale."

I do what he says, and it goes a little smoother this time.

"We won't be making a habit of this," he says as fair warning. "But for now, stay just like that."

I watch him curiously as he rises and takes to another blank canvas, repositioning it so that he can see me. When his intentions occur to me, it makes me nervous.

"Pretend I'm not here," he says.

It's an unmanageable task, considering he's naked. But I find it easier to watch him than to worry about my fears. The way his thighs clench as he tucks a paint brush between his fingers. When his arm sweeps over the canvas, his ass flexes too. I take another inhale, and he pauses to come fix the sheet that's half covering me. Pulling out my leg and revealing the curve of my hip, he gathers it just beneath my breasts. Now it's draped over me almost like a toga, and he's back to his canvas.

He dips his brush into the paint, mixing colors and using techniques that show a skilled hand as he works. It's a new obsession to watch him this way. The concentration on his face. The artist at work. I can't look away, and I never want it to end. But inevitably, it does.

He takes a step back, examining his work before he looks at me.

"Are you going to show me?"

He stalks back to our makeshift bed, mounting me with a hard dick that pokes into my belly. We kiss, and he takes me again.

When he comes, his face collapses on my breasts, and I stroke his hair.

"What will you call it?" I ask sleepily.

"Inamorata," he says.

CHAPTER 28
NIKOLAI

"I see that you've brought the Valentini girl with you this evening."

Viktor has cornered me on my return from the washroom, and his mood has soured now that the celebrations are winding down.

"Alexei asked me to bring her. It seems his wife is quite fond of her, and he thinks they might do well to become friends."

"Then she should be here with Mischa," Viktor says. "It does not look right, you bringing her here like this. In fact, I have tired of this whole charade. My Ana is waiting for your proposal, and I am ready to announce your intentions with her."

"I'm sorry," I tell him. "It was not my intention to disrespect either of you. I thought we had an understanding—"

"Time is up," Viktor growls. "Do you want to marry my daughter or not?"

I need a cigarette. Or ten. Any answer I may give him won't be satisfactory. Either way, the consequences will mean paying with my life. It's either death if refuse, or death if I give in. A life without Nakya is not a life I can imagine. I'm not ready to let her go, which is why my mother's file still sits unread in my vault at home.

"I would like more time to get to know Ana," I say. "So that we are both certain it's the right decision."

Viktor scoffs. "What else is there to know? She is beautiful, and she was bred for this life. She'll be loyal and faithful. And most importantly, she is Russian."

His words serve a purpose. He wants me to know that Ana is everything he thinks Tanaka isn't. The words of a hypocrite, considering we are here to celebrate the pregnancy of Alexei's wife. She is not Russian, nor does she have any of the traits that Viktor expects in a wife. But he has given Alexei his blessing. It would seem his good will is not equally distributed after all.

"Ana is very young," I remark. "I only worry that she will rush into this and regret it later. I want to be certain of her decision."

Viktor doesn't answer. Alexei has discovered us lurking in the hall, and he's coming our way.

"Are the celebrations over so soon?" he asks.

Viktor forces a smile for his benefit. "Of course not. We were just discussing some business, but I assure you, the celebrations will continue."

Alexei nods, and Viktor slaps him on the shoulder. "You're going to make an excellent father. Let's go see about a cigar, shall we?"

Before they leave, Viktor issues his final ultimatum. "One month. No more, Kol'ka. You will have your answers, or you won't. But either way, you will wed my daughter."

"It was a lovely party," Nakya says as we walk through the door.

She's made several attempts at small talk already, sensing something is off. After my conversation with Viktor, my mood soured, and for me, the celebrations were over. I drank simply for the sake of drinking, and now I can't see straight.

I send away the *bratok* who drove us home and lock up the house.

"You should go to bed, *zvezda*."

She moves closer, attempting to lure me back in with her honeyed lips. For one week, we have spent every night together. I have not tended to my Vory duties, forsaking all that is important because of her. And still, it is not enough.

"You aren't coming with me?"

"No."

Her shoulders sag, pieces of her hair falling around her face as she lowers her gaze. I think I liked her better when she refused to show her emotion.

"Did I do something wrong?"

"You shouldn't have been there." The words unleash from my tongue like a whip, and she flinches in kind. "You can't control your emotions. They are written all over your face for the world to see. For Viktor to see."

"I didn't think—"

"That is exactly the problem," I sneer. "You don't think. And I have grown tired of it."

Her chin quivers, and she clings to my shirt. "Please don't do this, Nika. I know that you care. This isn't you talking."

"You are mistaken, pet. It is exactly me talking. I'm bored of you, so do yourself a favor and get out of my sight."

She fractures as I knew she would, rushing away from me with broken sobs. Still, it isn't enough. I want her gone. Out of my sight and my mind. She is complicating my life and making it hell.

But it doesn't change anything.

Because even when she goes, I am empty.

CHAPTER 29
NIKOLAI

Over the course of a week, I've drunk my way through the liquor cabinet. Presently, I find that I don't much have a taste for Old Crow whiskey, but it does the job regardless.

Between chain smoking and drinking, I haven't got much accomplished. The brown file still sits in my drawer, unread, and Viktor calls to check in often, inquiring about my progress. The lies spill from my lips easily when I'm drunk, and if he notices my erratic behavior, he doesn't say.

Twice this week, I've been forced to sit through dinners with Ana. The *pakhan* has become obsessed with the prospective engagement on the horizon, encouraging every opportunity for us to spend time together. I speak very little during our encounters, asking only questions about her. She is happy to oblige with answers.

Unlike Nakya, she is not guarded. Ana is open and childlike, often choosing to reference celebrity gossip or other frivolous topics. She is girlish and giggly and far too naïve to be with someone like me, but it doesn't stop her from blushing every time I look her way. The worst part is that she believes she's in love with me because her father continues to nurture the idea.

My fate is sealed. Viktor will see me marry her, and I need to let go of the things I can't change. I have been a coward and a liar, and Alexei was right to say I'm undeserving of the stars I bear. I have forsaken my Vory brothers, and it's time to end this charade.

The house is quiet, and everyone is asleep when I settle into my office. Nakya has returned to the sanctuary of her own room, and I have made it a point not to see her during her waking hours. But every night, I check for her on the camera. I watch her restless sleep from the screen of my phone, and it's as close to her as I can get.

It's better this way. And regardless of what this file might hold, my decision has been made. If I'm entitled to my pound of flesh, it will come from Manuel himself. And then Nakya will go back to her life, free to do as she pleases. Free to starve herself or dance herself to death, or to marry Dante if she chooses.

The clock on the wall is the only soundtrack to my manic thoughts as I stare at the thick brown paper. *Tick, tick, tick.* For a moment, I choose to believe that Mischa was right. If I wanted to, I could let this go without reading the details. What difference does it make now? She is dead, and nothing will bring her back.

But it's only another lie.

She was my mother.

I drain my glass and smoke a few more cigarettes while pacing the length of my office. It can't be that bad. Mischa is always overly dramatic, I think. It's just a few pieces of paper, and I am a grown man. A Vor. And a Vor never backs down from anything.

I sit back down and retrieve the file I have tried to open so many times. It's just paper. Nothing more.

But upon opening it, I find that I am wrong. It isn't just paper. There are photographs too. Photographs I thought I would want to see, but I was mistaken. The grainy stills are from a surveillance video. And before I allow my eyes to settle on the main subject, I examine every detail of the room. A basement. A dirty sofa. A bucket. These living conditions aren't fit for an animal, let alone a woman.

Yet there she is. My mother. Strung out and naked.

I know I shouldn't, but I look at her face. Vacant eyes and hollow features are all that remain. An empty, sagging sack of skin and bones that a soul has long since abandoned. When I reach out to touch her, I feel her anguish in every cavernous inch of my body. This was the same woman who tucked me in at night and kissed me on the forehead. The mother who sang sweet lullabies and read lively bedtime stories.

These memories are all I have of her, and I loathe myself for being too young to stop this. I want to go back and fix it. I want to go back and murder every man who ever touched her. It's too late to save her. The only thing I can do for her now is rain down blood and fire on the animals who did this to her.

The report Alexei compiled is more detailed than I could have imagined. Everything is categorized, and the work has already been done for me. Dates, times, and the names of everyone who participated.

But it is the first on the list that leaves a permanent scar on my soul. A confirmation of what I've always suspected to be true.

Sergei.

My own father is responsible for this.

His ego has always been the most cowardly thing about him. And as the story goes, when he suspected my mother had betrayed him with one of his own men, he offered her as a gift to Manuel Valentini. But she was not a gift. She was a human sacrifice. A bonus to sweeten a gun deal between Manuel and my father.

He gave her away like she was a piece of garbage. Knowing the fate he delivered her to, he allowed her to be beaten and used by Manuel and his men for years. Yet every night, he would come to my room to watch me cry over her loss, insisting she had abandoned me.

I pour another drink and close my eyes. The images haunt me, and I know they'll never go away. I have been a fool. Allowing my dick to lead me, ignoring the cause I believed in the most. For months, their hearts have continued to beat. They have continued to breathe the air of this earth, when they should have been rotting in the ground already.

It isn't even the worst of it. That part is still yet to be read. And Alexei has not spared a single gruesome detail.

My mother left this world fighting. Fighting to escape. She slashed Manuel Valentini's dick with a shard of broken mirror.

And then he dissolved her in an acid bath.

CHAPTER 30
TANAKA

Crash.

My body jerks upright. Sleep blurs my vision, and I blink rapidly as I look around the room. My skin is clammy, and my heart is racing. Something isn't right, and my first instinct is to hide.

I scramble from the bed, but crippling pain shoots through my calf and paralyzes my leg. Hostage to the cramp, I have little choice but to wait it out.

Explosive noises reverberate down the hall. Glass shattering. Wood splintering. More animal than man, the grunting could only be coming from Nikolai.

A new fear blossoms inside me. Someone is here. Someone is attacking him.

He needs me.

I stumble down the hall, my leg dragging half useless behind me. I'm in nothing more than a nightdress, and I don't know how to save him, but I know I have to try.

Howls of agony erupt from the open doorway. In the short

distance, my mind conjures up so many different scenarios. But when I reach the threshold, nothing could prepare me for the reality.

He is shirtless. Bloody. Chest heaving as he sifts through an open storage container. A cigarette still hangs from his mouth, and there's an empty bottle of whiskey beside him. One by one, he removes glass framed photos, only to smash them to bits a moment later.

Murmured words rumble from his chest as he identifies the faces in the frames. Affection one minute, and hatred the next. And I think that an intruder would have been easier to handle.

There is no manual for a situation like this. He's hurting, and I want to help him, but I just don't know how. Knowing better than to approach a wounded animal, I call out to him from the door.

"Nika."

He freezes, and a chill moves over me. His head turns so slowly in my direction that it's like watching a horror movie.

"You," he sneers.

Frigid blue eyes carve into my face, anesthetizing my heart.

So much hate. I have never witnessed so much hate. And every fragment is directed at me. I have known Nikolai to be many things, but never this. Never this monster who looks so much like my own father right now.

I already know it's too late, but I run anyway.

The footfalls behind me are steady and thunderous, and before I can put any real distance between us, he has me by the hair. He yanks me back and pins me to the wall, and I cower before him, crumpling into myself. If any love for me ever existed in him, it's gone now.

"Please, Nika—"

Like a snake, his hand lashes out to wrap around my throat. "You don't deserve to live."

He's drunk. I can smell the whiskey on his breath, and I can see it in his bloodshot eyes. But it doesn't lessen the blow of his words. It doesn't make me feel any less dead inside. He made me fall in love with him, only to destroy me.

I don't feel sorry for him anymore. I want him out of my sight. Out of my life.

"Get off me!" I scream. "You are a savage. I hate you!"

He cuts off my air supply, and I claw at his hands. When that doesn't work, I scratch at his face. My nails tear into any flesh I can reach, and it only makes him more volatile. He releases his hold on my throat, only to reach for the cigarette in his mouth.

I watch in horror as he drags it a hair's breadth from my throat. Smoke wisps between us, and heat rolls off the flame red cylinder as I struggle to stay stock-still. He can't do this. He wouldn't scar me like my father scarred my mother.

I want so desperately to believe that there is good in him. I haven't fallen for a sadist. Emotion leaks from my eyes, forging rivers down my cheeks and betraying my weakness.

That weakness is also my salvation. My tears are the only thing to break him from his spell. His grasp on me falls away, but his lips relay his disgust with one final parting blow.

"It would be the least of what you deserve."

CHAPTER 31
TANAKA

"What do you think?"

Talia hands me a catalog, gesturing to a photo of a crib inside.

I offer her a gentle smile. "It looks like it would match the theme."

She nods and closes the catalog with a sigh. "I don't know what I'm doing, honestly. There are so many decisions to make, and just so much stuff. I don't know what's necessary and what's not, and I have no idea if any of it's safe. I think I'm going to be a terrible mother."

"You aren't going to be a terrible mother. You'll learn as you go. That's what mothers do."

She shrugs. "I guess so."

"You're excited, aren't you?"

She taps her fingers on the sofa next to her. "I never thought I wanted to be a mother. I'm anxious, and I don't know if that makes me an awful person."

"It doesn't."

I know this isn't easy for her. This culture is entirely new to her. But even for a veteran like me, it never gets any easier.

"Are you okay?" Talia asks.

I blink at her and nod automatically. I wasn't prepared for the question. We've been spending time together over the past two weeks, but we aren't at the stage that I'd consider divulging all my secrets. I've never had a friend before, and I hardly know what's appropriate.

"You seem different." Her voice is quiet, and I can tell this is foreign territory for her too. She's spent the past year of her life fighting for survival, and I'm sure it hasn't been an easy transition into her new life.

"I think I'm tired," I say.

In truth, it isn't just exhaustion. I'm one foot in the grave already. When I look in the mirror, I see a haunting reflection so reminiscent of my mother that it terrifies me. It's been two weeks since Nikolai's outburst, and if I were holding my breath waiting for an apology, I'd have starved of oxygen by now. As far as I can tell, he's only been home in the late hours, and he's made it a point to avoid me.

He might be fine, but I'm not. Inside, I'm withering. A slow death is torture, and I can feel it happening. Every night, I replay his words. I can't forget them. And I can't go on living like this.

I won't become my mother.

Mischa was right, and I should have listened to him long ago. If I don't get out now, I'm doomed to repeat history.

What Talia doesn't know is that these visits with her will be the only thing that saves my life. Today will be the last time I see her, and it isn't fair. I don't want to abandon her to this world without a friend, but I have no choice.

The truth aches to spill from my lips. She deserves that much. But I'm not naïve enough to believe that our every move isn't being recorded. Talia was quick to point it out on our first visit. I think the cameras bother her, but I also think she was trying to warn me not to speak out of turn. Our friendship can only be as deep as the words we're able to admit out loud.

"Solnyshko." Alexei enters the room, hand delivering some tea to his wife. "Magda sent this for you."

"Thank you." She smiles at him, and her love for him is not false. She does care for him. She sees him as her savior. And as happy as I am for her, it hurts me too.

"How is Nika treating you?" Alexei turns to me, his blue eyes roaming over my face with obvious concern.

Part of me feels like I could be honest with him. I could tell him the truth, and he would not hold it against me or betray me. But it would be a betrayal to Nikolai, considering how strained relations already are with his brother. As awful as he was to me, I can't bring myself to do that to him.

So, I smile and provide a default answer. "He's keeping busy. Honestly, I've barely seen him in weeks. But all is well."

Alexei does not look as if he believes me, but Talia saves me from further inquiries by interrupting.

"Tanaka is very tired. Would you mind getting the car?"

"Of course." He nods. "I'll walk her out."

We all rise, and Talia and I exchange hugs. She doesn't like them, but I think somehow she senses the dark clouds looming over us. When I hug her for a second longer than necessary, she doesn't let go either. I thank her for the visit, and she urges me to return next week if I'm able.

"The car is ready," Alexei informs me as he pockets his phone.

He follows me from the room and walks me downstairs as promised. When we reach the front door, he pauses.

"I know that Nikolai can be difficult. If you need anything, don't hesitate to ask. You are my wife's friend now, and there is always a safe place for you here."

My throat burns as I thank him. It's a nice offer, but the truth is, there is no safe place for me in this world.

Franco is waiting outside as promised, but I falter when I see Mischa standing there. I haven't seen him since the Christmas party, and he isn't supposed to be here now.

"What are you doing?" I ask.

He opens the door and gestures for me to get inside. I look at Franco. He is the one who drives me home, but today, he simply nods and walks back into the house.

"Just get in," Mischa says.

I hesitate for only a second before I read the urgency in his eyes. He isn't supposed to be here, but whatever's happening, I trust him. I get into the car and put my seat belt on while he walks around to the driver's side. He starts the ignition, and the car rolls down the winding drive of Alexei's private estate.

I'm waiting for him to tell me what's going on, but he doesn't. His knuckles are white against the steering wheel, and his entire body is rigid.

"Mischa?"

He glances at me across the car, and if I didn't know any better, I'd think he hates me a little right now.

"I shouldn't be doing this," he says.

"Why did you pick me up?"

"Nikolai doesn't know I'm here," he admits. "If he finds out, he'll kill me. You've got one chance, Nakya. Just this one. If you don't get out today, then you've signed your own death certificate. Do you understand?"

It almost seems too easy, considering the painstaking amount of time I've invested in planning my own escape. Franco was supposed to drive me today. I would have asked him to stop at the gas station, insisting I had to use the bathroom. Franco has always accommodated my requests, and I knew this time would be no different. But I wasn't going to use the bathroom. I was going to run.

That was the extent of my plan. There wasn't really any follow-through because I had none. I only knew I had to get out. But now Mischa is offering me an escape on a silver platter, and I'm still trying to discern if he's really as trustworthy as I thought.

"You have no choice," he says, reading my mind. "I'm the only option you've got."

"Why are you doing it?"

"Because it will destroy Nikolai if anything happens to you because of him."

I don't believe that, but there's no point in arguing. My focus is on the future. My focus is on escaping.

"How are we going to do this?" I ask.

"There's a bag in the trunk." He tips his head back. "Some food, money, and a coat. I'm going to stop in Pittsfield and drop you off at the bus depot. You buy a ticket. Whatever the first bus is, I don't care, you get on it. And then you keep getting on buses or trains to get wherever the fuck you want to go, preferably on the opposite side of the country."

"That's it?"

He glares at me. "What the fuck more do you want? I'm not a travel agent."

"I know. I'm sorry. I'm just ... I'm freaking out."

"Just be smart," he says. "Once you're off the East Coast, you'll be doing all right."

I wish I had as much confidence, but I just nod.

The drive is tense and quiet. And when Mischa pulls to a stop at a curb, I genuinely don't think I can do this. I've never gone anywhere by myself. I don't even know how to buy a bus ticket or figure out the schedules or pick a place to go.

"Nakya." Mischa shakes me from my thoughts. "The bus depot is just up the street on the left. I can't drop you any closer. You have to go now."

He pops the trunk and leaves the car running. This is it. He's not getting out, and I'm on my own from here. I know how much he's risking by doing this for me. He's already done enough, and my panic isn't the way to repay him.

I unbuckle and get out of the car, pausing to look at him one more time. "Thank you, Mischa."

He swallows and nods. "Don't forget your bag."

THIEF

I shut the door and grab the backpack from the trunk. Mischa is gone in a blink, and I'm left standing on the curb, feeling as lost as I've ever been.

I glance up the street. The bus depot isn't far, but I need to get to the crosswalk. It's a busy intersection, and the middle of the day, so traffic is thick. Attempting to blend in, I join the other pedestrians waiting to cross. My heart is racing, but I try to make it look like I do this all the time.

The light turns, and I move with the crowd. So far, so good. On the other side of the street, we disperse. I'm in the clear, but I feel more vulnerable walking down the street alone. The traffic is at a standstill, so I keep my head down and try to avoid attention as I pass the cars.

It feels like an eternity until I make it to the oddly shaped building, even though it's only a short distance. I'm almost to the glass door when an eerie feeling creeps over my skin. Something prompts me to look up, and when I do, my heart stops.

There's a blue sports car idling in the street, waiting for the light change up ahead. And it isn't so much the car, but the face behind the wheel that I recognize. I saw him at the Christmas party, and I remember him because he was one of the men ogling me at the door. He does a double take, and I know that he's seen me too. The tattoos peeking out above his shirt collar only confirm my fears. He's a Vor.

I duck my head and dart inside the building, walking as fast as I can. Every few feet, I pause to look over my shoulder. He isn't there. But he saw me, and I'm certain he recognized me. *Didn't he?*

I don't know what to do. It was always going to be a risk in any of these small towns. The Berkshires are crawling with Vory, and I should have known better. I should have walked faster. There were a lot of things I wished I'd done differently, but right now, I'm at a loss.

Adrenaline, not reason, has me walking to the ticket counter and glancing up at the bus schedules. It's late in the afternoon, and there aren't many left for the day, but I need to choose. The decision is suffocating, so I pick the first one that I see. There's a bus going to Boston and it's leaving in thirty minutes. From there, I can get another.

I get in line to purchase my ticket, clutching the straps of my bag in my hands. Every few seconds, I look around, and I'm certain it's probably only drawing more attention. I try to calm my nerves, waiting thirty seconds between passes. The people in front of me are taking forever.

Another glance out the window. It's quick, and I think I'm all right. But then I see him. He's on his phone, and he's got his hand up to the glass, his eyes squinting as he searches the faces in the crowd.

I'm screwed.

I'm so screwed.

I exit the line and force myself to walk normally to the opposite side of the station, moving with the flow of other travelers and praying he doesn't see me.

I need to get out of here, so I take the first exit I can find. Back on the sidewalk, I walk in the direction that I came from, making a right onto the first available cross street. I need to stay calm. Running will only draw attention, so I walk. And as I do, I retrieve the coat Mischa packed for me, shrugging it on and rearranging my backpack.

I don't know where I'm going. There are businesses along the way. Shopping marts, coffee houses, and even a medical center. But none of them feel safe. I need to get somewhere I can hide. And after fifteen minutes, I finally do.

It's a baseball park, and it's walled by trees. Enough that I can disappear and catch my bearings while I figure out another plan. The grass is cold and hard beneath my feet, but now that I'm off the main street, I decide to run. My ankle hurts with every jarring impact, and I worry that I might trip, but I also worry that if I don't run, I won't get there at all.

Behind the field, I find a heavy and full cluster of trees. It's the best cover I could hope for right now, so I pick the thickest one I can find. Flattening my body against the ground, I army crawl beneath it.

It isn't the least bit comfortable, and one thing is apparent now that I've executed my plan. Even if I do manage to go undiscovered, I won't survive the elements for long with the clothes I have on. My only hope is that I will be able to move from this area before dawn. I'll return to one of the shops I passed along the way and buy some different clothes, and then I'll go back to the station and take the first bus out of here.

But first, I have to survive the night. And with every passing second, a new doubt fills my head. It isn't baseball season, but the park still hosts the occasional dog and their owner. Every set of footsteps makes my breath stop. It goes on as the hours pass, and eventually, darkness sets in.

I rest my eyes and wonder what's happening back at Nikolai's estate. He would know that I haven't returned by now, and he would have contacted Alexei. It occurs to me that his brother must have known about this. Franco just let me go with Mischa without a second thought. They must have had some sort of plan for what they would tell Nikolai. He expected Franco to drive me home, so I assume they will say that I managed to escape from the car, much like I'd planned to. Nikolai will be none the wiser that his best friend helped me, and Alexei and his guard will receive the blame.

It's the best possible scenario for all of us. Nikolai can return to his life, and hopefully find peace without me. But I just have to force myself not to think about who that life will include.

It's for the best.

At some point, I fall asleep. I realize it when I'm startled awake by another sound of footsteps. Too late to be a dog walker, I think. It's dark, and it's blistering cold. My entire body feels like it's frozen, and it's only going to get worse.

I wait for the person to disappear like all the others, but they don't. The footsteps are getting closer. So close, that on one occasion, I can see shoes from beneath the tree. I hold my breath, dead certain I'm caught when a flashlight sweeps through the brush.

A voice calls out to someone else in Russian, and I swallow.

They've traced my steps, and this is the most logical conclusion. I have no connections, no car, no idea what to do. So where else would I go?

I wait for the guard to say he's found me. It's the longest minute of my life that he stands there, discussing what they should do. But through it all, it becomes clear he has no idea I'm here. And for now, I'm safe.

I still don't take a full breath until he moves again, and then I gulp the cool air in by the mouthful. Their footsteps grow distant, and eventually, they disappear.

Cold seeps into my bones, and I'm too afraid to move my limbs, even after it has gone quiet. I wait for them to come back. And then I wait some more. For what I would guess to be two hours, I lie as still as I can. Until I know that I have no choice.

It's now or never.

I have to move. I have to get to safety. I need a warm space, a phone, and every prayer in the world.

The lights in the distance feel close, but I know they are far away. This town is probably crawling with Nikolai's men by now. My only hope is to find a nice hotel where I can hide in the bathroom for the night. At least I'll be safe from the elements there.

But my nerves are shot, and my limbs are stiff as I travel through the park. I think I hear a twig snap behind me, and I freeze. Three seconds pass, and then four more. I want to believe it's my imagination. I want to believe I haven't made it this far in vain.

I forge on, and there isn't another sound. Not a single one. But the things that go bump in the night are not the most dangerous predators. It's the ones who are silent. It's the thieves who come to steal you away without warning.

And there is no thief more skilled than Nikolai Kozlov.

THIEF

I understand that when he cages me in his arms, his breath hot in my ear.

"And just where do you think you're going, pet?"

CHAPTER 32
NIKOLAI

Her pulse hammers against her throat as I drag her up the stairs to my bedroom. Filthy little liar. Covered in dirt and scratches, so desperate to get away from me. She calls me a sadist, and I laugh in her face.

"You have no idea, *zvezda*. I've been too kind to you. But if you wish, I can show you what a sadist really is."

Her bottom lip trembles, and she refuses to look at me as she pleads. "Just let me leave."

My palm blankets the delicate flesh of her throat. I could strangle her right now. I could end her life and this nonsense once and for all. Instead, my fingers wrap around her jaw.

"You don't get to leave me," I murmur against her lips. "The only way you're leaving me, pet, is through death."

"No," she protests.

I force her down onto the bed and pin her body with my legs. She gasps when I produce my switchblade and flinches when I cut her shirt in half. With a sudden and pointless case of modesty, the princess attempts to cover her breasts with her palms.

Her hands are removed with force, and best left tied to the

bedframe with the remnants of her shirt. She struggles against me, but already, her nipples are hard, and her tits are swollen for me. My palm flattens against her stomach and holds her in place while my teeth tug at her nipple.

She yelps and then whines when I lick her, soothing the hurt I caused. Her eyes squeeze shut because she is too proud to admit her defeat. It isn't necessary, regardless. I can smell the arousal soaking through her panties already.

She doesn't deserve my kindness. She doesn't deserve to come. But I will remind her who she belongs to. I will keep this little doll for as long as I wish, locking her up and bringing her out to play as I see fit.

"Nika," she begs.

I slap her tits. She cries out, and it stirs my cock, making me restless. I'm desperate to plunge inside her. I need to fuck her raw, over and over again, until she admits she is mine. It's the only cure for my sickness. She is the only source of calm I have. Her warmth, and her scent, and her tender touches.

I hate her for making me weak. I hate her for fucking up everything that I planned. And most of all, I hate her for being the daughter of Manuel Valentini. I close my eyes and try to block it out, but I can't.

My fingers move to her throat again, and this time, she looks into my eyes.

"Do it," she whispers. "Set me free."

I squeeze her and kiss her so violently she can't breathe. My teeth clash with hers, and I taste blood. I lap at the bitter sweetness, desperate for more.

She whimpers, and I thrust my pelvis against her. There are still too many barriers between us. A problem solved when I tug off her leggings and unzip my pants.

"You don't get to leave me."

I pry her legs apart and slap her clit. She sucks in a breath between her teeth, yanking against her restraints with all that she has. I rub my swollen cock against her, coating myself in her wetness.

She shakes her head in denial, and I crawl up the length of her body, smearing the leaking arousal from my cock against her lips. They are sealed as tight as can be, and it only makes me harder. My little doll is stubborn. My little doll is beautiful. And my little doll is a savage for denying me when I need her this way.

"Take my cock," I demand.

"Have your precious Ana do it."

I pinch her nipple, and she bucks against me. "Don't speak of her again."

"Ana, Ana, Ana," she screams.

I squeeze her jaw in my palm. "Take care of my cock, or I'll find someone who will."

Her eyes flare, and her cheeks color with crimson. She is jealous. She is possessive. And Nakya wants my cock all to herself.

"I hate you," she says.

I pet her face and rub my cock over her lips, groaning. "But not as much as you love me."

She stills, and in spite of her temper, a tear spills out of the corner of her eye. "Why do you have to torture me? Why can't you just let me go?"

"Because I need you."

It's the most brutally honest thing I've said to her, and I hate myself for it. But regardless, it's what she wants to hear. She wants me to be weak too.

"Nika," she begs. "Let me touch you."

"Suck my cock."

She opens her mouth and lets me inside. It's warm and it's wet, and it's my fucking heaven and hell all wrapped into one. She tries to do as she's told, but it does little good when I start fucking her face and using her.

It relaxes me to hear her gag and sputter and choke on my cock. Salty tears smear the mascara around her eyes, staining them with the evidence that I took her this way. I like her when she's filthy and mine.

"This is the only cock you will ever taste, *zvezda*. Your lips are mine. Your pussy is mine. And if you ever deny me again, I will fuck you up the ass to prove that it is also mine."

She moans, and I shove myself deeper. I could come right now. I could spill myself in her throat and make her swallow all of it. But it has been too long since I fucked her. I need to feel her pussy wrapped around me. I need to feel her slick with want for me. My balls are heavy, and I want to purge them inside her womb.

When I pull away, she whines. I stroke her cheek, and even though I shouldn't, I lean down to kiss her again. She arches up against my chest, her nipples stabbing against the material of my shirt. I wrap her legs around my hips.

"Let me touch you," she pleads.

"You ran from me, pet. Bad girls don't get to touch. They don't get to play."

I thrust inside her and sigh. Her pussy is tight and perfect, and the smug little brat knows it. I fuck her as though I'm half-drunk, and she watches me too closely, proud of herself for what she does to me. I'm half tempted to cover her face with a pillow so I don't have to look at her face. Or more importantly, so she can't see mine.

I want to fuck her like a whore. I want to put her in her place, but I'm out of fresh material. So, I pinch and slap her tits a few times because I can. I bite her throat and wreck her hair, and then I try the pillow idea, but it isn't the same.

I need to see her face.

"This is all you're good for," I growl. "A little doll that I can fuck and stuff with cum. You should be punished for asking for impossible things."

"You've already punished me," she cries. "There's nothing you could do that's worse than what you've already done."

The tremor in her voice gets to me even though it shouldn't. My touch softens, and my fingers roam over her face when I collapse onto her body. Instead of fucking her dirty, I end up fucking her nice. My lips find hers, and she sighs when I give her what she needs. My affection. My attention. My cum. All the things I don't want to give.

"You are poison," I tell her. "You're going to ruin me."

"So let me ruin you," she whispers. "It's the only way."

CHAPTER 33
NIKOLAI

The time has come for our monthly Vory meeting, and today, Viktor will demand his answers.

He will want a proposal for Ana, and he will want to know my prisoner's fate. If I tell him the truth about my mother, he will expect Nakya to pay. But to lie would mean sparing Manuel from the vengeance I rightly deserve. Already, I have waited too long. He should have been dead weeks ago, and if things were not so complicated, he would have been.

I would like to believe that in time, Nakya would forgive me for murdering her father. Their relationship is not without its own complications. She loves him, and she hates him, perhaps equally. It would be difficult at first, but she would come to accept my justifications. Not only for my own mother, but for hers as well.

Regardless, it should be the least of my concerns. For now, I must navigate the troubled waters with Viktor. He will not give me another extension. My time is up, and I still haven't decided what to tell him.

Slipping into the meeting at the last possible second is not my finest moment, but it gives me the benefit of extra time to make my decision. Viktor issues a sharp look when I arrive, the last Vor to take his seat. There will certainly be a discussion to follow, but for now, he directs one of the *boeviks* to the front of the room to operate the presentation Alexei has prepared. Today's agenda will be no different than every other month. Gambling operations, gun shipments, and whatever else makes the brotherhood money.

But when the presentation loads, it isn't the usual reports that fill the screen. It's a surveillance video from Alexei's home. A video that, by the expression on his face, he hasn't seen before. His housekeeper Magda is on the stairs, and beside her is Talia. His wife calls out to him from behind, but he does not turn, so she tries again.

Confused whispers begin to circulate around the room, but it only takes Alexei a moment to understand what's happening. Someone has betrayed his secret, exposing his hearing impairment for all the Vory brothers to see.

"Turn it off," he demands.

The *boevik* fumbles with the computer, but even when he removes the flash drive, the video doesn't stop. Alexei glances across the room, and his eyes land on Sergei, the accusation clear. It would be my first assumption as well, given the bad blood between them. But the embarrassment doesn't end there.

What happens next is worse. Far worse.

A sordid display of images emerges out of nowhere, flashing across the screen. Images of Alexei's wife. Strung out. Gaunt. Lifeless. And in every still, she's being fucked by a different man. They are from a time before Alexei took her into his possession, when she was still a slave. Logically, only two people should have access to these pictures. Talia and her former captor.

It's difficult to witness this insult to my brother. He is a man who loves his wife more than any other, and he's a man who has just been betrayed. One last slide presents itself, the final blow for all to see.

How does it feel to know your beloved Sovietnik is deaf and married to a whore?

Blind rage drives Alexei to smash the computer, and there isn't a single word spoken among us. Viktor is the one to clear the room, instructing us all to wait in the bar. I'm the last man to leave my place, eager to help, but understanding that in Alexei's present mental state, he won't see it that way.

Viktor stops me at the door. "Nobody is allowed to leave this building."

I nod, and the door closes behind him. My Vory brothers drink and speak quietly among themselves while we wait for a resolution. My eyes are fixed on Sergei, acknowledging the smug expression on his face. Soon, that smug expression will be replaced with a lifeless one.

If he did have his fingers in this, he's covered his tracks well. I have witnessed the genuine love between Alexei and his wife, and it's difficult to comprehend that she would ever do this, but that's how it appears.

I know my brother. Like me, he is quick to believe the worst in others. And I know when he emerges from the control room with Viktor, he has come to believe the worst of his pregnant wife.

Viktor moves to the front of the room with Alexei in tow, and there is no explanation needed for what happens next. The Vory way is simple, but brutal. By hiding his secret from his Vory brothers, Alexei has committed a betrayal. The brotherhood doesn't tolerate secrets, but Alexei has kept his for good reason. He considers his deafness a weakness.

It will not save him from punishment regardless. This is the Vory way. He strips his shirt and takes the drink that Viktor offers him first, draining it in one swallow. With a nod, he signals that he is ready to accept the consequences, and Viktor has the first honor of punching him.

He strikes Alexei in the gut, and then gestures for the rest of his Vory brothers to follow suit. Every man has his turn. Sergei takes pleasure in the act, pummeling Alexei twice. When my turn comes around, I apologize in advance, and then hit him where I hope it will hurt the least. He takes it like a man, and when the ordeal is over, he earns another tattoo. A symbol that he has earned his way back into the brotherhood with honor.

But there is no honor in what happened to him. I'm murderous on his behalf, but I don't know what I can do to help him. Viktor calls for Franco and sends Alexei home to recover.

It's only once he's gone that it occurs to me I still have my own problems to deal with. And Viktor is not in a pleasant mood now. When he approaches me, I'm almost certain he will demand either Nakya's death or Ana's proposal by midnight tonight.

Instead, he slaps me on the shoulder. "We will discuss the marriage later. For now, I need you to do what you can to see Alexei through this. I foresee a difficult road ahead."

I nod, but Viktor is quick to remind me that this isn't over.

"Soon. You will make your proposal soon."

VIKTOR'S ORDERS have given me a renewed sense of purpose. It's easier to focus on problems when they aren't yours, and I have made it my objective to prove to Alexei that his wife did not betray him. However, my brother has proven himself to be more stubborn than I initially gave him credit for.

He's too blinded by anger to listen to reason, and I stand little chance of redeeming Talia without proof of her innocence. Mischa is on surveillance detail, analyzing the video from the club that day, but his work takes time. Time is not a luxury I have when Alexei grows colder and more resistant from one day to the next.

He spends hours locked away in his office, obsessing over every piece of evidence. Cognac has become his only ally because he trusts no one. The natural and logical progression in this situation is a simple one. Alexei won't let this go. At the risk of his own life, he will determine that the answers lie with Talia's former captor. The only possible end to such a visit will be bloody and messy.

In many ways, his situation is reflective of my own. Impossible and doomed to failure.

This morning, I am reminded of business left unfinished when I study the pieces still waiting in my vault. It's been too long since I painted, and it's as if time has stopped, preserving the memory of that day for an eternity. Her image still rests on the easel, untouched, and I think if I could, I would hang it in my bedroom.

She catches me in a vulnerable moment when she enters the room, her eyes moving to the painting, and then to me. I avert my gaze to avoid the discomfort of this situation.

"Everything okay?" I clean up some odds and ends to keep my hands busy.

"You haven't been here." Her words are an accusation, and she is past the point of hiding it.

"I haven't been with anyone else, *zvezda*. I've been helping Alexei."

"Is Talia okay?" she asks.

"She is healthy, according to Alexei. But I imagine, given the circumstances, she could be doing much better."

"I thought better of him," she answers quietly.

"It's easier to believe the worst in someone, is it not?"

When she doesn't answer, I'm left no choice but to look. She has always been light on her feet, but today, she appears to carry the weight of the world on her shoulders.

"What's going to happen to us, Nika?"

I release a breath I didn't realize I'd been holding. She deserves to know the truth. She's waited for it so long. Nakya is not ignorant to the ways of our world, but it doesn't mean she will understand. There is no softening the blow of the only words I have to offer her.

"I have but two choices, my sweet. And you will not like either option."

"Tell me," she insists. "I can handle it. I want to know."

I've tried to stay away from her, but when she's close enough for me to smell her intoxicating sweetness, I can't remember why I needed to avoid her in the first place. When I gesture for her, she comes, and it only makes it worse.

"The truth is, *zvezda*, it was never our fate to end up together. The stars are not in our favor, and the only way this can end is in tragedy."

"I don't believe that." She shakes her head, hair falling loosely around her pretty face.

"You know this world. Nothing is ever easy, and choices must be made. I can either forsake you and marry Ana, or I can let you go."

"Forsaking yourself," she finishes for me.

I toy with her hair and kiss her gently on the lips. Her eyes fall shut, and she leans her forehead against mine, soft and sad.

"Why can't we change our fates? Let's realign our stars, Nika. We can do it together. You can use your talents for your own benefit. You can paint, and I can dance, and—"

"You speak of impossible dreams." I close my own eyes and inhale her, drowning in her innocence. "This is not the way our worlds work, pet."

"It can be. Whatever we have to do—"

"I'm going to kill your father, Nakya. I'm going to torture him slowly, and I will take his last breath. So tell me now that we can be together."

Her body turns rigid in my arms, and just as I suspected, she retreats. I feel the loss of her everywhere, but I don't force her to come back. I want her to know that when her father dies, it will be at my hand.

The man abused her, and for that alone, he deserves to die. But it is her blood. And just as I'm trying to make peace with killing my own father, she will not easily find peace with my decision.

"Why?" she implores. "The debt?"

"It was never about the debt."

She paces the length of the room, collecting her thoughts and shaking her head. "I knew it couldn't just be about the debt. You knew too much about my life. You were so angry with me, and ... tell me why. I deserve to know."

"He murdered my mother."

She stops, and her sweetness turns to venom. "His mistress?"

"His slave," I answer. "A forced whore."

She blanches and rubs absently at her arms, visibly choosing denial. It's easier for her to believe that the many women who stole her father's attentions away from her sick mother were by choice. She has made it a full-time job to resent them. Her childhood gifted her a front row seat to the damages of infidelity, ensuring that she would remain steadfast in her resolve that she will never be a mistress. But she never saw the opposite side of the coin.

"I choose the second option." She squeezes her arms around herself. "Let me go. Have mercy, Nika. Let me leave while I still have a chance."

"Nakya." I step toward her, and she retreats.

"No," she says. "I think this should stop here. Please, let it stop here. I can't do this anymore."

CHAPTER 34
TANAKA

"Where is he going?"

Mischa fiddles with the cigarette between his fingers, tapping it against the end of his thumb before flipping it over and repeating the action all over again. He's reluctant to answer, and it makes me fidgety.

"He's going to help his brother."

"He's been helping his brother for weeks. What makes this time any different?"

Mischa stuffs the cigarette back into the pack and sits down on the sofa. He says he came to check on me, but really, he came to deliver the message that Nikolai didn't want to give me himself.

"Please tell me," I insist. "What's happening? Is he okay?"

Mischa leans back against the sofa, kicking his leg up and tapping his foot on the coffee table. "Against my advice, Nikolai is going to help his brother track down Talia's former captor. It's a dangerous place where they're going, and there are only the two of them. There's a possibility he might not make it back."

I make an effort to reply, but nothing comes out of my mouth.

THIEF

Mischa nods. We are both quiet while I process. I haven't even looked at Nikolai in weeks, but the idea of losing him siphons every bit of warmth from my body.

"He could have said goodbye." I swipe at the anger leaking out of my eyes.

Mischa barks out a laugh. "And give you the chance to push him away again? That isn't his style, Nakya."

"I didn't push him away," I argue. "It's him. He's the one who won't make a choice. He could have avoided this."

Mischa shakes his head. "It was never his choice to make. And if you don't know that by now, then you will never survive in this world."

"If you love someone, then you find a way. It might not be easy, but you can if you want to. And it has become clear to me that Nikolai doesn't want to."

"That is only what a hypocrite would say," Mischa observes.

"I am not a hypocrite. You told me yourself I had to get away."

"Riddle me this, princess." He leans forward, humoring me with unrestrained animosity. "How do you believe this fantasy relationship of yours would work? You would go back to being a dancer, and Nikolai could paint pictures of flowers and ponies while traveling around the world with you?"

"Of course not. I know it wouldn't be like that—"

"There is the small matter of having a bounty on both of your heads to consider. In addition to the fact that no matter where in the world you went, you wouldn't be safe. But you don't think about these things in your fantasy, do you?"

"I'm not ignorant," I choke out. "I know it isn't that easy."

Mischa softens, the way he always eventually does. "It doesn't mean he doesn't care."

I fall onto the couch beside him, attempting to contemplate a world where Nikolai doesn't exist. But I can't. And I don't know how it happened. One minute, he was stealing me away from my life, and the next, I was falling in love with him. There are so many complications between us that we can never overcome. His impending marriage. My impending death. His desire to murder my father. Every possible card is stacked against us, but still, I would fight for it if he did too.

"You know what it's like to lose your mother," Mischa interrupts my thoughts.

"What does that have to do with anything?"

"He lost his mother too, you know. His entire life, he's been told that she walked away from him. Nikolai is good at holding onto things. He's good at pushing people away before they can hurt him like that again. It's why he's so quick to believe the worst in people. It's why he will turn on you when you least expect it."

"If you're trying to convince me that he's not good for me, you can save your breath. I already know these things."

"I'm not trying to convince you of anything," he says. "I'm just telling you that until you, his relationships were nonexistent. You were the first woman to get under his skin. If nothing else, you should know that it does mean something."

I offer him a weak smile, but it doesn't make me feel any better.

"I know that I need to go," I tell him. "I don't suppose you'd be willing to help me out with that again?"

"After what happened last time?" He shakes his head. "Not a snowball's chance in hell. Besides, he would definitely know it was me this time."

I shrug. "Fair enough, I suppose."

He gives me a sideways glance. "You'll figure something out. I'm sure of it."

DURING NIKOLAI'S ABSENCE, it has come to my attention that there is a two-hour gap throughout the day in which I'm alone with Nonna. At all other times, there is a Vory appointed guard loitering

THIEF

throughout the house. One who doesn't speak or dare to look at me.

Mischa drops in usually every other day, but his visits are unpredictable. My window of opportunity is a small one. Since Nonna has the house locked up tighter than usual, I'm not able to get to the office to use the phone. So I have two options. Either the guard, or Mischa. I've been studying their every move, attempting to predict the most opportune moment. But when it finally presents itself, I'm not prepared at all.

It happens on a Sunday, in the morning, on the happenstance occasion that I cut my time in the gym short because my ankle is bothering me. Nonna always comes to lock up when her timer goes off, so I don't bother to alert her. But when I leave the room, I bump into the guard as he's racing toward the bathroom.

He looks like hell, and it's apparent that he had no consideration for his duties this morning because he still reeks of alcohol from the night before. The bathroom door slams behind him and the sound of his retching follows me down the hall.

I'm content to continue on my merry way until I notice that he left his things behind on the sofa. Specifically, his cigarettes, some change, and a phone.

I glance back at the door down the hall. He could be in there for a while. This could be my only opportunity. Or it could backfire spectacularly. Either way, I know I have to try.

I scoop up his phone and dart into the closet, huddling into the corner among the coats, hoping I can be quiet enough. My fingers tremble as I dial Gianni, and it seems to ring for an eternity before he picks up.

"Hello?"

"It's me," I whisper. "I need your help. Can you get me out of here?"

He's quiet for a beat, and I hear shuffling on the other line as he moves somewhere so he can talk. "Tanaka?"

"Yes. Please, Gianni, I don't have long. I need your help."

"I can't come to his house. I've been trying to get to you another way, but you'll need to get out on your own first."

"How?" I hiss. "That's not going to happen. I've already tried."

"You have to, Tanaka," he implores. "I can't come there. It's too risky. Too much surveillance. You need to get out first. Just get as far away from the house as you can, and I'll come for you."

I want to scream out my frustration, but down the hall, the toilet flushes. "When, Gianni?"

"Tomorrow," he answers. "With Nikolai gone, I don't trust that you have much longer."

I'm not sure how he knows that Nikolai is gone, but he's right. I don't trust that I'm safe here any longer, and I know that this is the only way to save both of us.

"You have to be close by," I tell him. "It's the only way."

"I'll be close," he assures me. "Just get out of the house, and I'll come for you."

Down the hall, the faucet turns off.

"I have to go," I whisper. "Tomorrow."

"Tomorrow," Gianni agrees.

I press the end button frantically and race to delete the call but it's too late to return the phone. The bathroom door opens, and when he walks down the hall, his shadow passes over the crack in the closet door.

There's some rustling and a low curse in Russian before he's walking back down the hall to the bathroom. I bolt from the closet as quietly as I can manage and run toward the sofa, stuffing the phone into the crack between the cushions.

I won't have time to make it back up the stairs, so I run back to the gym. I barely have time to swing my leg up onto the barre before the guard pauses at the door, peering in. His eyes are narrowed, full of suspicion, but he doesn't voice it. I return his gaze, desperately hoping I'm not giving anything away. After two of the longest seconds in my life, he goes back to the sitting room. I wait for five breaths before peeking around the corner to watch him from the door.

After some digging, he retrieves his phone from the cushions and shakes his head, flopping onto the sofa. I collapse against the wall and gulp my next breath of air.

Tomorrow.

I just have to make it to tomorrow.

CHAPTER 35
TANAKA

"Tashechka."

The hand on my arm is persistent, and I'm confused when I wake to find it's Nonna shaking me. I sit upright in bed, noting from the darkness outside that it's not yet dawn.

"What's wrong?" I ask.

"Nikolai has asked for you."

"He's here?" I rub the sleep from my eyes and move the blanket aside.

Nonna doesn't answer, but she guides me to the closet and instructs me to dress.

"Where is he?"

"He's waiting for you, but you must hurry."

I don't understand what's happening, but I dress in the clothes Nonna hands me and when I'm finished, she leads me down the stairs and nods to the guard.

"She's ready."

He opens the front door and gestures me outside, but I hesitate. I'm supposed to leave today. Gianni will be waiting for me, and I won't be able to meet him because I don't know where we're going.

"Where is Nikolai?" I repeat.

The guard looks at Nonna, and she shrugs as if to give permission. When I look back, he's moved closer. I try to step away from him, but he reaches out and grabs my arm.

"Nonna?" I look at her for reassurance, but there isn't one to be found.

"It's time for you to go," she says. "Don't make it harder on yourself. Nikolai wants you gone."

"No." I throw an elbow and the guard grunts, but his grip tightens. The door is open, and if I can just get past it, I'll be okay. I can run and hide until daylight when Gianni comes to save me.

It's the only hope I can grasp onto, and it's snatched away before it has a chance to grow roots. The guard knocks me onto the floor and pins me down with his knee, forcing my wrists together behind my back. He gestures to Nonna, and she produces some rope and tape that he uses to secure me before propping me upright.

"Why are you doing this, Nonna?"

This woman has taken care of me. She has provided my meals and made my bed and showed her concern when I wasn't eating. I can't make sense of it.

"It's not me," she says. "It's Nikolai. I only do what he tells me. He does not want you anymore. If you accept this, it will be easier. Don't fight."

I don't want to believe her, but how can I not? Nikolai has gone and left me to my fate. The fate he warned me would inevitably end in tragedy. And I know before the guard even places the tape over my mouth that this is it. They are taking me to my death.

Gravel crunches beneath the tires as the car moves away from the house. Around us, there is nothing but wilderness. Even if I did manage to get out, I doubt I could outrun the guard in my current state. But I know I can't give up. I can't give up hope until I've exhausted every option. I wiggle my arms back and forth to loosen the rope, but it makes too much noise.

"Stop," the guard orders. "Or I will make it worse."

I meet his eyes in the rearview mirror. He is little more than a soldier, and his rank within the Vory is insignificant. Yet this is the man who Nikolai sent to bring me to my death.

Perhaps this is why he opted not to say goodbye. There is no goodbye when it's forever. He knew I would be gone when he returned, and he would be free to marry Ana and fulfill his duties as a loyal Vor. It's the only solution for him because he just couldn't let me go, thinking that I might have a life on my own without him.

A sob rips from my chest, and I continue to thrash against my restraints regardless of the guard's threats. If I must die, then I will go out fighting.

"I told you to stop," the guard bellows.

He pulls over, and I slide to the other side of the car, curling my knees into my chest. I'm prepared to kick him with as much force as I can manage when he wrenches the door open and comes at me. My legs heave toward him, clashing into solid flesh. It's a blind effort, since my hair is a mess, and I can't see past it. My ears, however, are still intact.

An explosive sound vibrates through my skull, and something wet sprays across my skin. I jerk backward, but there's nowhere to go, and now the weight on my legs is too heavy to move.

"Tanaka."

A hushed voice breaks through the chaos, and I shake my head, trying desperately to see through the tangle of hair.

"Gianni?"

The door opens behind me and strong arms drag me out. I'm still not sure if it's the enemy or my savior until the knife cuts through the restraints on my wrists, freeing me.

I scrub the hair out of my face and sniffle when I see his face.

Gianni.

THIEF

He came for me. He came like he said he would. And I am not going to die today.

"Quick." He grabs me by the arm and leads me through the brush to a waiting Jeep.

Before I can even thank him, he hoists me inside and takes his place in the driver's seat, firing up the ignition. The ride is a bumpy one, and it's left up to me to remove the tape from my face, which is also partially tangled in my hair. It hurts, but compared to what could have happened, it's nothing.

"How many other guards are at the house?" Gianni asks as he speeds down the dirt road and onto the highway.

"That was it. Just him."

He nods.

"Is he dead?"

Gianni glances at me and then back to the road. "Yes."

I take a moment to process that. "How did you know?"

"I came early," he says. "I've been camping out all night, watching the house. The panic in your voice yesterday concerned me, so I didn't think there was much time left."

"There wasn't." I swallow and look out the window. "They were going to kill me. Nikolai sent me to die."

Gianni looks at me incredulously. "Tell me you didn't fall for him, Tanaka."

"Of course not."

It isn't believable. Gianni shakes his head but makes a point not to argue about it. There are more important things to discuss, like my future.

"Where are we going?"

"That depends on you," he answers. "Your options are limited, Tanaka."

"I know."

"Does that mean you're ready?"

Reality settles over me, and it's heavy. What he's asking will change everything. It means letting go of my old life. Letting go of the memories of Nikolai, and any love that lives in my heart.

I close my eyes and lean back against the seat. The words don't come easily, but they do come. "I'm ready."

CHAPTER 36
NIKOLAI

"Kol'ka."

Viktor gets out of his SUV, and I step out of my car. After this week, this is the last thing I want to do, but I know why he's waiting here at my home.

"How is Alexei?" he asks.

I lean back against the car and cross my legs. "As good as you might expect. He doesn't want to talk right now."

"I don't imagine," Viktor says. "This changes everything."

The uncertainty weighs heavy on his face. As the *pakhan*, it is up to him to decide when we go to war. And when a sin like this has been committed, we have no choice but to go to war. Upon our return to the states, we got the news that Alexei's pregnant wife had been murdered in our absence. It's a crime too horrific to imagine, and I have no doubt that Alexei will be painting the city with the blood of our enemies in no time at all.

"Are you certain she's dead?"

Viktor sighs. "I don't know. It could be months before we know for certain. There is nothing left to identify, but it won't stop Alexei. He will need to be kept in check."

He believes me capable of keeping Alexei in check, but he's wrong. I will not be the one to stand in the way of his vengeance. I will be the one to hand him the gun.

"I need you to keep an eye on him," Viktor says. "Just help him come to terms with it. Let him kill who he wants, within reason. I don't need a war on our hands until we know exactly who's responsible."

"I'll do what I can."

Viktor nods, but he isn't finished. "About Ana—"

I am tired of this discussion and, more so, this dark cloud looming over me. I've had a very long journey and difficult news, and I'm not in the mood to feed him more lies. If there is anything I learned from Alexei's pain, it's that life is too short. It needs to be now or never.

Viktor wants the truth, and the honorable thing to do is give it to him. I will face whatever consequences he deems necessary, but I will not live another day under this oppression.

"Viktor, I can't marry your daughter."

His face mottles with red. "What do you mean you can't marry my daughter?"

"It wouldn't be fair to her. She deserves more than I can give her. She deserves a man who loves her."

"Are you telling me that my daughter is not worthy of you?" he sneers.

"Not at all. In fact, I'm telling you that I am unworthy of her. You've had your suspicions about the Valentini girl from the start, and I am sorry to admit that you were right. She isn't Russian, but she's mine."

There's a moment in which I think that Viktor might put a bullet between my eyes here and now. I wouldn't be surprised if he did.

"I should cut out your stars for dishonoring my family this way," he says.

"If that is what you must do, then I accept it. I will go to my death willingly, as long as you promise to leave Tanaka untouched."

He laughs. "And why would I promise that? The whore seduced you. She blinded you. And now you ask to cast my daughter aside and spare the life of the woman who will take her place?"

"You accepted Alexei's choice. Now I am asking you to accept mine."

"Ana is in love with you."

"Ana knows nothing of me. She is young, Viktor. Too young to marry someone like me. She should be with someone her own age. Someone who can give her everything she needs. I am sorry that I hurt her. I am sorry if I led her on, but I did not want to disappoint you. I did not want to insult the honor you had bestowed upon me."

He lights up a cigarette and smokes it in silence. Perhaps it was not the ideal time to bring it up, but I don't regret that I did. Even if it means I don't breathe another day on this earth, I won't regret it.

"What of Manuel?" he asks. "Have you found the answers you seek?"

"Yes." I kick the dirt beneath my shoe. This is the part he will not like. "I was correct. He beat and tortured and killed my mother, and Sergei gave him the honor of doing so."

Viktor shakes his head in visible disgust. "And still you ask to spare his daughter's life? Where is the justice in that? What about your mother? Will she have died in vain so that you may please your dick?"

"No," I force out. "I would ask for your blessing to kill Manuel myself, as well as any of the men in his employ who touched her."

"And your father," Viktor adds.

"And my father," I agree somberly.

Viktor tosses the butt of his cigarette on the ground and stubs it out with his shoe. "It would be a reasonable request, if it weren't for one small matter, Kol'ka."

"What is it?"

"Nonna called to report that some of Manuel's men broke into the house while you were away."

That isn't possible. That doesn't even make sense. I glance at the house, but Viktor goes on.

"They took the Valentini girl, and they destroyed your security system. It's what I came here to tell you."

I abandon Viktor for the stairs, determined to see it for myself, but the *pakhan* isn't finished delivering bad news.

"Before you think about storming into Manuel's compound, you should know that the feds got him. Everything is cordoned off. You won't get in there, and you won't get near him. She is gone, Nika."

CHAPTER 37
NIKOLAI

Manuel adjusts the phone closer to his mouth, breathing heavy into the other line. "Do you know where my daughter is?"

What a fucking joke. He is a vile cunt of a man, and if there wasn't inches of glass between us, I would jam this phone through his skull until his brains decorated the floor.

He wants to play stupid, so I'll humor him for now.

"You tell me, Manuel."

He closes his eyes and sighs. "I can't believe she would do this to me. It's you. You have turned her against me."

I silently pick apart his words, attempting to find logic in them. But I know that it can't be right. He can't be implying what I think he is.

"A fucking rat. My own daughter." His mood swings from violent to hysterical in the span of two seconds.

"Are you trying to tell me that Tanaka flipped?"

He levels me with vacant eyes. "It's fucking Gianni. My own man. I trusted him, and he was a goddamned fed. He's been playing me all along. They both have."

My fingers turn white around the receiver as Manuel comes unraveled on the other side of the barrier. He's losing his mind, but there is still some substance to what he's telling me. I just don't want to believe it.

I tap on the glass. "Pull yourself together. I need to know where she is, Manuel. Who took her?"

"Fucking Gianni," he roars. "It has to be him."

I shake my head. It can't be right. He's out of his mind. He's delusional.

"You're next," he says. "She will flip on you too."

"That won't happen." Tanaka wouldn't turn on me. Or maybe it's only what I want to believe.

"You know what you have to do," Manuel tells me. "I can't pay the debt. The feds took everything, so you have to take it from her. I just beg of you, be merciful."

I smile at him through gritted teeth. "As merciful as you were to my mother? You remember her, don't you?"

He blinks, unsettled, and I can see the gears turning in his mind. He is trying piece together which one she was, but I'm content to remind him.

"Irina Lemeza."

The color drains from his face, and his palm comes to rest on the glass, sticky and desperate. "No."

"Yes, Manuel." I lean toward him. "You know the Russians are fond of an eye for an eye. I know you worry about your daughter, but there's no need. She won't be the one to pay the debt. I think for once in your life, it's time to do the honorable thing, don't you?"

"Nikolai is here to see you," Magda says.

Alexei is slumped against his desk, drunk again. And though I have spent the past four weeks helping him slaughter every man he deemed remotely responsible for his wife's death, it has done nothing to ease his pain.

It has, however, come as a welcome distraction while I seek out Nakya.

"Send him away," Alexei murmurs.

"Too late." I step into his office so that he can see me. "I have something I believe you will want to see."

His eyes move to the drive in my hand, and for the first time in weeks, there is a spark of life inside him. He takes my offering and rouses the computer from sleep, bringing up countless images of his wife on the wall-to-wall monitors.

Alexei glances at the images, haunted, and breaks down all over again. I take it upon myself to bring up the surveillance video from the club. The same video of the day he was humiliated in front of his Vory brothers. When it begins to play, he makes an effort to watch.

"I had Mischa look at it." I bring the cursor to a time stamp on the screen and click on it. "It's on a loop. Whoever it was knew what they were doing. They were fast, and they came prepared."

"How long?" he asks.

"Thirty seconds maximum. You couldn't have noticed it, Lyoshka. It was very well edited."

He falls back into his office chair as reality settles over him. Someone wanted him to believe it was Talia who betrayed him, but in truth, it was one of his own Vory.

I take a seat across from his desk. "There is something else."

"What is it?"

"Katya's guard mentioned that she visited a security store a few months back. He didn't know what she purchased but found the trip out of character for her."

"Then we need to talk to her." Alexei nearly stumbles over himself as he tries to stand.

I signal him to sit back down. "I already tried. She was found dead this morning, *bratan*. Hanging from a rafter in her ceiling."

Alexei flops back into his seat and reaches for the bottle of cognac, only to realize that it's empty.

"She wasn't working alone," I tell him. "Someone is cleaning up loose ends. Katya is not smart enough to set up that slideshow, and she was not in the building that day."

My words settle over Alexei like a dark cloud, and it doesn't take him long to draw the same conclusion I have. He sinks back, eyes darkening as he utters the name we have both come to hate.

"Sergei."

CHAPTER 38
TANAKA

"Niki."

Gianni takes a seat on the park bench beside me, tapping out a message on his phone before he turns his attention to me. I grab another handful of oats from the plastic bag in my lap, carefully dividing it among the ducks as I throw it.

"It's a beautiful day," he remarks.

I look up at the clouds, clear and blue. The sun warms my face, and I think that it's always a beautiful day in Florida. It's a different kind of heat, though. Muggy and thick. It's hard to adjust to, just like everything else about my new life.

"How are you doing?" Gianni asks. "Anything new to report?"

"I'm fine." I shrug. "Nothing new to report. Every day is the same."

And it is. I go to work, and I don't talk to anyone over the age of eight. When I'm finished, I go straight back to my apartment and turn on the television or the radio just to avoid the numbing silence. My life in witness protection is not all that different than it was before. It's still a prison, just a different kind.

"It's an adjustment," Gianni insists. "It takes time, but things will get better."

"I thought it would be different." I crumple the empty bag in my hand and toss it into the bin beside us.

"Everyone has an idea of what it will be like, but it's important to follow the rules. They're in place for a reason, and they keep you safe."

"I'm not talking about the program," I mutter. "I'm just talking about the world."

Gianni takes a sip from his travel mug. Coffee black, just the way he always drinks it. I've come to know that about him. Recently, I've come to know a lot of things about him. For example, he chews with his mouth open. And he still wears a gold chain, even when he's not pretending to be a gangster. But the most obvious thing I've learned is that he really just wants to be a hero.

He sighs and leans back, drumming his fingers on the park bench. "I suppose it's a grass is greener on the other side sort of situation. In your case, though, the grass really is greener. But it'll take time to see that."

I don't know if I believe that. My new world is everything I imagined. I have the freedom to come and go as I please, within reason. I can choose my own meals. I can dance whenever I want. I have a job, and I have a purpose. But I had to sell my father out to get here. Something that when I was at home, suffering at his hands, seemed like a good idea. Gianni approached me when he knew I was at my lowest. He saw my vulnerability, and he struck like a python, squeezing until I caved in.

Does my father deserve to go to prison? Undoubtedly. But do I want to be the one to stand up and testify against him? Absolutely not.

I'm empty inside, and the worst part is that I feel like everyone I've ever loved has betrayed me.

"We need to talk in private," Gianni says.

I already knew that. It's why he's here, after all. But he's impatient and determined, so we make the walk back to my apartment to put him at ease.

After unlocking the six deadbolts on my door and keying in the alarm code, we're in, just like that. Gianni is familiar with the space and makes himself at home on the Ikea sofa, while I opt for the kitchen.

In truth, I've done very little with this space. I don't see the point when he says I might have to move again after the trial. I might have to move again any time they say for the rest of my life. That's how it works. I am a tree without roots. A flower that cannot bloom where its planted.

"Do you want some tea?" I reach for the kettle.

He declines with a shake of his head.

I busy my hands with the preparation, so I have something to do while he talks. Already, I expect the worst every time he comes here. I expect him to show up in the middle of the night to say they're coming for me.

"I'm ready whenever you are," I tell him.

"Are you sure you don't want to sit down?"

"No. I'm good where I'm at."

He sighs, but reluctantly agrees. "Tanaka, I don't know how to tell you this. But it's about your father."

"He's dead?"

"Maybe," he ventures. "But probably not. The judge released him on bail, and he's gone."

"How could that happen?" I demand. "You told me they wouldn't give him bail."

"I don't know," he admits, frustrated. "But if I had to guess, someone bribed the judge. Or threatened him. Regardless, it is what it is. I have an obligation to let you know."

"That's it?" I stare at him. "Just an obligation to let me know?"

"It isn't just him," Gianni adds. "Half of his crew was killed in prison. The rest have gone into hiding. Something's going down, and I suspect it's the Russians."

The kettle boils, and I remove it from the stove, pouring the water over my tea bag and watching it steep.

"I don't suppose you know anything about that, do you?"

His tone is accusatory and slightly hostile, and it pisses me off. He's been trying to get me to flip on Nikolai since he took me into WITSEC.

"How could I?" I reply. "I'm not there, am I?"

"This changes things," he says. "You won't be going to trial now, obviously. And the DOJ will likely determine you're no longer at risk, considering the circumstances. You'll be left to fend for yourself."

I drop the tea bag in the garbage and suppress the urge to slap him. In truth, I owe Gianni a great deal. My life, actually. But he hasn't done any of this for my benefit. It's about his name. It's about being a hero and what that will mean for his career.

"You can save your breath," I tell him. "I don't know anything about the Vory. I've told you that already. I don't know how many times I've told you that."

"Tanaka, you lived with him for months. You must know something. I don't know what sort of misguided loyalty it is that you have for Nikolai Kozlov, but I can assure you that he has none for you. If he finds you, he will kill you. Do you understand that?"

"I do," I admit. "I understand it better than you ever could."

He comes into the kitchen to demand his answers. "So why are you protecting him?"

"Was that all you came to tell me?" I ask. "That WITSEC might dump me from the program?"

"Tanaka." He reaches out in an attempt to soften me by touching my hand. "If you don't do this, they will kill you."

"Then maybe I will finally be at peace."

His lip curls, and I know he resents me for not doing this for him. He's a federal agent, but I'm honestly beginning to wonder if I can really trust him. But then I realize it doesn't really matter either.

I'm done running.

If any of my father's men want to come for me, they will. And if

Nikolai or Viktor want me dead, then there isn't a place on this earth I can hide.

I am tired of living a life where I worry about survival every day. And if there is not a place safe from that in this world, then maybe it is not the world for me.

CHAPTER 39
NIKOLAI

"Talia's death was quick," Alexei murmurs. "But I can assure you that yours won't be."

Sergei's lips twitch at the corners, offering his firstborn son a bloody gruesome smile. Even on the verge of death, his ego lives large.

Alexei gestures to the Irish Reaper, and Ronan hands him the small black case that will inevitably end Sergei's reign of terror. Already, he has been waterboarded, suffocated, and brought back to life with shock paddles several times. His eyes are cloudy, and his face is sallow, but he won't admit defeat.

If either of us expected an apology, it isn't coming. But I don't want Sergei's wasted words. I only want his death.

Alexei's fingers clamp onto the black case, and I know he wishes that he could be the one to end our father's life. Rightfully, he probably should. Though Sergei is responsible for the death of my mother, he has taken much more from my brother.

In the end, he hands me the case. "You can do the honors."

It isn't an honor at all to end a dishonorable man's life. But there is a purpose for everything, and the purpose of this is that it will hurt

Sergei the most. He doesn't care for Alexei, and he never has, but he does care for me, on some level at least. I'm the son he was proud of. The one who he claimed.

And I'm the son who will lay him to rest in the brutal fashion he deserves.

There is no reason to draw it out when I have a busy schedule ahead of me. I remove the syringe from the case without fanfare, and for a split second, there is fear in Sergei's eyes. Not equal to the fear my mother felt as a consequence of his actions. And not equal to what Alexei's wife must have felt before her death. But it's there, and it's enough.

Ronan assists me, instructing me where to inject the snake venom in Sergei's arm. It's too quick, and it isn't as intimate as it would have been to flay him in half with a blade, but it will be a long, painful death.

As the neurotoxins flood Sergei's body, he begins to convulse and foam at the mouth. When paralysis sets in, Alexei leans over him to whisper in his face. "It is only the beginning."

We sit, and for hours, we watch our father die. The room is quiet, save for the thrashing of Sergei's body on the table. Viktor is at Alexei's side, and Ronan is at mine. The event is entirely too short, and it doesn't bring my brother any peace when Sergei finally gasps his last breath.

In truth, it does nothing for me either.

I leave Alexei to process his grief, and Viktor follows me into the hall, shutting the door behind us.

"I'm sorry for your loss, Kol'ka."

"It's not a loss."

"But it does not bring you relief as you had hoped, does it?"

"It doesn't bring my mother back," I tell him. "Nor does it bring Alexei's wife back."

"No, it doesn't," he agrees. "Shall we get on with the next one then?"

I nod, and we walk upstairs together. Alexei's home is vast and well secured, but for this particular occasion, the event will take place in a secluded thicket located on the back half of the estate.

The walk is not a short distance, but the air is refreshing and despite the gruesomeness that awaits, it's a beautiful day. Already, Ronan has set everything up, and we find him waiting on a bench while Manuel squirms on the ground in front of him. This is just another day for the Irish Reaper, and there is none more skilled in the art of human torture than he is. It's why I've asked for his assistance, and because of our alliance, he was inclined to provide it.

Before I spare Manuel a second glance, my attention is drawn to the fifty-five-gallon barrel in the center of the clearing. A short distance away, there's also a fire roaring beneath a cast iron kettle straight from the history books. These items are Manuel's future, and not too far away is his past—a plastic tarp littered with bloodied power tools. In truth, I don't have the stomach for torture, but over the past twenty-four hours, I've checked in often to witness Ronan's work.

Like my canvases, he approaches every piece differently. While he stuck to the tried and true methods of torture for Sergei, he got a little more creative with Manuel. Specifically, he seemed to have some fun with a power drill. I watched him drill into Manuel's knees, which was enough for me, and I took his word for it that he also made some new holes in his hips and elbows.

That wasn't the extent of it. A sandblaster made quick work on half of his face, and a staple gun has been put to good use on the fleshier parts of his body. But I couldn't forget my Nakya in all of this. I couldn't forget the ways he made her suffer. For that part, I was the one to shatter his ankles with a hammer.

Manuel has reaped what he's sown in this life, and for that, I have no regrets. I can't bring my mother back, but I can send her tormentor to hell.

"Are you ready?" Ronan asks.

I nod in the direction of the large black cauldron. "What's the kettle for?"

"I wasn't particularly sure how you'd want to go about it," he says. "We could boil him or light him on fire. Your choice, really."

I look at Manuel—hogtied, dirty, sweaty, and covered in blood. Already he is unrecognizable. If Nakya knew the extent of what I did to him, she would never forgive me.

"Which one hurts the most?" Viktor asks.

Ronan scratches at his chin. "Ahh, I'd say they're about equal. Boiling takes longer, of course, but fire is as effective if it's pain ye want."

Viktor looks at me. It's my decision, and it's an easy one. I'm done with this pig, and it's time to bury him. "Let's make some stew then."

Ronan nods and gestures for some help. Between the three of us, we lift Manuel's mangled body easily enough. He can't move. He can't fight. But he can look at me with his one good eyeball, and he does.

"She'll rat you out too," he slurs. "Just watch."

I'm tempted to dunk his head into the boiling oil and hold him there for a few seconds before Viktor stops me.

"That's what he wants."

He's right, of course. Manuel would do anything at this point to end his suffering in the easiest way possible, including taking his daughter down with him.

"Easy does it," Ronan says as we lower Manuel into the kettle, legs first. "We don't want to splash, might hurt a wee bit."

As it turns out, he's quite comfortable with this method, and I'm almost positive it's not the first man he's boiled alive. On Ronan's instruction, we all pull away at the same time, and the natural weight of Manuel's body sinks him into the kettle.

His face bobs up and down in the oil, mouth split open in the shape of a silent scream. It's an image I won't ever forget, and a smell that will haunt me for eternity too. A price I'm willing to pay for vengeance.

Unlike Sergei, Manuel's death is much quicker. It feels like no time at all until his head disappears completely into the roiling liquid, and there's nothing left to do but watch the flames flicker beneath.

After enough time has passed to be considered appropriate, Viktor clears his throat.

"You've had your vengeance because I'm a man of my word. Are you ready to prove that you are a man of yours?"

"Yes," I answer.

I knew it would come, and I'm prepared to face my sentence, whatever Viktor determines it should be. Today, he will deem me worthy of my stars or worthy of the grave. It's the Vory way.

Viktor nods. "Very well. It's been a long day already. Let's go to the club. The brothers are waiting."

CHAPTER 40
Nikolai

Viktor takes his place at the front of the room, face solemn as he glances into the collective audience of my Vory brothers. Already, my offenses have been laid bare, and for the past five minutes, silence has entombed us as they've considered every possible punishment. Some of which include the removal of my tongue, fingers, hands, or other appendages. Other options are carving the stars from my skin, flogging, beating, burning, branding, and if that weren't enough, the room is always open for suggestions.

It's only the beginning, and even after my punishment is handed down, I could still be sentenced to death. At the end of the day, it is the *pakhan* I have offended, and he is who I must answer to.

"Is there anyone who would like to speak on Nika's behalf?" Viktor asks.

I am not surprised that Mischa is the first to stand. His eyes cut to mine as he testifies to my character, offering both my flaws and positive traits, and the loyalty he feels to me as a brother. He tells several stories that portray me in a positive light, and I'm not certain I deserve his kind words, but I'm grateful for them nonetheless.

"Thank you, Mischa." Viktor gestures for him to sit down.

The proceedings continue with testimonies from several of my Vory brothers, those who I haven't managed to piss off in some way or another over the years. When they have finished, Viktor directs attention to the front of the room again.

"Is there anyone who would like to speak against Nika?"

The room is quiet, and I half expect several of the men to air their dislike of my character, but none do.

"Very well, then." Viktor adjusts his watch and loosens his collar, already preparing for what comes next. "You have heard the laws that Nika has broken. He has made a mockery of our code, and therefore, we must make an example of him. Every Vor must place his vote. Let's start with Boris."

Boris tips his chin in my direction, a sign of respect. "I vote flogging."

The man next to him, an *avtoritet*, also nods in my direction. "Flogging."

The votes continue around the table, unanimous in their decision.

Viktor signals to a *bratok*, issuing him an order to retrieve the wooden device reserved for such occasions. "The first punishment will be flogging," he says. "Any nominations for a second?"

Again, the room is quiet. After enough time has passed, Viktor nods, and I breathe. Flogging is not a walk in the park, but it could be much worse.

The *bratok* wheels in the flogging station, and I take my place at the front of the room. Removing my shirt and tossing it aside, I step into position, facing the wooden crucifix. The *bratok* secures my wrists to each side, and my face rests flat against the wood as Viktor takes the whip in his hand. He will be the first and probably the worst.

Not one to draw it out, he steps behind me and cracks the whip in the air twice, testing the distance and loosening his wrist. The third is the one to hit me, and it feels like a tree branch cracking over my back. My body jolts forward on impact, but the wood prevents me from escaping the blow. The only thing to do is grit my teeth and bear it, aware that this too is a test. Should I show any emotion or weakness, I'll be sentenced to death without a second thought.

Twice more, the whip comes down on my back, splitting open my skin and raining fire on the wound. When Viktor is satisfied with his work, he calls the next man to take his place.

It requires a skilled hand to operate a bullwhip, and for this reason, the next Vor chooses the bamboo cane for his turn. Even though the sound is not as impressive as a bullwhip, the cane still feels like a punch to the kidney.

The level of severity is different for each man who steps up to take his shot, and I'm certain it doesn't last more than a few minutes, but it feels like an eternity. When I am finally heaved from the crucifix, it hurts to breathe. Several of my Vory brothers drag me to my feet and help me to a chair, and it's all I can do to lean forward and brace my weight on my knees.

There is no time for recovery. Viktor comes to stand in front of me, eager to finish the day.

"You have insulted me, Kol'ka," he says. "But worse, you insulted my daughter. And for this reason, I am leaving it up to Ana whether you live or die."

It's a fair decision, but it doesn't inspire any confidence that I'll live to breathe another day. Ana is young, and she believes herself in love with me. She will likely be scornful from my rejection, and there is nothing else to do but wait for her decision.

Viktor summons the *bratok* to bring her in, and he opens the door where she must have been waiting outside. Fighting the urge to pass out from the agony in my back, I look up as Ana walks into the room. Her face is pale, and her cheeks are pink, and she is uncomfortable with so many Vory eyes on her. But when her eyes find mine, the discomfort morphs to anger.

Her lip curls in contempt as she moves toward me, and Viktor repeats what he just told us. It's up to her to determine my fate.

For a long while, she just stares at me. I'm not certain what's going through her mind, and it would be out of turn to speak unless she asks me to. So I wait along with all my brothers to hear what she has to say.

"Why did you pretend?" she asks. "Why did you come to dinners with me, and let me think …"

Her throat bobs, and she swallows the emotion.

"I'm sorry, Ana." I hang my head in shame. "It was never my intention to hurt you. I only wanted to do what was right, but I should have been honest with you from the beginning."

Her chin quivers. "My father tells me you love someone else."

It's a volatile question, but I answer it anyway. The truth is all I have left to offer her. "I do. I'm sorry that it wasn't you."

She chews on her lip and squeezes her hands at her sides. "I hate you for what you did. I'm humiliated. You could have saved me this pain by being honorable."

"I know," I agree.

She looks at her father. "I don't want to see him again, but it isn't my place to take his life. Please don't kill him, Papà."

Viktor's eyes settle on me when he answers. "Very well, then. Nika will live to see another day. I only hope you can appreciate this gift my Ana has given you."

VIKTOR HANDS me a glass of whiskey and takes a seat across from me while the *bratok* cleans my wounds.

The room has cleared, and now there is only one final item on our agenda. The most important item we have yet to discuss. I down my drink and reach for the bottle, helping myself to another.

Viktor lights a cigar and leans back to study me. "Your Valentini girl is a snitch, and I want her dead."

I'd be lying if the thought hadn't occurred to me. Every day, I've waited for the feds to show up at my door and arrest me. She had every opportunity to give them the ammunition they needed. I'd been careless during our time together, exposing too much of myself and the things that I do. I put my brotherhood at risk, but I believed in her loyalty. Perhaps it was falsely given, or perhaps this is what I deserve.

"I can see how this might present a problem for you." Viktor flicks his ashes onto the floor. "Given your lovesick condition."

"I can't allow you to kill her." It's a bold statement, considering the circumstances, but Viktor humors me nonetheless.

"She ran out on you. She betrayed you, yet you would still protect her?"

"She snitched on Manuel," I answer. "Not me."

"It speaks to her character," he says. "A rat is a rat. And I wouldn't hedge your bets just yet. You don't know what she's told them."

It's true, but I still don't believe she betrayed me. Not like that.

"I know her character. She is loyal to those who deserve it. Manuel did not."

Viktor is quiet, and I worry that I'm too late. There's no telling if he knows her location. If he already has men watching her. His resources are vast, and mine are not. I have left no stone unturned, but it does me little good if she's in witness protection. She has a new name, a new life, and it isn't with me.

Viktor sighs and stubs out his cigar, leaning forward onto his elbows. "I don't think you deserve such kindness from me, Kol'ka, but if you are determined to save her life, there is one other option."

I nod, anxious for the answer. "What is it?"

"It's a last resort," he utters. "And in truth, you must be prepared to accept that she will not like it."

CHAPTER 41
Nikolai

"Have you found anything?"

Mischa grunts a useless response from the computer. "I can't find anything when you are constantly hovering. The answer is no. They fucked up your entire surveillance system. Everything's been destroyed."

I swallow two more painkillers and wash them down with vodka. It still doesn't make sense. "How long would that take for a novice, you think?"

He snorts. "It wasn't a novice. They knew what they were doing."

"Nonna said they took her in a matter of minutes."

Mischa looks up from the computer, glancing toward the hall.

"She's not here," I tell him. "She went to visit her sister."

"Why didn't you tell me this before?"

"What?"

"When did Nonna leave to visit her sister?" he asks.

I try to recall, but everything has been blurry lately. "I don't know. A while ago."

"Around the time you killed Sergei?"

The implication makes my gut churn, but there is only one way

THIEF

to know for sure. I retrieve the calendar and look for the last note Nonna left with my messages. It was dated two weeks ago. *The day after Sergei's death.*

I want to believe it's a coincidence, but now that Mischa has pointed it out, I can't.

"What she told you is physically impossible," he says. "This would have taken them an hour to destroy, bare minimum. How can you be sure that she wasn't working with Sergei? And the guard too? It's difficult to know who he swayed. If he could get Katya to plant cameras in Alexei's house, there's no telling what else he did."

"Fuck." I kick the bottom of the desk and fall back into the chair. He's right. Everything he said is right, and I was too blind to see it for myself. "If it's true, she'll be in the wind by now."

Mischa shrugs. "Still couldn't hurt to put the word out."

My phone chimes, signaling an incoming text message from Alexei. Mischa yammers on about Nonna, but I'm not listening. My eyes are fixated on the message. I read it three times over to make sure I'm not mistaken.

"What is it?" Mischa asks.

I hand him the phone. "What does it say?"

He reads it silently before looking up, his face pale. "It says Talia is alive."

MISCHA MEETS me outside the hospital room, his eyes cutting in front of me. "What is that?"

"What?" I look down at the gift in my hands.

"Did you bring an Aston Martin Stroller?"

"He's a Vor." I shrug. "He should be riding in style."

Mischa wiggles the stuffed teddy bear in his own hands. "You make my gift look pathetic."

"That's because it is pathetic." I slap him on the shoulder.

"I'll get him a stripper and some vodka for his eighteenth birthday to make up for it," he says.

"Good luck with that," I mutter.

We walk into the room. Already, Talia is surrounded by other Vory visitors, and beside her, Alexei holds his son. I pause, almost feeling like I'm intruding on this moment as the new parents speak to each other in hushed whispers, gushing over their firstborn child.

The natural chain of thoughts makes me think about Nakya. I think about what she would look like here beside me, my babies in her arms. It's an empty fantasy, and I am grateful when Alexei breaks the spell and gestures me farther inside.

Viktor whistles when he sees the stroller. "Very nice, Kol'ka."

"Limited edition," I say. "Only the best for our newest Vor."

Alexei rises to greet me, and to my surprise, he reaches out to shake my hand. "Thank you for coming, *bratan*. And thank you for the gift."

"Of course."

There is an awkward moment of silence between us, but it's a moment of understanding. Alexei isn't just thanking me for the gift, he is thanking me for my help during the past month. But more importantly, he is forgiving me.

CHAPTER 42
TANAKA

"Are you ready, Niki? You're on in five."

I rise en pointe to test out my shoes. A hard-won lesson. "I'm ready. Thank you again for this opportunity."

Louis nods, his eyes moving down to my ankle. I know he's worried it won't hold up, and in all honesty, it might not. But I'm grateful he gave me a chance, even if it's a small one. My days of being a soloist are over, but for tonight, I have a guest spot at the local ballet company, performing in *A Midsummer Night's Dream*.

One last dance.

While my days spent teaching children are fun, it isn't the same, and it will never be the same. My love for the ballet cannot be fulfilled through teaching. A dancer who can't dance is as good as an artist who can't create. I don't know what my future holds, but I know that I'm ready to say goodbye to this chapter of my life.

"Niki?" One of the stagehands waves to get my attention.

"Yes?"

"Someone left this for you."

My hand trembles when she offers me the solitary white lily. She smiles, and I think I smile too, but my mind has just gone from zero to sixty, and I think I might throw up. When she disappears back down the hall, I open the attached note, reading the words with deliberate care.

Shine bright little star before you burn out forever.

A tingling sensation expands my heart and out through my limbs. One lily. Alexei mentioned to me once that it's considered bad luck to give anything but odd numbers of flowers in Russian culture. The message is cryptic, and it could be from any of the Vory. But the flower itself has meaning that can't be ignored.

In ballet performances, white lilies signify purity. It could only be from *him*.

"One minute," someone tells me.

I need to think about so many things, but there isn't time. I set the gift aside and take a breath. It's my turn, and to say that I'm nervous as I make my entrance onto the stage would be an understatement. The last time I did this, it ended horrifically. But I can't let that night stain this memory for me. Before I retire my shoes forever, I want to pay tribute to everything that ballet has given me. And if that note is any indication, it might be the last thing I ever do on this earth.

I throw everything I have into the performance—body, heart, and soul. Magic is real, and it exists on the stage. Around me, butterflies and fairies twirl. Tinkers and tailors and weavers enter the fray, hair whipping and arms swaying as they perform their duties. Lovers quarrel, and a forest is born. Stars cross, and chaos ensues. Kings and queens fall, and I learn how to fly again. Leaping through the air with slicing jetés and bounding across the stage with the lightness of a feather. It's the most painful performance I've ever given, but it's also my best.

Because I am free.

Tears cling to my cheeks as the final curtain falls, and when I exit the stage, I'm limping but at peace. I collapse onto the closest chair I can find and bask in the adrenaline high. Several of the dancers congratulate me on a job well done as they exit the stage behind me, everyone buzzing with the excitement of our collaborative effort.

"It appears that the angel has found her wings again."

Ocean eyes crash into mine, and his name exalts from my lungs before I can stop it.

"Nika."

He smiles, and it feels like sunshine after an eternal winter. Everything else falls away, and there is only the chaos in my heart when I look up at him.

"Come." He holds out his hand for me.

My relief falters. It can't be him. I can't look into those eyes as he bleeds the life out of me. He should have sent Viktor. He should have sent anyone else.

"Do you no longer trust me?" he asks.

"Should I trust you?"

"Does it matter at this point?"

I shake my head. It doesn't. He's here. He found me. And whatever he decides, my fate is sealed.

"Come, *zvezda*," he urges. "It's time."

"What if I say I don't want to?"

His hand wavers, but he doesn't retreat. "Then it would break my heart."

"I didn't realize you had a heart to break," I whisper.

"Even monsters have hearts, my sweet."

I know it's true because a monster lives inside me too. I take his hand, and his fingers close around mine.

"You are sore?"

I nod, and Nikolai wraps his free arm around my waist. We walk together, and he takes me into the room where the stage props are stored. Behind the larger-than-life trees and one-sided building displays, he corners me.

When he touches my face, my eyes fall shut, and my chest heaves. He will probably strangle me. It's an intimate way to die, and Nikolai is nothing if not intimate. He will want to see my face. Burn my skin with his fingers. Feel the last dull thump of my beating heart beneath his hands. His scent will be the last thing I breathe. His lips, the last thing I taste. And his skin, the last thing I feel.

A fresh tear leaks from the corner of my eye, but it's bittersweet. I'm afraid that even in death, he will find a way to haunt me.

"Don't cry, pet." He wipes away the salty emotion with his thumb, smearing the evidence

into my skin.

"Will you make it quick and painless?" I ask.

His body cages me in, and his lips hover over mine. "It will be painless," he murmurs. "But it won't be quick."

My heart leaps into my throat when he jerks me around and presses my face against the wall, his hands mauling my body as his lips come down on my throat.

"Nakya." He grinds his erection against my ass while his fingers slip down between my legs, cupping me through the leotard.

"Tell me that you're mine."

"You already know I am," I rattle.

His thumb drags over my clit while his teeth graze my shoulder. "I'm going to fuck this pretty little ballerina. You better be quiet if you don't want anyone to hear."

The thought of someone catching us leaves me panting. Ragged breaths wrench from my chest when he yanks my leotard aside, ripping a hole in the tights. I'm scared, and I'm so swollen for him it hurts. Nikolai yanks me around like a doll, forcing my hips back and arching my spine forward.

The position drags my nipples against the fabric of my suit as he jostles me forward, rubbing his cock against the hole of my tights.

"Are you still pure for me?" he asks. "Are you still mine?"

"I haven't been with anyone else."

"Good girl, *zvezda*." He pets my face and wraps his hand around my throat, forcing my head to arch back until my eyes meet his.

We stay like that while he squeezes his cock inside me, and I whine as my body adjusts to the size of him all over again. He is impatient, and my nerve endings scream when he drags himself out only to stuff me full again.

"Please, Nika," I beg, unsure of exactly what I need.

"Don't say please," he growls. "Don't cry or beg or tell me that this is wrong. Just be sweet and come on my cock."

I don't have a choice when he touches me with his fingers. I come for him, and it is without mercy. The orgasm leaves me in a state of total devastation, clutching his forearms to stay upright as he drives into me over and over again.

"My pussy. My tits. My ballerina." He punctuates every declaration with a thrust. "Tell me yes."

"Yes," I shout.

He groans and buries himself as far as I can take him, his dick pulsing jets of hot cum deep inside my womb. His hands come around my waist, and he continues to fuck me, long after he has come, until his dick has gone soft and he has too.

His hands are gentle, and his lips are full of worship. I'm still holding my breath, afraid of what happens next. He will probably tell me he's sorry before he ends my life. He will probably even mean it too.

"Nakya." He kisses my ear. "Are you happy with this life? Are you happy with the freedom you have always wanted?"

His questions throw me off balance, and I revert to my natural protective instincts. "Yes, I'm happy."

"You haven't been taking care of yourself," he murmurs.

"I ... I'm fine."

He removes himself from inside me and adjusts our clothing to a more appropriate state before turning me in his arms. There is no hiding from him now. Not when I face his eyes.

"Lie to me again," he dares me.

"What do you want from me?" I ask. "Why did you come here, Nika? Is it not enough to kill me? Must you torture me too?"

He kisses me like he's defusing a bomb, and it works.

"You didn't betray me," he says.

"Only your ego would allow you to say so."

"Don't trifle with me, Nakya. You couldn't give me up, so just admit it."

"And look what good it did me. You found me anyway. You came to take your pound of flesh."

"I'm not here to kill you." He reaches for my hand, pressing it against his heart. "I'm here to keep you."

"What does that mean?" I croak. "What about Ana?"

"Tell me the truth, *zvezda*," he says. "It's the only time I'm going to ask you before I leave your life forever. If you love me, say it now."

My throat burns. My eyes burn. Everything burns, and I'm afraid that what he says is true. He will walk away forever, abandoning me to this existence without him. But what he's asking isn't fair.

"You tell me first," I demand.

He grabs me around the waist. "So stubborn, pet. You want to hear me admit it first?"

I nod.

"Very well then. I love you, my sweet. I love you more than the stars in the sky love the moon. I love you more than I love my Vory brothers, and I would die to prove it. Is that what you want to hear?"

I cling to his shirt, desperate for his assurances. "You said it wasn't meant to be. The stars weren't in our favor."

"So maybe I've rewritten our stars."

"Don't play games with me." My voice wavers. "I can't take it, Nika. Are you really here to collect me?"

"You should know that we have many customs." He releases me and falls away from my arms. "The stars on my knees dictate that I should bow before no man."

Nikolai lowers to his knee and takes my hand in his. "But I will bow to you, Nakya, if it means that you will agree to be my wife."

Emotion steals my voice. It steals my ability to breathe or think. What he's asking seems impossible. This is the life I swore I would do anything to leave. I promised myself I wouldn't be a mafia wife, and that I'd rather die than live that way.

But when I search Nika's ocean eyes, he is not just mafia. He is not Dante or my father, or any man who I have ever known before. He is my artist. The color of my life. My thief, and the stealer of my heart. I don't know how I could possibly go forward in this life without the other half of my soul.

I get down on my knees to meet him, grasping his face in my hands. "Do you promise to be loyal to me? Do you promise that I will be your only warmth? The only woman in your life?"

"You are the only woman in my bed, my heart, and my life," he assures me. "My loyalty is with you, now and forever."

His eyes plead with mine. Blue to my amber. Until now, I didn't know that I was dying of a thirst I never knew I had, and he was the bluest water I ever tasted. For eternity, I could drink him, and for eternity, I would never be satisfied.

"Tell me that you're mine," I whisper.

He drags me against him, tipping my chin up so he can taste my lips. "I'm yours, Nakya."

"And I'm yours," I assure him.

CHAPTER 43
NIKOLAI

"How did you find me?" Nakya asks.

I squeeze her knee and reach for her fingers. She hasn't been still since we left her apartment. It will take time for her to trust that this is real, but I've only got time to give.

"Gianni told me where you were."

"He did?" Her voice stings of betrayal.

"I thought you knew better than to ever trust a fed."

She glances out the car window, watching the scenery fade from view as the highway eats up miles behind us.

"He was the only option I had at my father's. And then you came in and wrecked that plan."

"Lucky for you."

She looks back at me, and I think it's too soon for jokes. "You sent me to die. What did you expect from me, Nika? He saved my life."

Mischa glances at me in the rearview mirror. And though I would prefer that he wasn't here for this conversation, I am grateful that he's driving right now.

"Is that what Nonna told you?"

THIEF

Nakya's foot beats an anxious rhythm against the floorboard. "She said you were done with me, and then the guard took me."

I squeeze her hand, probably too hard. "And you believed them?"

"Why wouldn't I?" she questions. "You left me no choice but to believe them. And if Gianni hadn't come along—"

I kiss her because I can't allow her to say it. I can't and probably won't ever be able to accept that I failed her in this way. She is right about Gianni in that he wasn't completely worthless. If he hadn't been there, Sergei would have taken her away from me.

"I'm sorry," I tell her. "I should have done more to protect you, but *zvezda*, you should know that I would have never let you go."

She curls into my chest, breathing me in. "What happened to Nonna?"

"She's gone," I answer. "And she won't be coming back. She betrayed me for Sergei, and so did the guard. But they are all gone now."

She looks up at me with cloudy eyes. "Sergei is dead?"

I nod. Someday, we will speak of it, but it won't be today. I have no intention of inviting that darkness into the new chapter of our life. But Tanaka is quick to remind me that there is still darkness between us.

"My father is dead," she says. "Isn't he?"

Lying to her would be easy, but it isn't what I want. I need her to love the darkest parts of me. I need her to love me when I'm at my worst.

"Yes, my sweet. I'm sorry, but he is dead too."

"I thought so," she says. "And you killed him?"

"Yes."

I think that there will certainly be more, but instead, she lays her head against my chest and falls to sleep.

CHAPTER 44
TANAKA

I find Nika on the dock, face up to the sky. He's watching the stars, and I would give anything to know what he's thinking at this moment. The world stands still, and I find that I can breathe again as my eyes move over the man who came into my life like a wrecking ball.

He's wearing a white button-down, gray slacks, and his motorcycle boots. A silent laugh shakes my chest when I think about how much I hated those boots the first time I saw him. Now, I know that it's just Nika. I love his bullheaded, boorish ways, and I'm probably crazy for it.

I take a breath and utter the most important words of my life. "I'm ready."

He turns to look at me, nostrils flaring. Warmth spreads through me, and I smooth my hands over the gauzy white fabric.

"It's a beautiful dress." I swish back and forth.

"The dress is nice," he agrees. "But I'm looking at you, Nakya. Only you."

He insisted I wear white, and I insisted that I didn't want a fuss.

This dress was our compromise. Light and breezy, it's perfect for our beach nuptials.

"I regret that I'm the only one who gets to see it," he says.

"The minister will see it. And Mischa too."

Nika moves into my space, tipping my chin up with his fingers. "Trying to make me jealous?"

"What is there to be jealous of?" I ask. "You will be my husband tonight. I will have your star on my hand. We will be together, and everyone else is just white noise."

He growls into my mouth. Nikolai loves the idea of being my husband, but I think he still feels some regret too. The Vory way would be to show me off. To have a grand, extravagant wedding in front of all his brothers. But when he confided that we would need to be married before our return to Massachusetts, I was relieved to tell him that I wanted no part of a big wedding. It isn't for anyone else. Just us. And it doesn't get any more private than having our own beach in the Florida Keys. For the next five days, we will do nothing but sleep, and eat, and make love in our bungalow over the water. It's perfect, and it's important that he knows I wouldn't have it any other way. It doesn't matter where we get married. It doesn't even matter how. All that matters is that we do. When we go back home, Viktor will give us his approval, and our lives can go on.

I know what I'm signing up for. Life with Nikolai won't always be a fairy tale, and once I'm in, there aren't any take backs. But if I'm going to do hard time, I want to do it with him.

"I'm ready," I say again.

Nikolai takes his time pawing at me before he finally gestures for Mischa and the minister to come down to the beach.

Against the backdrop of the water, and beneath all the stars in the sky, we say our vows. They are simple, and they are traditional in the mafia way.

Nikolai vows to protect, cherish, provide for, and remain faithful to me for all the days of his life. He vows to let no other woman come between us and also adds that he will ensure my health, even when I might not like it. When we fight, and we will fight, he declares that we will use our words and not our fears to work things out.

In return, I vow my undivided loyalty, respect, and honor to him. I tell him that my virtue will always belong to him, and that I will proudly wear his star on my hand and in my heart.

The ceremony is completed by the minister's official seal of approval, followed by the application of my new tattoo by Mischa. It's an odd thing, when I trace over the letters of his name etched into my skin, how much I like it.

"Thank you." Nikolai dismisses the minister, and then turns to Mischa. "You can go now too."

I laugh when he scoops me up into his arms and starts striding down the dock toward our bungalow, but his face has never been more serious.

"It's time to consummate this marriage."

EPILOGUE
TANAKA

"To strong women." Sasha holds her shot glass in the air, toasting all of us gathered around her today.

"The strongest," Mack agrees. "We have to be to put up with them."

Our gazes collectively move across the lawn where our husbands are gathered with small children nipping at their feet like dogs, begging for their attention. Two of the men, Nikolai and Mischa, are presently hovered over Mack's latest addition to the Irish syndicate.

"And to think they still don't know how to change a frigging diaper," she hoots.

All the women break into laughter, and Talia leans over to reassure me. "Don't worry, they figure it out eventually."

My hand comes to rest on the top of my bump, and I give her a relaxed smile. "I'm not worried. I already know Nikolai will be a good father."

"Pfft." Mack pours another drink. "You are still in the honeymoon phase. Don't let him get out of his daddy duties just because you're all starry-eyed now. Trust me, you'll thank me for it later. You have to put your foot down. Make him get up in the middle of the night. Let him change a few diapers. And most importantly, don't give him any nookie unless he's pulling his weight."

"Don't let her scare you," Sasha says. "She isn't as tough as she sounds. One look from Lachlan and she turns to mush."

I'm not scared. But I am grateful when I look around me. In the span of such a short amount of time, my life has changed so much. The thing that I was most afraid of has turned out to be the best thing that ever happened to me. This isn't just a group of women and their husbands. They are my family. The family I never thought I would have.

We look out for each other. We laugh, and we cry, and we poke at each other. And even though I am still relatively new, they have accepted me with open arms.

Ronan, the Irish Reaper, comes to collect his wife, Sasha, and the other men are quick to follow suit. Lunch is ready, and there is a celebration to be had for baby Franco's birthday. But while the others filter into the garden at Alexei's request, Nikolai holds me back, taking my hand and sneaking us into the house.

"What are we doing?" I whisper as he closes the bathroom door behind us.

He props me up on the vanity, his hands roaming over my body. It has changed so much, and I'm still struggling to accept it. Every day, my belly grows, and not just that but my breasts and my hips too.

"You're beautiful," Nikolai murmurs as he gropes at my breasts. "And these are magnificent."

"We're going to get caught," I laugh.

"So let us get caught." He grabs the bulge in his jeans and shows it off proudly. "I want to fuck my wife."

"Mmm." I want to resist him, but it's hard when he knows all my weaknesses. Particularly when he kisses my throat. And before I know it, he has the top of my dress pulled down, rubbing his face all over my breasts.

"You are obsessed."

THIEF

"Large or small, I'll never get enough of them, Nakya. Get used to it."

"Soon you will have to share."

He grunts and rests his hand against my belly where his son grows. "In that case, I won't mind. It will be good for me to learn moderation."

He's right, but I don't voice it, because it's just occurred to him that his opportunities are limited, and now he's back to molesting my breasts again. Sucking them and squeezing them and licking them while he fumbles with his zipper.

He's been taking me so often since I told him I was pregnant that I joked he would keep adding babies if he didn't stop. But he has no intention of stopping. He tells me so when he wraps my legs around his waist and stuffs himself inside me.

"*Zvezda*," he says it like a prayer. "You are having my baby."

"I know." I kiss his throat.

"I still can't believe it," he groans.

He says it every day. And every day, I agree. It has been an adjustment, learning to love my body as it changes for motherhood. Nikolai is careful not to let me slide back into old patterns, and he is also quick to point out everything that he loves about me often and passionately.

"Come for me, my sweet," he begs.

I come twice. My nerve endings are more alive than they've ever been. Nikolai loves it, and so do I.

Someone knocks on the bathroom door, and Nikolai grunts. "I'll be out in a minute."

"You better not be desecrating my house," Alexei calls through the door.

I smile up at Nikolai, and he shudders out his release. Something I have come to realize about him is that he likes the thrill of getting caught. He seizes any opportunity he can to take me in public places, including his own brother's home.

"Just tending to my pregnant wife," Nika says even though Alexei can't hear him. "Right, pet?"

"Apparently, I'm very needy."

He brings my hand to his lips, kissing the place where his star resides. "Are you happy, *zvezda*? Have I given you a life worth living?"

"You have given me a life worth loving," I amend. "Always, Nika. Because I am yours."

In the end, I let him ruin me. It was the only way.

THE END.

BOOKS BY A. ZAVARELLI

Boston Underworld Series

CROW

REAPER

GHOST

SAINT

THIEF

CONOR

Sin City Series

CONFESS

CONVICT

CONTEMPT

The Society Trilogy

REQUIEM OF THE SOUL

REPARATION OF SIN

RESURRECTION OF THE HEART

The Rite Trilogy

HIS RULE

HER REBELLION

THEIR REIGN

Ties that Bind Duet

MINE

HIS

Bleeding Hearts Series

ECHO

STUTTER

Standalones

KINGDOM FALL

BEAST

STEALING CINDERELLA

PRETTY WHEN SHE CRIES

HATE CRUSH

TAP LEFT

For a complete list of books and audios, visit http://www.azavarelli.com/books

About the Author

A. Zavarelli is a USA Today and Amazon bestselling author of dark and contemporary romance.

When she's not putting her characters through hell, she can usually be found watching bizarre and twisted documentaries in the name of research.

She currently lives in the Northwest with her lumberjack and an entire brood of fur babies.

Sign Up for A. Zavarelli's Newsletter:
www.subscribepage.com/AZavarelli

Like A. Zavarelli on Facebook:
www.facebook.com/azavarelliauthor

Join A. Zavarelli's Reader Group:
www.facebook.com/femmefatales

Follow A. Zavarelli on Instagram:
www.instagram.com/azavarelli

Printed in Great Britain
by Amazon